AMANDA LEES

THE MIDWIFE'S CHILD

Published by Bookouture in 2023

An imprint of Storyfire Ltd.
Carmelite House
50 Victoria Embankment
London EC4Y 0DZ

www.bookouture.com

ISBN: 978-1-80314-683-6
eBook ISBN: 978-1-80314-682-9

For Ann
In memory of Frankie and Arthur

PROLOGUE

29 DECEMBER 1944, AUSCHWITZ-BIRKENAU

She was laid out on the brick stove in the centre of the block, her breath coming in short gasps, forming clouds in the freezing air. The stove was never lit, which made it the perfect place to deliver a baby. Especially a baby like this – a Jewish child. The yellow triangles on the mother's tattered clothing had the letter F in the centre of them. A French Jew. A countrywoman. Her eyelids were fluttering as she drifted in and out of consciousness, the bones in her chest protruding above her belly, her lips moving as she muttered a name.

'Antoine. *Mon cher*. Antoine. *Aide-moi.*' Help me.

'It's breech,' said the nurse. At least, that was what she'd been in a former life. Now, like the midwife, she was assigned to Mengele's squad, forced to report a baby like this so it, too, could be taken and killed. Or worse. Except that, somehow, they had managed to conceal this pregnancy. It helped that the mother was young and strong. It also helped that she was so thin her bump barely showed beneath her baggy striped uniform, the baby in her womb as undernourished as she.

The midwife felt for the baby's feet, tucked by its bottom as it sat, cross-legged, reluctant to enter the world.

'I don't blame you, little one,' murmured the midwife. What kind of world was this to enter anyway? A rat-infested concentration camp riddled with disease and ruled by cruelty. The baby was better off dead, even if it somehow managed to survive the birth. The mother, though, that was a different story. She could still be saved so long as she looked fit for work.

She was muttering again in French, her eyes open now, staring somewhere beyond the filthy hut, seeing someone who wasn't there.

'Antoine.' She smiled, in spite of her agony. 'You came.'

'She's delirious,' said the midwife. 'Feel her skin – she's burning up. We need to get her to the infirmary.'

'No!' The woman was staring at her now, lucid, eyes focused, pain creasing her brow. 'Don't take me there. They'll kill my baby.'

The midwife looked at her, taking in the blue eyes, the hair that was stuck to her forehead with sweat, darkened by it, although beneath it looked blonde. The short curls that sprang from her head appeared to be about six months' growth from when they'd been shaved off. She must have been pregnant when she got here.

The midwife unconsciously touched her own curls, shaved when she'd arrived back in August, copper bright still in spite of the grey numbness that lay all around. Most of the inmates gave in to it, the fight seeping from them. That was when you knew they were done for, halfway to the gas chambers and the crematoria that belched death into the sky.

This woman wasn't like that. She was still fighting. Delirious with pain and fever, yes, but crying out for her beloved while she did all she could to save their child.

'What's your name?' asked the midwife.

'Eva. My name is Eva.'

'And your husband's name?'

Although she already knew, she wanted to keep her talking, keep her conscious.

'Antoine.'

The midwife smiled. 'I have a friend called Antoine. Back in Lyon.'

'You do?'

She was drifting again, her eyes sinking back in her head.

'Stay with me,' commanded the midwife. 'Come on, Eva. For Antoine. For the baby.'

She looked at the nurse. 'I should really perform a caesarean, but if I do that, she'll almost certainly die, one way or another.'

The nurse stared back at her helplessly. 'So what do we do?'

'There's nothing else for it. I'm going to have to get this baby out. Let's sit her up so you can support her.'

Cradled in the nurse's arms, Eva looked little more than a child herself, so thin was she from the months spent surviving on watery soup and a tiny morsel of bread each day. Emaciated as she was, the midwife could see that she had once been beautiful, that she still was, perhaps even more so now. The spark was back in her eyes, and there was a determined set to her mouth. She was back with them, back with her baby.

'When I say, I want you to push,' said the midwife. 'Push as hard as you can.'

She felt for the baby's feet, pulling them gently, seeing the grimace on Eva's face as she bit back a howl of agony.

'Hush now,' the nurse soothed her, terrified the guards would hear and come running.

'That's it, Eva. And again.'

She knew what to do. It was clear this wasn't her first baby, but the midwife knew better than to ask about her other children. If they weren't here with her then they were gone, turned to grey dust like the other innocents. All the more reason to make sure this one lived, that Eva had at least one child remaining.

'Oh God. Antoine.'

A scream stifled by the nurse then another cry – the lusty song of a new-born.

'It's a girl,' whispered the midwife. 'You have a daughter.'

A daughter who wanted to live, judging by her lungs. Breech babies were normally slower to cry, but not this one. She searched hungrily with her mouth, her tiny fists flailing.

The midwife looked at the woman's breasts. She doubted there was any milk in there, but she had to try.

Eva reached out her arms. 'Give her to me.'

The baby latched on, sucking hungrily at what little there was. 'Leah, that's her name. We always said if we had a girl, we would call her Leah.'

Midwife and nurse exchanged a smile. There was nothing like it, the euphoria at delivering a new human being, despite the circumstances. It spoke of love and of renewed hope. Where there was hope, there was life. Even here, in Auschwitz.

Bang.

The barracks door flew open.

Two guards marched over and tore the baby from Eva's arms.

'You, get up,' ordered one, ignoring the midwife's protests.

'I can't,' whispered Eva, her face greyer than all the dust that swirled over the camp. That was when the midwife noticed the blood pooling around her hips, flowing from the place where the baby had emerged moments before. So much blood. She was haemorrhaging – and badly.

As Eva slumped, unconscious, back into the nurse's arms, the midwife screamed defiance.

'Leave her alone,' she roared. 'Or I'll kill you myself.'

ONE

Hoarse shouts from outside the ward, the sounds of doors slamming, of feet pounding on floorboards and the frozen ground outside, those that were barefoot near silent.

'What's happening?'

I took Eva's hand, feeling her wrist for her pulse. It fluttered under my fingers like a moth, barely detectable. Her eyes were closed, the veins on her eyelids a tracery of blue, all too clear against the paper white of her skin.

All of a sudden, those eyes snapped open, bluer than her veins, bright with fever and something else, something I'd seen before. She seemed oblivious now to what was happening outside, her face alight for someone only she could see.

'Hello, my love,' she whispered, reaching out one frail hand from under her blankets. She struggled to sit up, and I gently pushed her back down. She had been like this since they'd brought her back from Mengele, mostly unconscious, occasionally semi-lucid. She had lost so much blood it was a miracle she was still here. Maybe less a miracle than the sheer determination of a mother to stay with her child.

'You need to rest,' I said. 'Try to get some sleep, Eva.'

More shouts, closer now. I squinted out of the window at the far end of the ward but all I could see were blurred shapes moving in the distance, dozens of them. All at once, Dr Laba appeared, uncharacteristically out of breath.

'They're marching everyone out,' he gasped. 'We have to pack what we can carry and be ready to go. You must come now. They'll shoot you otherwise.'

Someone grabbed my hand. I looked down to see Eva's fingers, marble white, entwined through mine, gripping with surprising strength.

'Go and find my baby,' she said. 'Find Leah. Take her with you. Take her to my Antoine, to her father.'

Her voice was full and resonant as it hadn't been since the birth, eyes blazing with a fierce insistence that I do what she asked.

I squeezed the hand that gripped mine. 'I'll find her,' I said. 'I promise.'

'Antoine Melville. He was last in Lyon. Working with the Resistance. Take her to him. I know you'll find a way.'

I stared at her, dumbstruck. 'Antoine Melville,' I repeated.

She was already sinking back, the effort sapping what little strength she had left. I felt her fingers slacken and then slip from mine. She let out a long, shuddering sigh and then she was gone, unconscious once more. It wouldn't be long now, from what I could see. I tucked the blanket tighter around her.

'Sleep well, Eva,' I murmured. 'May God save you.'

I didn't believe in God, and certainly not a god who could do this, but it seemed the only thing to say.

'Hurry,' hissed one of the nurses. 'We all have to report now or they'll start shooting.'

I had no doubt she was right. They'd been shooting for weeks now as part of their killing spree. Dr Laba was standing there, wringing his hands.

'What about the patients?' I asked.

'I'll stay here with them.'

'You can't do that. They'll kill you.'

Dr Laba thrust his knapsack at me, the one he carried everywhere. 'They won't. They need me to be here. Now you take this and go. Get the baby. I'll look after her mother.'

There was nothing more I could do for Eva. It was between her and her god.

I grabbed some extra blankets, throwing a couple over her and then flinging one around my shoulders. I stuffed another inside the knapsack.

People were surging past me in the corridor, and I slipped in among them, hearing the guards bark orders, turning and pushing through them back towards the nursery, moving as fast as I could.

'What are you doing?' snapped a guard, stepping out to block my path. 'Everyone is to go to the square.'

'I'm a doctor,' I said. 'I have patients in the nursery. Dr Mengele ordered me to see which of them could be moved.'

'Go on then,' he grunted, waving his gun in the direction of the nursery.

I fought my way through to the door and stopped, looking over at the nurse in the corner, praying it was Hanna. Suspicious eyes glinted at me from a doughy, stolid face. Damn. It was the local woman, specially chosen for her unquestioning obedience to her Nazi overlords. They must have already moved Hanna and the other nursery nurses out.

'I need to check on the infants,' I said. 'Dr Mengele's orders.'

She carried on staring at me, saying nothing, as I checked first on Anna then on Leah. If she even suspected for a moment why I was really here, she would raise the alarm and the guards would come running.

'They've both deteriorated,' I said. 'Dr Mengele won't be pleased. He wanted them well enough to take with him for his experiments. See here, both their rashes are worse. How long have you been in charge of them?'

'What? Where?'

She scurried over, cheeks flushed in alarm. As she bent over Anna's cot, I scooped Leah from hers, grabbing a couple of full bottles as well.

'Look. It's spread. This one is much worse.'

The nurse crossed herself and let out a wail.

'Don't worry,' I murmured, eyes flicking to the door. 'You stay here and I'll deal with this baby. We can say it died. I'll come back and do the same with the other.'

I could hardly bear to leave Anna, but there was no alternative. I couldn't carry two babies, and Leah had to come first.

Wordlessly, she nodded, fingers plucking at her apron.

I placed Leah inside my knapsack, pulling the blanket up around her, and made for the door again, walking briskly back down the corridor, which was empty now, looking neither left nor right and praying she wouldn't cry out.

We were nearly at the door when one of the SS doctors appeared.

'What are you still doing here?' he asked.

I instinctively gripped the knapsack tighter. 'Dr Mengele's orders. I was checking on the babies before leaving.'

Another shot in the dark, one that seemed to satisfy him. 'You'd better get moving and join the others.'

'Yes, indeed.'

I was halfway out the door when he called after me. 'Wait.'

I turned to see him thrusting a coat at me. His coat. 'Take it,' he said. 'You'll need it.'

I slung it on over my blanket. Now the knapsack was well concealed. 'Thank you,' I said. A decent man. There were some.

'Good luck,' he murmured.

Then I was trudging across the snow, joining the others

lined up in rows, sliding in at the back in the hope the camp commandant wouldn't notice me. He was far too busy shouting orders at the guards standing by, organising the rows into columns as you would in a school playground. Except this was no school and there was nothing playful about it. You could sense the fear in the air and, for once, it wasn't just from the prisoners.

'The Soviets are nearly here,' murmured the woman next to me. 'That's why they're moving us out.'

My heart lifted in my chest then slammed back down as I saw Mengele making his way down our column. He was pointing left and right, just as he'd done when I'd first arrived. Only this time, those sent to the right were being lined up in yet another queue that stretched behind two guards at its head, those to the left herded back into the nearest hut, many of them so weak that some collapsed before they got there, only to be roughly hauled to their feet and shoved through the door.

I glanced at it with foreboding then stared straight ahead, my heart hammering now beneath my coat, beneath baby Leah. I dared not breathe in case it made it race even faster.

The right. Ignore the coat. Please, please to the right, I silently prayed, seeing his arm move, his finger extending. His eyes locked on to mine and then passed over me as if we'd never met, let alone conversed in his office barely an hour before. His finger flicked to the right, his eyes already on the next prisoner, far too immersed in his selection to notice or care about the coat over my prison uniform. Thank the god that didn't exist.

At that very moment, Leah let out a tiny cry. In the same split second, I heard a blast and then another. The hut where they'd herded the sickest and most emaciated prisoners was on fire, the fists of those trapped inside thudding uselessly against the locked windows and doors, their screams of agony ripping me apart.

As the flames caught hold, even those muffled sounds

ceased, and all we could hear was the crackle of fire, their cries and shouts dying along with them. But there was no time to stand and stare. We were already moving, marching towards the gates of the camp which, for once, stood open as we streamed through them, heading for we knew not where, eyes front as ordered. Even now they were trying to hide the evidence of what they'd done here from the Soviets. The thought gave me hope. The Nazis were afraid.

I risked a final look back as I passed through those gates I'd entered over five months before, spilling from the moving cesspit that had been the final transport train from Lyon. Then, as now, the camp spread stark under lowering skies, the yellow mud on which it sat extending as far as the eye could see between the rows of blocks. The sun never seemed to shine on Auschwitz. It knew better than to try. The brightest illumination came from the searchlights that blazed night and day above the electrified fence.

We were marching along the train tracks now, the wrought-iron words above the gate scarcely visible from here, but that didn't matter because they were etched on my soul.

'Arbeit macht frei.' Work sets you free.

A car roared past, and I caught a glimpse of Mengele in the passenger seat, the rest of the vehicle piled high with his boxes of notes. More evidence of heinous crimes. I had no idea where he was going or what he would do with them.

'I'll find you and your precious notes,' I muttered under my breath.

I eased the straps of my knapsack over my shoulders under my coat, wrapping my arms around Leah inside it, her tiny body held in my grip.

They're wrong, you know, Leah, I said to her in my head. *It's not work that sets you free. It's love.*

I felt her move against my chest, the smallest wriggle that told me somehow, she understood. My feet moved in rhythm with all the rest, trudging through the snow towards our unknown destination. Behind us, her mother lay close to death, if she hadn't passed already.

'I'll find him too, Leah,' I whispered. 'I'll find your daddy.'

Her heart beat against mine, echoing every breath I took. We lived and died together except that I was going to cheat death yet again. If it took everything I had, I would make sure that Leah had the life she deserved, the one her mother had lost, the one her father could still give her.

TWO

20 JANUARY 1945, UPPER SILESIA, SOUTHERN POLAND

We'd been marching for three days. Three days through the snow with the briefest of rest stops, those who fell by the wayside left where they lay or finished off by a bullet. Many were barefoot, the shoes they'd once had too small to fit their swollen feet, their striped prison pyjamas too tattered and thin to keep out the bitter cold. I felt the woman beside me stumble and falter, reached out and grabbed her by the elbow, hauling her back up.

'Keep going,' I muttered. 'Or they'll kill you.'

It was pot luck whether they left you to die slowly in a snowdrift or dispatched you in a flurry of gunfire. The guards looked nervous, their eyes constantly shifting, searching for the advancing Red Army. I could hear them snapping at one another, their jitters getting the better of them, their dogs barking and leaping at the slightest shadow, picking up on their anxiety. Good. The Germans were on the run again, just as they had been in France.

I let my mind drift away from the unending trudge, seeing them all clearly in my mind. My comrades in arms; my friends.

Marianne, Jack, Antoine. Poor Antoine. He had no idea his Eva was dead and so were his twins.

'Yes, but he has you,' I whispered, feeling the warm bulk of Leah against me, knowing that I had no milk left for her. So far, I'd managed to feed her in the dead of night as we marched, the constant rhythm and cold lulling her into a semi-comatose state. Her vitals were fine for now, but she could deteriorate at any moment. If she stirred, I coughed or sang or laughed. Let the guards think I was crazy. So long as I didn't slow the convoy down, we were safe, but the moment they discovered Leah, all was lost.

At the next rest stop, the woman who had stumbled slumped against me, her head resting on my shoulder, clearly unable to go on.

'I'm so cold,' she mumbled. 'So cold.'

I looked about, taking in the nearest prisoners to us, looking at their exhausted faces. Leah was my responsibility, but I could spare one blanket. I still had my coat and Leah the other. But who needed it most? An impossible choice. Everyone deserved it.

I felt the woman's head slide further down my shoulder and then the weight fell away as she slumped to the ground, her lips turning blue, her breathing slowing as she succumbed to the cold and starvation. I glanced at the woman on the other side of her, then further down the line where I suddenly recognised someone. Hanna – it was Hanna.

I stared at her until she looked at me too, our eyes meeting. She gave me a startled smile, and I beckoned to her, keeping one eye on the guards. She shuffled up the line while the guards were looking the other way, taking the place of the woman who'd slumped to the ground.

I slipped the blanket from my shoulders under the coat and passed it to her. Survival of the fittest.

'Take this,' I murmured.

'Thank you,' she whispered. 'I'm so happy to see you.'

'And I you. I have someone else with me.'

Her eyes widened as I lowered mine to my coat. 'Leah?'

'Yes. I only wish I could have brought Anna too, but there was no other choice. Her little face haunts me, but at least I managed to save this one.'

'Bless you. You did.'

She wrapped the blanket around her like a shawl just as the guards ordered us up on our feet again.

We set off without a backward glance, the woman who'd rested her head against my shoulder now lying, already half-covered by the falling snow. At least they hadn't put a bullet in her. Probably thought she was already too far gone. And three days out, they needed to conserve ammunition.

They sounded increasingly worried as we trekked on, with no end in sight. I knew we were heading west from the direction of the rising sun, giving me fresh hope each morning as it edged the clouds behind us with a faint silvery glow that penetrated the grey. We passed through towns and villages, the road and shop signs written in Polish, people staring as we passed. We must have been quite a sight.

Hundreds of walking skeletons clad in rags, the stripes barely visible beneath the grime, our hair matted and filthy, some with frostbitten feet and fingers, most reeking with the stench of despair. At least Hanna exuded determination.

We kept pace with one another as well as the women in front, stepping over anyone who fell, terrified of tripping too. I could feel the humanity seeping from me with every hour that passed. It had come down to this. To ignoring the suffering of someone I could have saved.

Except you can't, Maggie, I told myself. *You have no medicine, no implements. If you stop, they'll shoot you too.*

More than that, they would shoot Leah as well, although given what faced us, that might prove preferable. At least it would be a quick death rather than the slow, agonising one served up by starvation.

I would smother her before that happened. I couldn't let her suffer like that.

I glanced right and left – there had to be a way to escape.

The guards were up front and at the back, others spaced in between, barking orders and nudging us with their weapons, but there weren't enough of them to cover the entire convoy, not even with their dogs and horses. And there must be others marching too from the men's camp. Thousands of us being herded away before the Red Army could reach Auschwitz and, no doubt, the other camps.

I'd heard tales from prisoners who'd been sent on from those camps. Unbelievably, some were worse. But then, none of this was believable. I knew because I'd heard and seen the reports before I, too, was transported and had dismissed them as impossible. No one could be treating human beings like this. Except that they were.

A local woman ran up to us, trying to hand us bread. One of the guards barked an order at her and then raised his gun, shouting at her to back away. She cowered and ran, dropping her bread at the side of the road. We stared at it, knowing that if we tried to grab it, the guards would shoot.

It was too much for one woman, who staggered towards it, reaching down to snatch it up, driven half-mad by hunger. Her arms were still outstretched, fingers scrabbling for a loaf, when the guard unleashed his machine gun and she fell to her knees and then forward, face down into the snow, her blood seeping into the bread she'd tried so desperately to grab.

I averted my eyes, sickened.

'Bastards,' murmured Hanna.

No one else had the energy or will to say anything – all we had was this relentless march.

We rounded a bend in the road, and I looked over my

shoulder at the line snaking behind. It seemed to go on for miles, a moving caterpillar of misery, silent except for the muffled footsteps, the shouts of the guards and the barking of their dogs. But even they fell silent too as we started to pass through a wooded area with trees on either side, their eyes darting ever faster as they sensed others watching them, guns facing out now to protect themselves rather than to goad us.

'There's someone there,' whispered Hanna. 'People. In the woods.'

I peered as hard as I could through the fir trees, their thick covering concealing whatever she might be seeing. Or thought she was seeing. Except that the guards could see it too. The Red Army? It couldn't be. Or could it? All we'd heard were rumours passed along the line like Chinese whispers as we marched. The Red Army were still miles away. They were defeated, vanquished by Hitler's might. No. It was Hitler who was beaten. And so the words whirled, changed and embellished, until fiction became fact and I had no idea what the truth was anymore.

'Look. In there.' Hanna nudged me, her elbow digging into Leah instead of my ribs, startling her awake so she let out a wail. I froze, my mind racing, desperately looking for a bird, a beast, anything to blame for that feral sound, but the guards were already staring at me, turning, heading back, their guns pointed now at me instead of the trees, their eyes murderous.

I wrapped my arms around Leah tighter, jiggling her, begging her in my head to stop, but she kept on crying with the catlike yowl of a very young baby, her arms flailing against me as she screeched. And still the line kept moving, relentless.

We were emerging from the trees, open fields on either side, when I heard another shriek, this one louder than Leah's. Then a plane swooped low overhead and started shooting, the red star on its side visible. We all crouched, instinctively ducking until I saw what they were doing. They were shooting not at us but at the guards, expertly picking them off.

More cries, this time from men. Men who were running out of the trees, weapons raised, trained on the Germans, shouting at them to put their guns down, to surrender.

'They're speaking Russian,' I said. 'That was a Soviet plane.'

It was a small detachment, not large enough to take on the entire column with its eighty or so guards. Big enough, though, to splinter it.

'Come on.' I grabbed Hanna by the hand. 'Run.'

We raced towards the trees from which the Russians had emerged, plunging into them, pushing our way through the branches, hearing the sounds of shots and shouts from behind, never once hesitating.

At last, we came to a clearing where we stopped to catch our breath, the snow drifting through the canopy of trees, falling on my face as I lifted it to try to get some bearings.

Crack. A twig snapping.

I whirled, wishing I had a gun, anything to defend us. The man who stepped out from the forest had one, and he was pointing it straight at us.

Slowly, I raised my arms, and Hanna did the same. He was staring at us, a look of disbelief on his face that turned to pity and then compassion. He lowered his weapon and motioned to us to drop our arms. I could see the red epaulettes on his field jacket, the flashes on his collar.

'Red Army,' I murmured.

At that moment, Leah let out another howl, and the expression on his face turned to shock. He took a careful step towards us and then another, all the while trying to tell us with his eyes that he meant us no harm.

As he got within arm's reach, he held his out and nodded to me.

I shook my head. 'She's mine. I'm not giving her up to anyone.'

More soldiers started to appear from the woods, all of them dressed in the same uniform except one who was wearing British commando fatigues. He was taller than the others, his chestnut-brown hair curling back from his forehead, the same colour as his close-cropped beard and moustache. He stood like a man who was used to issuing orders, but there was no arrogance about him, simply a quiet confidence that was immensely reassuring.

The Soviet soldiers held back as he approached us and then, to my astonishment, saluted.

'Captain Maclean at your service. Don't worry – you're safe now.'

It was the first time I'd heard a British accent since I'd seen my comrades in SOE all those months ago in Lyon.

I looked into his kind, calm eyes and burst into tears.

THREE

She looked like a fawn that had burst from the forest, so thin her
limbs trembled and yet so alive. Even her hair was the colour of
the trees in autumn – copper bright, short curls framing a face
that burned with a fierce determination. She might be afraid,
but she was damned if she would show it. He could see that in
the set of her shoulders, the way she stood, protecting the other
woman and the baby strapped to her chest, swiping at her tears
as if they were an embarrassment. A baby. Out here. What the
hell had happened?

'It's alright,' he said, kicking himself for saluting. This
woman was a civilian in need of help. The last thing she wanted
was to be treated as if she was one of the troops.

He tried again, dropping his arms so she could see he was
no threat. 'I'm a British soldier. I can get you to safety. What's
your name?'

She stared at me, her hackles rising. 'I don't have a name
anymore. Just a number.'

'What do you mean?'

'Nothing.'

She turned and said something to the woman behind her in German. *'Keine Angst.' Don't worry.*

'You speak German?'

'Yes, but I'm not a Nazi spy, if that's what you're wondering.'

God but she was beautiful, standing there with her chin lifted, refusing to give in or give up. And the baby... Was she married? Why the hell did that matter?

He cleared his throat. 'I didn't think that for one moment. I was wondering where you've come from.'

'Auschwitz,' she whispered, her eyes clouding.

'The camp?'

'Yes.'

The break in her voice undid him. He wanted to pull her into his arms and never let her go. Her dignity, her strength after what she must have gone through – what they'd all gone through – was heart-rending.

He'd seen the endless column marching through the snow from their hideout, women who looked half-dead dragging shoeless feet, some stumbling and falling, being dragged up by their companions so those Nazi scum wouldn't shoot. It had made it all the sweeter when the plane had swooped, firing at them so they got a taste of their own medicine. His squad couldn't save them all – there simply weren't enough of them. And if they'd tried, the Germans would no doubt have turned their guns on them, but at least they had these three.

'Here,' he said, taking off his jacket and draping it around her shoulders, signalling to one of the men to do the same for the other woman. 'Come with us. I promise nothing bad will happen to you.'

She stared at him with a clear-eyed gaze that dared him to lie, eyes the colour of opals set in a face that some might call gamine and he would call beautiful, not least for the fire that burned behind it.

'That's an impossible promise to make, Captain.'

Later, he thought it was that moment he fell in love with her. Or maybe he was already in love with her – had been since the first moment he'd seen her. Who could say? It wasn't a sensation he knew well. All he knew was that this woman was someone he'd been seeking his entire life. And there was no way anyone or anything would ever hurt her again.

FOUR

Suzanne looked around the faces staring back at her across the table. In the centre of it, a map was spread out, a location on it marked with a red cross.

'You're sending us back to Lyon?' said Marianne, her expression almost as dark as her hair. Lyon was where they'd not just taken on Klaus Barbie but lost Maggie. It was a place that held too many memories for all of them, especially her. She could only imagine what Maggie had suffered since she'd been arrested and transported to Auschwitz, always supposing she was still alive.

'To another chateau just outside,' said Suzanne, tiny figure as poised as ever. 'Although this one is the headquarters for the US 7th Army OSS Detachment.'

'Are we running an op with them?'

'We're working with OSS on their mission to send German prisoners of war back into Germany as spies. They've been running it for a couple of months. You're going in on the final drop.'

Christine arched a perfectly plucked eyebrow and crossed her long, slender legs. 'Sounds interesting.'

'It is. It's all due to the Battle of the Bulge. They managed to surprise us then because we had no direct intelligence coming from inside Germany. We need that tactical intelligence to push on with the advance, but it's far too dangerous for foreign agents behind enemy lines. Which is why OSS came up with a plan to insert German prisoners of war instead.'

Jack exchanged a look with Marianne. 'How do we know we can trust them?'

'We don't. Not for certain. But we had little choice. This is it, the final invasion of Germany itself. The big finale. And, for you, an even bigger mission. We want you to identify and find those responsible for Nazi war crimes before they have a chance to escape.'

'And before the Soviets can get their hands on them?'

'Something like that.'

A silence fell, pregnant with so much that remained unsaid. They all knew that those war crimes included summary executions along with torture and other unspeakable acts that defied the Geneva Convention. Then there were the concentration camps like Auschwitz. Marianne swallowed. They might not like what they discovered about Maggie's fate, but they had to know.

'The German POWs will act as your frontline field operatives on the ground, gathering intelligence on who ordered and carried out the crimes as well as identifying them for you. You will train those POWs and ensure they don't betray us or any other Allied force.'

'What do we do with the war criminals when we find them?'

'You make sure you keep eyes on them so they don't leave Germany.'

'I thought you said it was too dangerous for agents like us?'

Suzanne smiled. 'I meant it was too dangerous for most agents. You're not most agents. Some of your colleagues are already working with OSS, but this mission is especially dangerous. You'll be heading straight into the lion's den. It's the only way we can end this war, by stealth as well as force.'

'My specialty,' said Christine. 'When do we start?'

'Right now. Go and pack. We leave for Lyon in one hour. All except you, Christine. I have another mission for you. You're going to Berlin.'

Her eyes shone. 'Berlin? Just my kind of place.'

'I thought it might be. I'll be briefing you separately. For now, you're all dismissed.'

As they stood to leave the room, Suzanne motioned to Marianne to wait.

'I thought you should know that Auschwitz has been liberated by the Russians.'

Marianne stared at her, hope flickering in her eyes. 'Any news of Maggie?'

Suzanne shook her head. 'Not yet. But the Red Cross are there now along with a British detachment. I'll let you know as soon as I hear anything. I thought we would keep this between ourselves for the moment so you can all focus on the mission.'

'Of course.'

The mission. Always the mission. But Auschwitz was liberated, which meant that maybe, just maybe, Maggie was free. If she was still alive.

Of course she was alive. She had to be. She was their Maggie. She wasn't allowed to die.

FIVE

He looked exactly as he had the first time I saw him – boots shining, white gloves immaculate as he flicked a finger to send one to the right, another to the left, all the time humming Wagner under his breath. He smiled as he did so, almost benevolent. He was smiling now, but I knew him better all these months later. Josef Mengele could smile as he offered candy to a child and seconds later inject that same child with phenol to the heart.

'Dr Bendel tells me you were his student at the University of Paris.'

'That's correct.'

'As you know, Dr Bendel assists Dr Epstein in running my research laboratory. I want you to help them. We need to speed things up.'

Of course they did, with the Red Army almost at the door. For weeks now they'd been destroying evidence, burning camp records and even some of the barracks. Rumour had it they were going to blow up the crematoria, although I'd believe it when I saw it. One thing that was certain was that Mengele would carry on with his ghastly work until the bitter end. Another thing I was sure of was that there was no way in hell I was helping him.

'T-That's a great honour,' I stuttered. 'But I don't believe I have the right experience or skills to be of any use in the laboratory.'

'Nonsense. Bendel tells me you were his star pupil. I understand that you were training to be a paediatrician.'

'I was.'

'Then you're perfect. You may have heard that I have a particular interest in twins. Most of the ones we get here are children. You understand their anatomy, their physiology.'

'I believe I can be of greater use by actually delivering those children as well as treating those who're sick. You... you want healthy specimens – let me get them for you.'

I could see his mind working as he began to hum under his breath. That same tune, from *Tristan and Isolde*. The one that accompanied his selections, sending most people to their deaths.

'You make a good point,' he said at length. 'I believe you delivered a healthy baby only yesterday. One with blue eyes.'

I stiffened, forcing myself not to touch the bruise on my face where the rifle butt had landed. I might be a prisoner doctor, but that meant nothing to the guards. They'd only stopped when the block Kapo, one of the good ones, shouted Mengele's name at them.

'I did. Although, as you know, all babies are born with blueish eyes.'

'True. Let me know if they stay blue.'

Now I had to suppress a shudder. Mengele's collection of blue eyes was infamous. He kept it in his office, a grisly selection of trophies from his experiments. And I was damned if he was adding little Leah's eyes to it. 'I will.'

'Very well. You may go.'

I had my hand on the door handle when he snapped, 'Wait.'

When I turned, he was smiling once more, his benign

expression at odds with his tone. 'The mother of this baby is still alive?'

'Yes. She was haemorrhaging, but we managed to stop it.'

'I understand she had twins before this one.'

I kept my face carefully composed. 'She did?'

'Yes. I have it here, in my notes, under her prisoner number. Twin boys. Three years old. They didn't yield anything of interest.'

I could feel the bile burning my throat, bitter. The boys weren't tattooed with their own numbers. They didn't get to live that long. I swallowed. 'Ah.'

'But yes, good that we keep her alive. She may provide some genetic clue for my research. I'll take some samples from her when she's fit enough.'

I nodded, unable to speak let alone protest.

'Off you go then. Check on that mother. Get her some extra rations. Keep me informed about the baby too.'

'Yes, of course, Dr Mengele.'

He wasn't worthy of the title, let alone my courtesy, but I had to play along, not least for Eva and little Leah. He could turn in a trice like a striking cobra. Better to keep him sweet at the same time as keeping them out of his reach. We did it with other prisoners, falsifying experiments so that they survived, and Mengele was none the wiser. A dangerous game, maybe but one that meant the difference between life and death, between the right and the left. And I would keep Eva and her baby alive, no matter what it took.

SIX

'It looks just like Auschwitz.'

I gazed up at the gates and the barbed wire. All that was missing was that damn sign: '*Arbeit macht frei.*'

'It might be better inside,' I said, although both Hanna and I knew that was unlikely. We were still on German soil, albeit in the area now occupied by the Western Allies. The mud might be different to the Polish mud, but it was still mud, and the buildings were depressingly similar to those we'd left behind.

'Did they say this was a German army barracks?' muttered Hanna.

'Yes.'

'Well, at least they treated their own soldiers like shit too.'

I couldn't help but laugh, although there was precious little to laugh about. We'd spent days on trains and trucks to get this far, rammed in with hundreds of others now that Auschwitz was liberated along with people fleeing the advancing Red Army, terrified by the tales of rape and murder that preceded them. They came from across Eastern Europe as well as from within Germany, those who'd been persecuted during the war as well as those who'd persecuted them. It was an unholy mix and a toxic one. Now we were here, at our destination, I could see that same mix all around me and feel the tension in the air. It didn't seem as if we'd come to a safe place at all, let alone one that would offer any more comfort than the camp we'd left behind.

As we passed through the gates, I cast wary glances at the men in uniform ticking names off lists and trying to instil some kind of order. I stiffened as one waved the woman ahead of me to the left, relaxing again as I realised he was simply sending her to her allotted barracks rather than to her death.

'Name?' He was looking at his clipboard rather than me.

'Marguerite Dubois. Dr Marguerite Dubois.'

A glance and then a pause as he referred again to his list, reading what appeared to be a note next to my name. I could feel my heart slowing too as I wondered what this meant.

'You're in there, Doctor,' he said, indicating what appeared to have been the officers' quarters, a more spacious and better-kept building to one side of the other barracks.

'The baby too,' he added, shooting another look at Leah strapped to my chest.

'What about my friend here?'

'Name?'

'Hanna Weber.'

'Yes, you're in there as well. The room next to Dr Dubois.'

Room? We had rooms? I wanted to shout aloud at this luxury. Instead, I smiled and thanked him, hustling Hanna with me towards the building he'd indicated before he could change his mind.

Inside, it was cheerless, the rooms cramped and sparse, but I didn't care. We had some small sanctuary in our own space.

I threw my knapsack down on the narrow bed, beside the cot someone had already set up for Leah. Thankfully they'd been organised enough to do that.

'Welcome home, sweetheart,' I said as I unstrapped her

from me and laid her carefully in it. 'Or at least home for now. I promise you we'll find something much better and very soon. Just as soon as I can contact London and let them know we're here.'

The trouble was, I had no idea how to do that. I had no radio crystals, no radio and no clue how to get in touch with my former comrades. All I could do was try to find someone who did or who could give me access to a radio. Until then, I was on my own. Except I wasn't because I had Leah to think about as well. We would both have to wait until I could reunite her with her father, with Antoine.

It was still so strange to think that, by a quirk of fate, I'd delivered his daughter. Every time I thought of her mother though, I felt a red-hot poker pierce my heart.

'I hope you're in a better place now, Eva,' I whispered as I tickled her daughter's tummy.

Leah gurgled at me, and I shook off my gloom to smile in return. She was such a good baby. Maybe we could start to recover a little here before the next stage of our journey.

'We're not staying long,' I said, wiggling her toes now. 'Just long enough to get some weight on you before you meet your papa.'

Those blue eyes sparkled at me, delighted to be seeing me face to face rather than endlessly strapped to my chest, although at least on the journey here I hadn't had to hide her under my coat. The other women had been kind, happy to see a baby, although I could also feel their pain. So many of them had lost their own infants, torn from them at birth in Auschwitz, drowned in buckets before they could even have a chance at life. Then there were those who'd survived selection but their children hadn't, herded off to take a shower from which they never returned. The unluckiest fell into the hands of Mengele.

At the mere thought of him, my heart shrivelled into a cold, hard ball of hate. Somehow, some day I would make him pay for what he'd done. But now wasn't that time. We still had to get out of Germany and to Paris. From there, I had to find a way to be reunited with my comrades. It was a long, arduous road ahead, but I was determined to take it and put the horrors of Auschwitz behind me.

A burst of shouting from the corridor outside my room interrupted my thoughts. Instinctively, I stiffened, my ears pricked, listening, waiting for a guard to burst in – or worse. And then I remembered where I was, slowly relaxing, the terror seeping away.

Someone knocked on my door, and I opened it to see Hanna standing there. Behind her, more women were carrying what meagre possessions they had into their rooms, almost all of them either older or with children.

'Look,' I said. 'They must have decided to put the most vulnerable in here.'

'Don't know what I'm doing here then.'

She smiled as she saw Leah happily staring at dust motes from her cot. 'Hello, sweetheart. Do you like it here?'

Leah cooed in response.

'Maybe he organised it. That British officer who helped rescue us. He put us on the transport after all. Captain Maclean.'

She was busy blowing pretend bubbles for Leah. 'Maybe.'

I could see him now, handing us our travel documents, a rare blast of sunlight turning his hair russet rather than chestnut brown, green eyes glinting as he looked at Leah and then me. 'Will you be alright?' he'd asked.

An irrational thought had flashed across my mind as I'd stared at the shaft of sunlight. If we had children, at least one would probably have red or auburn hair. It was a recessive gene, as far as I remembered, and we evidently both carried it.

I'd torn my eyes from his hair, aware that he was looking at me with a mixture of concern and something else, something I couldn't quite name. 'Yes, yes, of course we will, thank you. And thank you for everything you've done. You've been so very kind.'

'Not at all. It's my job to see that you're safe. Your transport will be escorted all the way to the camp so you'll be protected until you get there.'

He must have seen me flinch at the mention of the word 'camp' because he'd added, 'It's not like the one you've just come from. It won't be luxurious, but at least in there you'll be looked after as free citizens rather than caged up as prisoners.'

I wasn't too sure about that free part now. From what I'd already seen, those high fences and the guards were designed to keep us in as much as keep the enemy out. Yes, the Allies had captured this part of Germany, but that could still change at any moment. Hitler might be on the verge of doing so, but he hadn't quite lost this war yet.

I glanced at my watch, the one I'd been given as a camp prisoner doctor. It could never replace the one my parents had given me for my graduation, the one they'd torn from my wrist when I got to Auschwitz, but it would do. I sometimes looked at it and wondered from whose wrist it had been taken. Whoever it was, I wanted to do them proud.

I moved over to the window, another small luxury, and peered through it. It was set high so I had to stand on tiptoe, but I could see people milling around outside, some being directed into other barracks, others just loitering, wondering what to do.

'This place is chaotic,' I said.

'They only just requisitioned it,' said Hanna. 'Or at least that's what the woman in the room next to me said.'

'Then they need to get a grip. If they don't organise it properly, there'll be anarchy. I expect they don't even have an infirmary set up. So many people are already sick. This simply won't do.'

'Yes, but what are you going to do about it?'

'I'm going to go and see the camp commandant, that's what.'

Hanna looked at me, open-mouthed. 'He's not going to listen to you. We're basically prisoners here too.'

'Watch me.'

I flung on my coat again, pausing to splash water on my face from the basin in the room. The water was stone cold and the basin covered in stains, but it was another luxury compared to the facilities in Auschwitz. To have my own washbasin was unimaginable. But then, to be alive and out of there was unimaginable too. I'd never stopped believing it could happen even while a tiny part of me whispered it might not. I ignored that doubting voice now as I scraped my fingers through my hair and turned to Hanna.

'Will I do?'

'You'll more than do.'

'Look after Leah for me. And wish me luck.'

'You don't need it, but I will. You can do anything, Maggie. I've seen it so many times. I'm in awe of you, truly.'

Her sweet face was shining with sincerity, giving me the strength I needed.

I took a deep breath and pulled the door open, looking back to wave at the two of them before striding out of the block. I could see one of the guards with a clipboard directing yet more new arrivals.

'Where can I find the camp commandant?' I asked.

He ignored me.

'I asked you where the commandant is.'

'I know you did.'

'So where is he?'

'He's busy.'

'He's going to be even busier if I don't talk to him. Urgently. This place is a shambles. Do you even have an infirmary?'

He looked me up and down, his upper lip curling. 'You should be grateful you're even here.'

'And you should be grateful I'm trying to help. I'm a doctor. This camp will be overrun by disease within days unless you start checking and segregating these people. You need to make sure they don't have typhus before you put them in blocks together. That they're deloused.'

I was shaking with fury, not just at his expression but at the sheer stupidity of it all.

'Perhaps I can help,' said a voice behind me, a more cultured one. He stepped forward and I took in the stripes on his uniform along with the intelligence in his eyes. 'Captain Ross. Deputy camp commandant.'

'My name is Marguerite Dubois. Dr Marguerite Dubois. I've just come from Auschwitz where I worked in the prisoner hospital and I can promise you that unless you listen to me, you'll have a disaster on your hands.'

'I am listening to you, Dr Dubois, and I'm grateful for your advice. Maybe you'd like to accompany me to the commandant's office so we can discuss this in private?'

I fought back a surge of that familiar fear. *It's alright, Maggie. It's not a trick. These are the British.*

'I'd be delighted,' I said.

At that moment, I caught sight of the next person who moved to the head of the line to be processed. Was it? Could it be? I wasn't sure.

As I followed Captain Ross, my mind was whirring. I was pretty sure I recognised him – one of the Kapos who'd meted out such brutality to their fellow prisoners in Auschwitz, doing the bidding of the Nazis in return for food and favours. This one was worse than most, carrying out Mengele's orders as well as being a good friend of the female guard we called the Beast.

'Where's your friend now?' I muttered under my breath. No longer here to protect him. But revenge would have to wait. Right now, there was another camp to organise or more lives would be lost. Once we'd done that, I'd go looking for him. In the meantime, his face – and the faces of all the others – was etched on my soul.

SEVEN

30 DECEMBER 1944, AUSCHWITZ-BIRKENAU

'How's she doing?'

Dr Laba looked at me, his benign expression hiding the heart of a lion. Along with the other staff in the infirmary, he enabled a quiet but effective resistance to the Nazi rule.

'No change. The birth and the bleed took a lot out of her. She's stable but that's about all I can say. We've given her what we can.'

Thank goodness we had a decent supply of medication, most of it smuggled into the camp thanks to local women who acted as couriers. It was one of the reasons the hospital now saved lives rather than ending them.

'Mengele wants her kept alive. She's to have extra rations. We're to make sure her baby survives as well.'

Every word I said was loaded with meaning.

The doctor nodded, his eyes simmering with fury behind his round glasses, his voice still carefully neutral. While most of the staff in here were part of that resistance movement, there were still those who couldn't be trusted. 'I understand.'

I picked up Eva's wrist and felt for her pulse. It was weak but regular.

'Come on, Eva,' I murmured. 'I know you're a fighter.'

She moved her head slightly on the pillow, her lips working although no sound came out.

'Let her sleep,' said Dr Laba. 'God knows, she's been through enough. I'll call you if there's any change.'

'Thank you, Doctor. I'll go check on her baby.'

I hurried along to the nursery section, passing a couple of the orderlies I recognised along with a nurse I didn't. She was in SS uniform, her white apron pristine. 'Can I help you?'

A risk even to ask the question but her presence here sent a clutch of fear through my gut. The SS nurses generally kept to their own hospital, only accompanying the SS doctors when they came to inspect prisoner patients and select those that should be gassed. With the evacuations building up, more and more were being gassed rather than waste space on the transport.

She glanced at me as if I was a cockroach that had crawled out from under the floorboards, her lips pursed in annoyance, hair swept back from a pretty face that was soured by a scowl. 'No.'

'Very well,' I muttered. 'Have it your way.'

'What did you say?'

'I said I hope you find your way. Please do let me know if I can help.'

She stared at me, aquamarine eyes frigid. She had that bovine quality many of them possessed – an unquestioning cow-like acquiescence to men who snapped out orders and no doubt made other demands as well. Come to think of it, there was something about her that was familiar.

A memory swam to the surface. I'd seen her before, with Mengele, accompanying him on his rounds, standing primly a couple of feet behind him as he made his selections, yet again choosing those who would live or die. It struck me then that her gaze never shifted from him. An adoring gaze at that. I had heard the rumours. This must be her – the mistress. Apparently she was called Clara.

'Well, I'll be going.'

I turned and marched briskly along the corridor towards the nursery, all the while begging her in my head not to follow, to go in the other direction.

No such luck. I could hear her footsteps behind me as I tried to increase my speed.

'Wait,' she called out.

There was nothing for it but to stop and turn once more.

'There is something you can show me. A baby. Dr Mengele has asked me to inspect it.'

I choked back the words I wanted to spit out. 'A baby?'

'Yes. A new-born with blue eyes.'

'We have a few of those.'

She tutted. 'This one was born yesterday. You must know which one I mean.'

'I'm not sure. It's not really my department.'

'Surely you can direct me to the nursery section?'

I waved vaguely down the corridor. 'It's down there.'

'You are going that way. Show me.'

I gritted my teeth and forced a smile. 'Of course.'

As soon as we entered the nursery, I scanned the cots laid out in rows. Only two of them were occupied. Births had dropped off along with new inmates. The Nazis were busy emptying the place rather than filling it.

She glared at me. 'I thought you said you had a few?'

'We must have discharged some.'

I kept my eyes on her, forcing myself not to look at Leah, throwing the nursery nurse a look so she would keep quiet too. I'd known at once which one was Leah, the baby in the other cot far darker and even smaller.

The SS nurse strode over and stared down at that one. 'Wake it up so I can see its eyes.'

I wanted to slap her. Instead, I bent over the cot and gently stroked the baby's cheek. It was such a thin little cheek, far too gaunt for a new-born baby. But then, this child had been starved along with its mother and, by the look of things, would probably not last much longer, barely moving in response to my touch.

The nurse tutted again and reached into the cot, poking the baby in the stomach with her thumb. This time, the child let out a mewling cry, sounding more like a kitten than a human child. Still, its eyes stayed tight shut, scrunched up even more now in pain.

She forced one open, grunting as the baby began to properly howl.

'Not this one.'

She marched over to Leah's cot. I was hard on her heels and surreptitiously kicked the cot as we got there rather than have her lay a finger on Leah. Sure enough, the sudden movement startled Leah from sleep, and her eyes flew open. Like the other baby, they were blue-grey in the way of almost all new-borns, although hers were lighter.

Another grunt from the SS nurse. 'This must be the one. I have orders from Dr Mengele to check on her and make sure she's thriving until she's ready for him. I'll be back tomorrow to see how she is.'

My heart plummeted. 'Very good.'

'You will call me Nurse Clara.'

'Very good, Nurse Clara.'

So it was definitely her – Mengele's mistress.

The moment she was gone I would speak to the other doctors and nurses. Make sure Leah was protected as much as we were able. For now though, all I could do was smile politely into her cold, hard eyes and wish her dead with all my heart.

EIGHT

1 FEBRUARY 1945, DISPLACED PERSONS CAMP, GERMANY

The commandant's office was situated in a Nissen hut near the main gate. Captain Ross held the door open for me and then stepped smartly in to salute the man sitting behind a plain but serviceable desk covered in files and boxes of papers. For half a second I was back there, in Mengele's similarly crowded office. Then I shook off the momentary surge of revulsion. These were just lists of the people in the camp along with files on their logistical requirements. By the look of things, their needs were enormous.

'Major Nicholson, this is Dr Dubois.'

The major regarded me levelly from under bushy, greying eyebrows. 'What can I do for you, Doctor?'

I took a deep breath and plunged in. 'Major, I want to talk to you about the organisation of the camp, specifically to do with prevention of disease and medical provision.'

The major sighed. 'Dr Dubois, let me stop you there. We're doing the best we can in very difficult circumstances. We took over this camp two days ago and my men have worked day and night to get it ready for you people.'

I bridled at his 'you people', but this was no time to argue. 'I realise that, sir, but the thing is, this is urgent. If you put in place the measures I suggest right now, it will save you a lot of trouble later. As well as a lot of sick or dead people.'

His eyes narrowed, disappearing even further under those eyebrows. 'What do you mean?'

'I'm talking about typhus along with other diseases that spread in crowded conditions such as this. Dysentery for one. I've just come from Auschwitz, where I worked in the hospital. We managed to contain typhus outbreaks by implementing strict hygiene measures such as delousing inmates along with their accommodation. I believe we should do the same here.'

I didn't mention the other measures Mengele had taken at Auschwitz to deal with typhus, including gassing the occupants of an entire block before sterilising it and then moving in deloused prisoners, scrubbing down all the other blocks and repeating the exercise until the disease was under control.

'What are you suggesting? That we make people shower and disinfect their hair when they arrive?'

I gaped at him in horror before it struck me – he had no idea what had gone on in Auschwitz. Few people did. I knew that reports had got out, but the problem was that no one really believed them. If they had, they would have done something to help us in there. Or perhaps they didn't care. I was starting to believe that was the case.

'Sir, you can't ask people to shower the moment they get here, not if they've come from a camp like Auschwitz or any of the others that have been liberated.'

'Why not?'

I swallowed, my eyes darting to Captain Ross and then back to the major. 'In Auschwitz, people were routinely sent to the showers when they arrived. At least, that was what they were told. They were even given a bar of soap after they were ordered to strip naked and herded into the shower room. Only it wasn't a shower room at all but a gas chamber. Hundreds of thousands of people died in them. They had four, right next to the crematoria they used to burn their bodies afterwards.'

I could feel the silence that fell after I finished speaking. It pulsated as if I'd thrown a live grenade.

The major cleared his throat. 'I see.'

'But do you? Do you really, sir? Those people out there are all traumatised in one way or another, if not by being in a death camp, then by being forced to leave their homes and lives behind as they tried to escape this war. Some of them have been raped. Most have lost everyone they ever loved or knew. They're weak and tired and many are suicidal. The least you can do is make sure they have basic healthcare and that you do your best to stop them catching something that could kill them after all they've been through.'

I stopped dead, aware that my impassioned speech may have gone too far but not really caring. It was about time people knew what had been happening while they'd been waging their precious war.

I sensed the waves of sympathy coming from Captain Ross and the more measured response from the major. At length, he spoke.

'You make a good point, Dr Dubois. Actually, several. Perhaps you can suggest how we may set up these measures to ensure new arrivals do not contaminate others and that everyone stays as healthy as possible?'

I could feel the weight lifting from my chest. 'You'll do it? Really?'

'Dr Dubois, I may be a soldier, but I'm a human being too. I want to run a tight ship here, but I'm aware, thanks to you, that we may need to be more sensitive in our approach, especially as people continue to arrive from liberated camps. I welcome any suggestions you have that will help.'

I stared at him, speechless, and then gathered myself. 'What medical facilities do you have already?'

He spread his hands. 'They're very basic. We have a first aid room and an army doctor on standby. We can also call on the Red Cross, but they're very overstretched, as is everyone. We need all our resources for the front lines.'

'I understand, so why not use the expertise you already have here? I'm a doctor. My friend in the room next to me is a nurse. I'm sure there are other trained professionals among the residents.'

I forced myself not to call them inmates. This might look like yet another prison camp, but I was determined not to think of it like that.

'I'm sure there are, Dr Dubois, but how do we identify them?'

'Simple. You implement a system of daily assemblies where you call together everyone in the camp. You can then make important announcements as well as ask for volunteers with particular skills to turn this into a much better place for everyone. Just please don't turn them into roll calls. That was another thing they used to break people in Auschwitz.'

'Noted. What else do you need?'

'Somewhere to set up a proper infirmary. Medical supplies such as drugs and dressings. I can make you a list. Disinfectant and DDT for delousing, although we must be very sensitive about the way we use and refer to it.'

'Of course.'

'We also need things to help the people here recover from their trauma and move on with their lives. Books. Musical instruments. A space to run a school for the children. Somewhere for those children to play and other places where adults can socialise. Then, perhaps, they'll learn that they're not so different from one another after all.'

'These are all excellent suggestions. We can't implement them overnight, but we'll do our best – you have my word on that, Doctor.'

There was a new respect to his tone now, along with an appreciation in his eyes. He saw me not just as yet another refugee among thousands. In time, I hoped he and his men would see every single person here in the same way. Well, perhaps not every single one.

'There's one other problem that needs to be dealt with straight away. I recognised a man who I know worked as a Kapo in Auschwitz – a prisoner who aided the guards in running the block. This one was particularly cruel, beating up his fellow inmates as well as carrying out Dr Mengele's orders. There are others who did far worse. They must be held to account.'

The two officers exchanged a glance.

'Let me handle this,' said Captain Ross. 'I'll have a word and see what we can do.'

I had an inkling then that Ross wasn't all he seemed. He had that air about him, the same one my friends and fellow agents had. That I'd once had. The air of someone who was self-contained and yet on high alert at all times, ready to do what it took.

Major Nicholson tapped his pen on the sheet of paper where he'd been making notes of my requirements. 'Will that be all?'

'For now.'

'In that case, dismissed.'

He saluted me, and I automatically saluted back. So I hadn't forgotten everything then.

I turned to see Captain Ross looking at me with new inter-est. 'I'll escort you back to your quarters,' he said.

'We'll organise an assembly for 9 a.m. tomorrow morning,' Major Nicholson called after me.

'Thank you, sir.'

He harrumphed and made another note, his walrus mous-tache stretching upwards in the semblance of a smile. I left his office with a spring in my step.

'Well done,' said Captain Ross. 'You lived up to expectations.'

I faltered, my footsteps slowing as I looked sideways at him. 'What do you mean?'

'Your reputation preceded you, Dr Dubois. Captain Maclean said you were a remarkable woman, and he was right.'

'Captain Maclean? You know him?'

'Indeed I do.' He held the door open for me again. 'I'll be in touch, Dr Dubois.'

'Maggie. My name is Maggie.'

A salute. 'Maggie then. It's been a pleasure. *Au revoir.*'

'*Au revoir.*'

I watched from the doorway as he made his way back to Nicholson's office. Now there was an enigma. And one who knew Captain Maclean. The thought of him sent an unfamiliar sensation flooding through me, making my heart dance in anticipation.

Don't be an idiot, Maggie. You'll probably never see him again.

But somewhere deep down I knew I would.

NINE

'That nurse. The one who was here. She's Mengele's...'

'Yes. Yes, I understand.'

Dr Laba cast a glance at the guard who was standing at one end of the ward, watching. She was young and very pretty too, as Aryan as they come. Another one Mengele favoured although we all knew about her. We called her the Beast.

'What's she doing here?' I whispered.

'Looking for new victims.'

The Beast was only in her early twenties but already a supervisor, the highest rank for a female SS guard. Whatever she was trying to prove, it was never good.

I watched her out of the corner of my eye now as she strode between the beds, her feral eyes raking the faces of the female patients.

Just as she reached Eva's bed, Dr Laba made his move. 'Ah, Rapportführerin. I believe Dr Mengele was looking for you.'

Those bestial eyes lit up, ignited by Mengele's name. 'He was?'

'So I am informed. He was here not so long ago. Perhaps you can still find him.'

Without another word, she scurried off, eager for her mentor and erstwhile lover. The Beast liked nothing more than to carry out her selections once he was finished with his. No doubt she sniffed another opportunity to do so.

'Bravo,' I murmured.

'She'll be back,' he sighed. 'There's a meeting in the administrative office in ten minutes. Why don't you join us?'

I looked at him. A meeting in the administrative office meant a meeting of the resistance leaders. 'I would be delighted.'

'Excellent. Now look – your patient is awake.'

I spun round to see that Eva was trying to push herself up against her pillows. 'Lie still. You need to rest.'

'Where's my baby? Where's Leah?'

'She's asleep in the nursery. I saw her myself not ten minutes ago. She's absolutely fine, Eva but you must recover your strength, and that means complete bed rest.'

She glanced at the IV tube snaking out of her arm. 'What's this? What are you giving me?'

'Relax. It's to prevent infection and to keep you hydrated. It's all good, I promise.'

She eyed me warily, with the mistrust of someone who'd seen and endured too much in this hellhole. We all knew what the showers really were, the same as we all knew of Mengele's vile experiments. It might be a vast camp, but whispers spread fast, helped along by the resistance. Knowledge was power. The more we could spread, and the more we could get the word out to the wider world about what was actually happening in here, the better. The Russians might be advancing, but every day the Nazis kept us in here, subjected to their inhumanity, meant more lost to the gas chambers, the bullets and the lethal injections. The trouble was the world already knew. It just didn't care.

But we did. It was written across every face as we crammed

into the administrative office, the door shut to keep out prying ears, doctors, nurses, orderlies and administrators all gathered as one to work out what more we could do.

Dr Nowicka, one of the senior Polish doctors, opened the meeting. 'First, the good news. I'm happy to say that we've managed to get our last known Gestapo informant moved to other duties. This gives us more scope for resistance here in the hospital. We've also managed to speak to more of the German physicians, suggesting that they may wish to consider their prospects if Germany loses the war.'

'Not if. When.'

Dr Nowicka glanced at me. 'Indeed.'

'And what about the bad news?'

'As I'm sure you all know, five prisoners who attempted to escape were hanged this morning during roll call. Three of them were Austrian, two Polish.'

One of the nurses crossed herself. Another began to openly weep.

'Have we heard any more about the preparations to blow up the gas chambers?'

'Only that they're happening. We just don't know when.'

I flexed my fingers, aware that I'd been digging my nails into my palms. Only a couple of months before, the Sonderkommando who worked in those gas chambers removing the bodies and crushing their bones had revolted in one glorious outburst of defiance at the news the crematoria were to be blown up, taking their lives with them. Of course, their revolution had been crushed. Hundreds of them had died anyway, along with hundreds more innocent prisoners. What a wonderful sight it would be to see those gas chambers blown to the skies just as they'd belched the lives, hopes and dreams of so many into them.

'It's a new year in two days – 1945,' I said, half to myself. 'We've been at war for six years. Surely we're near the end now.

You can see it here. Feel it. All these things we've been talking about. The Nazis are running scared. Isn't it time we tried for a bigger revolt? One where we all break out of here?'

My words fell into a pool of silence, the ripples from them spreading through the room as people either sat, seemingly transfixed, or shifted in their seats.

'It's too dangerous,' said a man sitting opposite me. 'We've evaluated the risks many times. Look how many have died trying to escape. Think about those five hanged only this morning.'

'Yes, but things are different now. The ones they hanged tried to escape months ago. They only hanged them now because the Soviets are so close and the Germans know it. They want to make sure we keep quiet while they scramble to conceal their crimes. That means they're not keeping such a close eye on us. If there was ever a time for a mass breakout, it's now.'

My face was flushed with the heat of my words and the passion behind them. I could feel it, the warmth flooding my skin, clashing no doubt with what remained of my hair. I didn't care.

'That's precisely why it will fail,' said the same man, his accent marking him as maybe Czech or Polish. 'We are the living evidence of their crimes. At least for now. If we break out and give testimony, everything is lost for the Nazis. They would gun us all down rather than let that happen.'

He had a point.

'They might do that anyway,' I said. 'They're already executing those they consider surplus to requirements. What are they going to do with the rest of us other than take us somewhere else? Somewhere that could be even worse than here. Our biggest chances are when they blow up those crematoria and when they evacuate those of us that are left.'

'Why do you say that?'

'Because that's when their normal routine changes. The

Germans love routine. Disrupt it and they don't cope so well. Both situations create chaos. We can take advantage of that.'

I could sense them all hanging on my words now, listening hard.

'We can only plan that if we know when either or both events will take place.'

I looked at him, at his earnest, clever face. He was one of the doctors I'd seen in passing, I was pretty sure of that. 'We can start now. Plan for every eventuality. Then, when we know for sure they're about to blow up those crematoria or march us out of here, we know exactly what to do.'

'What about the other prisoners? There are around seventy thousand of us. How are you going to let them know about these plans?'

'We don't. Not until the last moment. What we do is identify a trusted prisoner in each block and warn them to be ready. Then we alert them to organise their block as we give them the final plan.'

'It will take a lot of organising.'

'It's better than dying.'

'True.'

He looked at the group, then at Dr Nowicka. 'I say we give it a go. Let's plan one final revolt.'

Then he looked at me and our eyes held, saying more than words ever could. Here was a comrade in arms. A like-minded thinker. Maybe we really could get out of here. Or at least die nobly in the attempt.

TEN

'There's someone here to see you.'

I looked at the guard. Over his shoulder I could see yet more people carrying bags and bundles of clothing. Since Auschwitz had been liberated, there were new arrivals every day. The camp was becoming overcrowded, those arriving the weakest who'd been left behind, now even sicker, some starved beyond repair. The new infirmary I was standing in was already over-run, although there was little we could do apart from give them a bed to rest in, fluids and basic medicines. At least we had those now, although getting supplies was frustratingly slow. That went for food too, which was still not sufficient for our needs.

'Who?'

'Never you mind. You must come to the commandant's office now.'

The man was surly, his manner abrupt. But he wasn't going to shoot me on a whim or march me off to the showers like the Nazi guards, and for that I was thankful.

I looked down at Leah again, gurgling on the mat we'd laid out for her on the floor, her face pink where it had been ghostly pale when we got here, her vital signs now strong and healthy. I had also regained some strength, in spite of the meagre rations. I was lucky – I'd only been in Auschwitz for five months and, thanks to my work in the hospital, I hadn't become a walking skeleton like so many others.

I handed my stethoscope to Hanna, one of the few items of equipment we had, and followed the guard across the camp, feeling a brief burst of early spring sun on my face, nodding at my fellow inmates along the way, clad now in proper clothes and shoes donated by the Red Cross. I could see one of the women reading aloud to a group of children through the window of another hut we'd designated the schoolroom, and hear someone else playing a violin, the sweet notes rising above the harshness of our surroundings. We were coming back to life slowly but surely, although the wounds sustained inside and out would take longer to heal.

'Hurry up,' the guard snapped as I paused to smile at the children. 'The commandant is waiting.'

I shot him a look. We might have been liberated, but we were not yet free.

'Marguerite Dubois, sir,' he announced, opening the door and saluting.

'That's Dr Dubois to you,' I said, walking briskly through the door. I caught sight of the figure standing by the commandant's desk and stopped in my tracks.

'It's you,' I gasped.

Captain Maclean smiled. 'Good to see you too.'

'I didn't mean...'

The commandant cut across my fumbled words. 'Captain Maclean is here to invite you and some of the other ladies to a dance.'

I stared at him, dumbfounded. 'A dance?'

'Yes, a dance this evening at our barracks. We're stationed nearby but we're not allowed to fraternise with the local women. We thought perhaps you and your friends would give us the pleasure of your company.'

'Why? You think we're easier than the local women?'

It came out harsher than I'd intended, but the long months in Auschwitz had eroded any social pretence I'd once had. I no longer had the patience or the will to please or placate, unless it was for a patient. Even then, I relied on my medical skills, saying little. The truth was that I'd run out of words for what I'd witnessed, what we'd been through. And now here was this man asking us to come to a dance. It was so absurd that I laughed.

'Not at all,' he said. 'I – we – just thought you could do with some fun for an evening. I can assure you that my men will treat you ladies with the utmost respect. Many of them haven't seen their sisters or sweethearts for years. It would be wonderful to have some female companionship and conversation.'

Instantly, I felt ashamed. He was so patently sincere, and he was, after all, one of the men who'd saved us. He was also, truth be told, rather handsome with those sage-green eyes that smiled at me from his strong and yet tender face. It was a face I wanted to touch, my fingers longing to run over the dimples in his cheeks, his jaw.

What on earth was I thinking?

A pang of guilt jolted through me. But along with the guilt was an urge to do something so normal. So innocent. Where so many others had died, I now had the chance to... dance? The ache would always live with me, but I knew life had to go on. I had to go on.

'Very well. I'll ask the others. What time does this dance start?'

'The dancing starts at eight o'clock in the village hall, but we'd be honoured if you'd be our guests for dinner beforehand. I could send transport to pick you up at six. Major Nicholson here has graciously agreed to lift the curfew just for tonight.'

Dinner. Proper food rather than the slop doled out in the mess hut.

I returned his smile. 'I'll go and tell the other women,' I said. 'How many of us can come?'

'As many as wish to. We wouldn't want to leave anyone out.'

He was trying so hard – I could see that. I could also hear the nervousness in his voice.

'That's very kind of you,' I said. 'I'm sure many of us would love to come.'

His face lit up. 'Really? Then I look forward to seeing you later.'

It may have been my imagination, but he seemed to put some emphasis on that 'you'.

I walked back across the camp in a daze. They were never going to believe this.

As it turned out, they did, which was why forty of us were ready and waiting when the transport arrived, dressed in the finest outfits we could muster, women lending each other a lipstick here or a necklace there, the excited chatter more of a tonic than any medicine I could provide.

'I'm going to dance their socks off,' declared Hanna, stretching out a leg to admire the high-heeled shoes she'd snaffled from the Red Cross store. Mine, too, were three-inch high block heels, black in contrast with the deep green dress I'd found. Hanna had insisted I apply lipstick, expertly making sure my smile was as bright as hers.

I ran my hand through my hair, trying to ruffle up my curls. It was still too short to twist into any kind of style. Too bad. I would simply smile all the wider.

I felt a ripple of excitement run through me. *It's just a dance*, I told myself. A bit of fun, as he'd called it.

Ah yes. Captain Maclean – our saviour. I could see him now, standing outside the village hall, ready to greet us as we hopped down from the truck, aided by the soldiers offering helping hands.

His eyes took in my dress, my heels, the lipstick. 'Good evening. Thank you for coming.'

'Thank you for inviting us.'

All at once, I was swept with a rush of shyness. Where was my charm when I needed it?

I felt Hanna tug at my hand. 'Come on, Maggie. Let's join the party.'

As we burst through the doors, I stopped dead. There, laid out on trestle tables, was a feast, or as much of one as they could muster, given their rations. And it looked as if they had given us all their rations, seeing the plates piled high with food. I stared at the tureen of stew in the centre of the table as if I'd never seen one before.

'May I have some of that?' I asked the soldier standing ready to serve us.

'Of course.'

He ladled out chunks of meat along with carrots, potatoes and what smelled like gravy from heaven. Never mind the odd lump of gristle – this was food from the gods. I could feel it sticking to my ribs, filling up my stomach, still shrunken from the months of starvation.

'Oh my God,' I mumbled. 'This is so, so good.'

Beside me, Hanna silently shovelled in her stew, concentrating fiercely until every morsel on her plate had disappeared.

'Would you like some more?'

It was the young soldier who'd served us, bringing around second helpings to the table where we sat.

Hanna looked at me, then at him in disbelief. 'There's more?'

'Eat as much as you like.'

I glanced up to see Captain Maclean also making his way round the tables, offering extra potatoes to go with the stew.

Tears sprang to my eyes. I quickly bent my head to my plate again.

'Maggie?'

'Ah, yes. Yes please,' I whispered, looking round to make sure that there really was enough for all, that this wasn't some kind of mirage.

'Is that enough?'

I stared at my plate once more, now magically refilled with stew, a neat pile of potatoes steaming beside it. As I did so, my appetite disappeared. There were people still starving out there in camps along with the corpses of those who'd starved to death. While I was here, gorging myself.

'I'll never be able to dance after this,' I said, feeling just as bad at leaving it.

'That's to give you the energy to dance all night.'

He hesitated, as if there was something more he wanted to say but all he did was give me a little nod and a half-smile. I gazed after him as he carried on serving the others, my wit apparently having deserted me.

Hanna nudged me and giggled. 'He likes you, that one.'

'Don't be ridiculous.'

Still, when they cleared away the tables and the band struck up, I was disappointed when Captain Maclean didn't materialise. Instead, a subordinate stood before me.

'The captain wonders if you would like to dance.'

It seemed I wasn't the only one who was lost for words.

'Does he now? Tell the captain to ask me himself. I don't dance by proxy.'

Thirty seconds later, Captain Maclean was by my side, his face flushed in embarrassment.

'You must think me an awful coward.'

'Not at all. Or at least not now you've turned up.'

'So would you give me the honour of this dance?'

'If you insist.'

'I do.'

He laced his arm around my waist, taking my hand with the other, guiding me in the unfamiliar steps.

'This is the St Bernard's Waltz,' he explained. 'It's a traditional ceilidh dance.'

'Ceilidh?'

'It means a social gathering. We're a Scottish regiment so the band is playing traditional Scottish ceilidh tunes.'

As we whirled together around the room, I could feel the awkwardness between us melting away.

'Thank you for organising this,' I said. 'You don't know what it means to these women.'

'I hope it means something to you too.'

There was a twinkle in his eye now, a hint of a teasing note in his voice.

'Oh, well, I love to dance.'

'Is that all? I hoped you might enjoy the company as well.'

I loved the way he spoke, so properly.

'Are you Scottish too?' I asked. 'You don't sound it.'

He laughed. 'I was born in India, educated in England, but my parents are Scottish. How about you?'

'I'm French, though my mother is half-English. I was born in Normandy and training to be a doctor in Paris when the war broke out.'

'Why did they send you to the camp?'

I bit my lip. The war wasn't quite over yet. He might be a British soldier, but I lived by the code that had kept many of us alive. *Say as little as possible.*

'I'm sorry. That was idiotic of me,' he added, seeing my face. 'Forgive me?'

'There's nothing to forgive. I was caught sabotaging railway lines.'

He looked at me more closely. 'You were with the Resistance?'

'Something like that.'

'Well, good for you.'

'No more questions. Let's just dance.'

And so we did, on through the evening. Never mind the first dance, I gave him all my dances. No one dared cut in on the captain.

Over his shoulder, I could see Hanna laughing up into a soldier's face, as carefree as any young girl. Which was what we were of course. It was just so hard to remember that sometimes.

'Your friend looks to be having a good time,' he said.

'Hanna? I think she is. You know, you haven't told me your first name.'

A flash of a memory – the forest, him asking me my name, my response. I felt a rush of shame. He hadn't deserved that. This time I would keep it light.

'I thought you said no more questions?'

'Very funny.'

'Jamie. My first name is Jamie.'

'Jamie? Is that short for James?'

'Yes. But only my mother calls me that!'

'Then I'll make sure I never do.'

'And you're Marguerite?'

'Maggie. Everyone calls me Maggie. Including my mother.'

He drew me to one side, off the dance floor, handing me a glass from the makeshift bar.

'A wee dram,' he said.

'A what?'

'Try it. It's whisky.'

I took a gulp. Then another, feeling it sear the back of my throat, bringing tears to my eyes.

Jamie laughed. 'Not so fast. This is a Macallan. My favourite. You're supposed to sip it.'

'Or light fires with it,' I muttered.

'She'd like you,' he said. 'My mother.'

'I'm not sure if that's a compliment or not.'

He threw back his head and laughed. 'Trust me, it is. My mother is from Glasgow. They don't suffer fools gladly there.'

'Well, I'm no fool.'

'I can see that.'

He clinked his glass against mine, and somewhere within me, I heard an answering echo. The first note, perhaps, of happiness. A sound I'd thought I might never hear again.

ELEVEN

He caught up with me as I was leaving the meeting. 'My name is Aleksandr,' he said, extending his hand. 'But everyone calls me Aleks.'

'Maggie.'

Names, not numbers. A tiny spark of humanity.

'You're a doctor here?'

'Yes.'

'I've seen you around.'

He had the Slavic eyes and fine bone structure I'd observed in so many Poles around the camp. But there was something different about him – an air of complete self-assurance coupled with a quiet but palpable courage. He reminded me of my older brother, so much so it hurt to look at him.

'I've seen you too.'

The others were milling around us now, heading off to their various wards or offices. Meetings had to be short and sharp in case the Nazis realised we weren't just discussing the everyday business of the hospital. The last Gestapo informer might have been weaselled out, but there were always more where he'd come from.

'Where can I find you?'

'Mostly with the women and children. My specialties are obstetrics and paediatrics.'

'Mengele tapped you up yet?'

'Only this morning.'

'That figures. He wants to get what he calls his research done before the Soviets come knocking.'

'What do you call it?'

'Murder.'

'Me too.'

A tacit understanding passed between us along with something more. Solidarity.

'We need to do this,' I whispered.

'We do.'

'Maybe we could talk some more? I'm going to the nursery now, to check on one of my patients, but I'll be free later.'

'Why don't we meet in the dispensary? Shall we say in one hour?'

I smiled. 'See you there.'

As I made my way to the nursery, I realised it was the first real smile I'd managed in months.

The moment I entered the room and scanned the cots, my smile vanished. 'Where is she?'

'They came about thirty minutes ago and took her.'

While I was in the meeting. 'Who took her exactly?'

'That nurse who was here earlier along with another woman.'

Nurse Clara. 'Oh my God.'

Mengele's willing accomplice had Leah and there was nothing I could do. I stared at her empty cot as if I could find some inspiration there, looking up at the nursery nurse again as she let out a tiny gasp.

'Are you looking for someone?'

I whipped round to see Mengele smiling broadly at me.

Beside him, Nurse Clara was holding Leah in her arms. It took everything I had not to run over and snatch her back. Instead, I waited, watching as she marched over to her cot and dumped her back in it none too gently. Of course, Leah let out a lusty cry, her fists flailing.

'She's a strong one, that one.' Mengele smirked. 'She'll be excellent for my research.'

I could taste the vomit in my mouth again, sour. I clenched my teeth to keep it from spewing out.

'Not quite ready yet though,' Mengele went on as if he were discussing a prize lamb being readied for slaughter. 'Another week or so when we can be sure about her eye colour.'

'Of course,' I muttered.

Nurse Clara shot me an evil look. Mengele made a tiny motion with his finger that signalled she should follow him as he turned on his heel and departed without another word.

I held in my breath until I was absolutely sure they were gone and then let it out in one, anguished groan. Another week. Maybe two. That was all we had.

I pulled back Leah's blanket, making sure she was alright, before tucking it back tight around her.

'Keep a close eye on her,' I said to the nursery nurse. 'Call me if she seems any different. I have to go to the dispensary.'

I glanced at the other baby as I left, lying completely still. I bent over that cot too, feeling for a pulse, observing the child's breathing, then pulled back the blanket. Another girl, her nappy soiled and hanging off her. I palpated her stomach – it was distended and hard.

'Change this child,' I said to the nurse. 'And make sure you wash your hands between touching her and the other one.'

I didn't want her to know how much Leah meant to me. It surprised me how much she did. The staff in here might want to be considered trusted colleagues, but I preferred to stick to what

I'd learned the hard way. Trust no one. Not fully. Not even someone like Aleks.

I thought of him now as I hurried to the dispensary. Beyond the barbed wire and blazing searchlights, out there in the world where people still fought for peace, we might have fought along-side one another or at least in the same way. I could smell it about him, that same sense I got from my friends and comrades.

Marianne's face flashed before me, along with Juliette's and Antoine's. My colleagues in the Resistance and SOE. What were they doing now? Still fighting, I hoped. Doing everything they could to sabotage the Germans and win this war.

He was waiting for me in the dispensary, chatting to the pharmacist who was studying his prescription chits.

'Got any farming done?' he asked.

The pharmacist smiled. 'Plenty.'

It was the camp farm detail who helped smuggle medicines into the camp, collecting them from the animal feed troughs and hay bales where the local resistance concealed them. Other medicines were plundered from the SS hospital or sent concealed in parcels addressed to fictitious or dead prisoners which were intercepted by inmates working in the parcel room. The pharmacy shelves now had decent stocks, but it was those that were hidden or pulverised on arrival that were especially important. It was how I managed to ensure Eva had the right antibiotics to counteract any infection that would have killed her, although the faster she recovered, the sooner Mengele would get his hands on her too.

'Are you alright, Doctor? You look a little distracted.'

I shook off my thoughts, flashing another smile at Aleks. 'I'm both, thank you.'

'Well, let me distract you a little further. There's a patient I want to discuss with you, if I can take a few moments of your time?'

'Of course.'

I could sense the pharmacist watching us, listening to every word. Another of his colleagues joined him, waving a piece of paper which he handed to Aleks. 'Your test results.'

'Thank you. Were they as expected?'

'Absolutely.'

I had no doubt that meant they were falsified to protect a patient and potentially save their life.

'Come,' said Aleks. 'We can talk in here.'

He took my arm and guided me towards a small room off the pharmacy, barely more than a cupboard, its walls lined with shelves which held yet more stock. I perched on the stool that was used to reach the higher shelves while he sat on a crate. Once the door was closed, only the pharmacists would know we were in here. I glanced at it now.

'Don't worry,' he said. 'They'll make sure no one disturbs us. They're good folk, the pharmacists. People like us.'

'What do you mean by that?'

'I mean that they resist in any way they can while protecting and preserving the life of the patients.'

'Is that what you do too?'

'Yes, and I'm sure I can say the same for you.'

All of a sudden, I couldn't breathe. This place, the horrors we'd seen. Trying always to fight back. To remain human. It was all too much.

'Are you alright?'

'I – yes. No.'

'Here,' he said, pulling a flask from his pocket. 'I carry this with me for emergencies. Take a sip.'

I gulped down a little. It tasted like rough cognac, razing my tongue and making me splutter.

He laughed. 'Don't worry. It's good stuff. The couriers send it in along with the medicine. Home-made and very potent. You look as if you could do with it.'

I wiped my hand across my mouth. 'Thanks.'

'Let's face it, we all look as if we could do with it.'

'That's true.' Except that, in his case, he'd somehow managed to keep the fire alight behind his eyes. This was a man who would go down in flames, still fighting, although I hoped he never had to.

'What are you thinking?'

'Me? Nothing. Nothing important. Now, what was it you wanted to talk to me about?'

He sat straighter, pulling back from where he'd been leaning towards me, his elbows resting on his knees. 'Ah yes. The crematoria. Plans.'

'Do you have one?'

'Not yet but you got me thinking in there, at that meeting. Why do you think it's one of our best opportunities?'

'Think about it. The crematoria are all situated on the edge of the camp, next to the woods and fields beyond. We know that they plan to blow them up. They've already dismantled part of them, and they got prisoners to do that. We have all kinds of experts in here including engineers. I know a fair deal about explosives, but I'm sure there are others who know more.'

'Go on.'

'I'm also sure that they'll get prisoners to blow up the crematoria too, or at least do the donkey work. During the Sonderkommando revolt, they used gunpowder that some of the women had smuggled out of the munitions factory. That's too risky now, but it got me thinking. What if we get the same locals who help smuggle in medicines to also drop off the components we need to make extra explosives? Explosives we can use to blow holes in the fence at the same time as they blow the crematoria.'

He was looking at me as if I'd lost my senses. Perhaps I had. Then I saw his mind start to churn, turning over the possibilities.

'It's a crazy idea but it might just work. Although you realise we can't possibly get everyone out of the camp? There are just

too many. We would have to choose perhaps a few hundred at
most.'

I swallowed. 'I know. I suppose, in my dreams, I'd like to
save everyone.'

'In my dreams too, Maggie, but it's not going to happen.
This, however, could. Let me talk to my pharmacist friends out
there and find out when the farm detail is next making a drop.
We need to talk to them so they can get a message to the locals. I
will also speak to one of my patients. He's an engineer, and he'll
know of others.'

'If we can get hold of plastic explosives, we can stick them
as close to the fence as we can. They're more stable. Otherwise,
we'll have to use dynamite or TNT. Then we need detonators
or at least the parts for them. Anything those women smuggled
out for the Sonderkommandos was used or destroyed.'

His eyes sharpened. 'Where did you learn all this about
explosives?'

I pointed to my red political prisoner triangle with the F
stamped on it. 'Where do you think?'

'The French Resistance?'

'Something like that.'

'Well, wherever you learned it, I'm impressed. I'm
impressed by you too, Maggie. You're an amazing woman.'

Tears pricked my eyes as I tried to swallow the lump in my
throat. His words were raw. Real. I could hear the sincerity
behind them. 'Thank you.'

'I mean it.'

'I know.'

Something was forming between us, something more than a
pact. As one, we rose to go about our business, Aleks holding the
door for me. As I passed him, I felt it again, that sense we were
almost the same person, comrades in arms prepared to fight to
the death. Whoever and whatever Aleks was, we were made of
the same stuff.

TWELVE

'I want to ask you something. A favour.'

It was a week after the dance and somehow Jamie had contrived to see me every day. At first it was a polite check to make sure we'd enjoyed ourselves. Then his men appeared with extra sacks of potatoes they'd set aside for the camp. After that, a suggestion we might take a walk, albeit in the snow. It was a very different walk from the one I'd taken only a month earlier.

Now here we were, standing outside the infirmary he'd asked to inspect to see if he could help with more supplies. In reality, it was little more than a hut we'd transformed as best we could, dividing it up so that infectious cases were at one end, in a separate area, while others were in old but serviceable beds at the opposite end, the whole separated by a nursing station with an outpatient clinic operating in another, smaller hut behind.

I held my breath, hesitating before I went on. My gut was telling me I could trust him, but my stomach still lurched as I framed my request. I had no idea where the others were or if I was somehow betraying them by trying to get in touch, but there was nothing else I could do. It was now or never.

'Anything.' He smiled. 'Anything that I can do to help.'

I looked around. There was no one else within twenty yards. People preferred to keep their distance from the infirmary hut unless absolutely necessary, fearful of what they might catch, especially the typhus that had run rampant through the camps.

'I need you to get a message to someone in London.'

'A friend?'

'In a way. More like family.'

He looked at me intently. 'Someone you worked with?'

'Yes. In France.'

We might be on liberated soil, but I was keenly aware that we were still in Germany. Eyes and ears were everywhere, even in a place like this, but it was a risk I had to take. If anyone could get a message to them, it was this man.

'I'll do my best,' said Jamie. 'What do you want me to say?'

'That I'm alive. That I'm here and I want to rejoin them, but first I need to deliver something to a colleague in France. I need their help to do that.'

'Something?'

'Someone. Would you like to meet her properly?'

Curious now, he followed me into the hut and through to the nursery we'd created, a separate room that held three cots also supplied by the Red Cross. One was empty, the baby who'd occupied it succumbing to pneumonia in spite of our best efforts. I went over to Leah's and lifted her out, cradling her in my arms. She was safer in here than in our room during the day, where there was always someone to keep an eye on her.

'She's beautiful,' said Jamie. 'Is this the baby you had strapped to you when we rescued you?'

'It is.'

'She looks so much better. Is she yours?'

'No. Her mother died in Auschwitz. She asked me to take Leah to her father who was – is – a colleague of mine.'

'May I?' He held out his arms.

I passed her to him, noting the way he cradled her head, supporting it as he rocked her.

'You've done this before.'

'We're Catholic. I have hundreds of cousins. I've held babies all my life. She's so tiny. How old is she?'

'Nearly two months. She was born on the twenty-ninth of December.'

'Not even three weeks old when you were on that march. It's a miracle she survived. That's thanks to you, Maggie.'

'You'd have done the same.'

'I'm not a doctor. I don't have your skills or, I suspect, your courage.'

Leah sighed softly, content in his arms. I looked at him, at this gentle warrior, holding that tiny baby as if she were made of glass. Yet I knew those same arms could haul a gun through a Polish forest and use it to kill Nazi guards without hesitation. He was an enigma, my Jamie. Ruthless and yet compassionate. Tough when he had to be. Strong enough to show his feelings. I could see them now, in his eyes, in the way he looked at me.

My Jamie. What was I thinking? If there was one thing I'd learned in Auschwitz it was to guard my feelings. To go it alone. To never care too much about anyone in case they weren't there the next day or even the next moment. Or in case I wasn't there. I would carry the guilt for leaving Eva and Anna there to my grave.

'She needs feeding,' I said, handing him the bottle.

He looked at me, obviously taken aback at the sudden coolness of my tone. Still, he didn't hesitate, holding it to her lips, encouraging her to suckle. Once she was feeding, her small, sucking sounds only matched by her fierce concentration, he looked at me again, more warily this time.

'You have to deliver her to France?'

'I promised her mother that I would take her there, to her

father. My colleagues in London will know where he is. Leah is all he has left.'

'Does he know that?'

I shook my head. 'The last time he saw his family was just before they were taken. Their other two children were twins. Dr Mengele used them in his experiments.'

'Who is Dr Mengele?'

Of course. It was easy to assume that everyone knew about him when, in fact, no one did save the Nazis.

'One of the senior SS doctors. He has a special interest in what he calls research although there's no scientific basis to it that I could see. He especially loves to experiment on twins. What he calls experiments, anyone else would call torture and murder.'

'And he did that to your friend's children?'

'Yes. I saw the notes of what he did. I'll never be able to forget what I saw. He also experimented on their mother, Eva, who was already very sick from Leah's birth. I had to leave her behind, knowing she was dying.'

'Dear God, Maggie, I'm so sorry.'

He took a step towards me, and I instinctively backed away. I saw a shadow flit across his eyes, but I couldn't help myself. 'I don't need your pity.'

'It's not pity. Alright, part of it is. But I am deeply sorry that happened to you, to your friend's family and to everyone else he hurt. He sounds like a monster.'

'He is. And I'll tell the world all about it, I can promise you. I'll find him, whatever it takes. He took his precious notes with him when he left Auschwitz. I'll find those too.'

Jamie stood, keeping a careful distance, as my heart raced, resounding round my head. I hated myself at that moment perhaps even more than I hated Mengele.

He held out Leah to me. 'Here, Maggie. Take her. You need

to hold her for a moment. You're safe now, both of you, and I'll do what I can to help you get her to her father.'

I looked at him through the tears that were dappling my vision, seeing him as if through a prism. 'Thank you.'

'No need to thank me. I'll get a message to London today even if it means I might be losing your company.'

I managed a watery smile. 'No great loss.'

'On the contrary, Maggie. I think it will break my heart.'

I dropped my head and buried it in Leah's shawl. It would break my heart too if I let it. And that was the last thing I was going to do.

THIRTEEN

1 JANUARY 1945, AUSCHWITZ-BIRKENAU

The ward was quiet, the patients unconscious or sleeping. I glanced at the clock on the wall – 12.02 a.m.

'It's a new year, Eva. A new beginning,' I whispered. She was breathing more evenly but was still very weak. Every day she remained in here gave her a better chance of survival than out there, in the main camp, but it also kept her in the sights of Mengele.

I heard a whisper in my ear. 'Happy New Year.'

'Aleks. You startled me.'

'I'm sorry. Come – let's talk.'

He beckoned to me to follow him into the corridor and from there into the ante room that served as a linen cupboard, if you could call it that. The thin blankets scarcely kept out the cold, and the sheets were rough and worn, but we did our best, piling them on patients and keeping them clean. I could smell the laundry soap now. Such a normal smell. One that reminded me of other hospitals. Of home. Of a life beyond electrified fences patrolled by dogs and guards.

'You have some news for me?'

'I spoke to the leader of the farm detail. They have an engineer on their crew as well as a couple of men who are Cichociemni.'

The elite Polish soldiers and airmen who'd trained with SOE, forming their own unit.

'Cichociemni? They built the tower we used for parachute training. We weren't allowed to get to know them or their code names, but they seemed to be excellent fighting men.'

'They are some of Poland's best, and they learned sabotage techniques from your SOE too. These guys are perfect for what we're planning. They're going to make a list of what they need and get it out to the local resistance just as they do with the medicines.'

'I hope they're careful.'

'They've never failed yet, and they encrypt all their lists, so don't worry. They're going to conduct discreet reconnaissance of the area and especially the fences. We want to make sure they'll blow apart at the same time as the crematoria, so we need to be precise with the position of the explosives. We also need to ensure we blow them wide enough to get as many people as we can through at the same time. My patient in here also knows some others who can help. It looks as if we can make this plan work.'

'God, I hope so. It relies on so much luck. We don't even know yet when they plan to blow up the crematoria.'

'That's a problem but one the resistance in here is working on. The Gestapo aren't the only ones who have spies.'

His voice was surer now, ringing with certainty. I held a finger to my lips. 'Did you hear that?' I whispered. 'Footsteps.'

We waited, listening.

Silence. Then the sound of someone walking away, treading slowly and carefully. I wrenched the door open, sticking my head out into the corridor just in time to see one of the orderlies disappearing around the corner. I raced after him, not caring what noise I made, with Aleks hard on my heels.

I caught up with the orderly as he was about to exit the building. 'Where are you going?' I demanded.

He gaped at me. 'Back to my block. My shift is over.'

'If you're on night duty, your shift runs until dawn.'

'My shift has already overrun. I was supposed to finish at 10 p.m. but no one came to relieve me.'

'I see.'

I was panting, my breath coming in short gasps. I took a deeper one, steadying myself, trying to appear more in control. The man was now regarding me with something approaching suspicion.

'Don't worry,' said Aleks. 'We've just been trying to save a patient and the doctor here thought you might be someone else, if you get my meaning. Someone a little less sympathetic.'

The orderly's face cleared. 'Ah, yes. I do. Luckily, I am not.'

'Luckily, you're not so we'll bid you goodnight. And a happy New Year.'

'Happy New Year to you too although let's be honest, it's unlikely.'

The man sloped off, the picture of exhaustion. Although we had it better here in the hospital than most, it was still gruelling work. Especially when every day we had to protect the patients from the SS and men like Mengele. When we talked about trying to save a patient, everyone knew that meant from the clutches of people like them. The falsified test results, diagnoses and even treatments were all designed to keep the Nazis at bay, but we couldn't do that forever. We needed to do something more.

'We have to make this plan work, whatever happens,' I murmured as the door swung shut behind the departing orderly.

'We will, Maggie, we will.'

I wished I could be as certain.

FOURTEEN

22 FEBRUARY 1945, DISPLACED PERSONS CAMP, GERMANY

Hanna nudged me. 'He's here again. Your captain.'

'He's not my captain.'

She glanced at me. 'Something wrong?'

'Nothing. Well, nothing apart from the fact we're still trying to get basic medicines, that this place is overcrowded and there are more people arriving every day with all kinds of infections and injuries.'

'Yes, but think about what we have achieved. What you've achieved, Maggie, as it's mostly down to you. We have an infirmary, the camp is as clean as it can be and people now have enough food thanks to your captain.'

'Like I said, he's not my captain.'

'Oh come on, Maggie. You like him. It's obvious. There's nothing wrong with it, you know. You need some fun after everything that's happened.'

I rounded on her. 'I'll tell you what I don't need and that's fun. How can I have fun when people are still out there, dying? When someone like Josef Mengele is alive and free to carry on killing them?'

Her jaw dropped. 'I'm sorry,' she muttered. 'I didn't mean to upset you.'

I sighed. 'No, it's me that should be sorry. I had no right speaking to you like that. I'm just so very tired and I need to get out of here and get Leah to her father. But then, I'm worried I'll be leaving you all in the lurch. I'm not sleeping well, Hanna. Forgive me.'

'There's nothing to forgive.' Her hand on my arm was warm, her grip firm. 'Now you listen to me. Don't worry about us in here. I can run things along with the other doctors. Yes, I know they're elderly, but they're competent. What's important is that you get Leah to her papa. I also think you should go easier on yourself.'

'That's never going to happen.'

'I know, my friend, I know, but you deserve happiness too. Remember that please.'

I managed a rueful smile. 'I'll try.'

Hanna's eyes widened, and I turned to see Jamie standing just inside the infirmary door.

'Captain Maclean, what can I do for you?'

If he was disquieted by the formality of my tone, he didn't show it.

'No word back. I'm sorry, Maggie.'

'No word back *yet*, Captain.'

He studied me for a few seconds, his easy smile still in place, then bent to throw a fresh log on the stove. Every week now, another supply of logs appeared from the barracks, cut down by Jamie's men to keep the growing numbers of refugees, or displaced persons as we were officially called, warm in the bitter weather.

'It's good to be optimistic, Maggie, but what happens if they don't send a message?'

'Then I'll go and find them. These are my friends as well as my colleagues. If they haven't sent a message back, there's a very good reason. Any more news from the front?'

A swift change of subject that evidently didn't fool him for a moment.

'General Konev's army is less than sixty kilometres from Berlin according to the latest reports. Now, how about I take you and the little one here for some proper grub? Sausages and beer at the local inn? It's rustic but clean.'

I gazed at Leah, curled contentedly against me, tiny fists opening and shutting in her sleep. 'That's a kind offer but I don't think so. Leah's not exactly going to want sausages and beer.'

I would have eaten an entire pig if it meant a change from the camp's dismal fare. But I had made a promise to myself. A promise was a promise.

From further down the hut, Hanna cleared her throat loudly, obviously listening to every word. 'I can look after Leah,' she said. 'Go on. It will do you good. I'm sure you and the captain have business to discuss.'

Her meaning couldn't have been clearer.

I stared at my hands, rough and chapped from constant washing as well as use, my thoughts churning. Would it really be so bad to get out of here for an evening? We could just be colleagues, the captain and I. Perhaps even friends, although that would be as far as it went. Curfew was no longer an issue now that Jamie had the commandant in his pocket thanks to the deliveries of wood and sacks of food brought by his men.

Captain Maclean. Not Jamie.

'Alright,' I said, realising almost immediately how ungracious that sounded. 'I mean, thank you. That sounds like a lovely idea.'

'Excellent. I'll be back to collect you at six sharp by the gate.'

'See you then.'

I ignored Hanna's triumphant smile and the acceleration in my pulse rate. This was just a meeting between acquaintances, that was all. We'd discuss what we could do next to try to get in contact with my comrades as well as how to get me and Leah to Paris in any event.

I was at the gate promptly at six sharp, but there was no sign of him. I tugged my coat tighter round me, breathing in the faint but sweet tobacco scent that sometimes rose from it. At least, I preferred to think it was tobacco. That was all I would let myself think of Auschwitz.

'Eva,' I murmured.

I could see her still, eyes on fire as she demanded I take Leah to Antoine, a mother fighting to the last for her child.

'I won't let you down,' I whispered.

Jamie's voice cut through my thoughts. 'Sorry I'm late, but I have some news.'

I looked up to see him striding up to me, offering me his arm before he led me through the gate, gallantly holding open the door of the jeep he'd borrowed for the evening. In spite of myself, I let my arm linger in his, luxuriating in his touch, his body next to mine, the faint scent of soap and cologne rising from his neck, so close I could kiss it. Not that I would.

'What news?'

'All in good time.' He grinned as he shoved the jeep into gear and we roared off towards the village.

My spirits rose. It must be good news then.

The tavern lights beckoned to us from across the street, a welcome beacon in an otherwise bleak landscape. The local people were friendly enough, but there was always an overlay of tension. We saw it with the ones who'd worked at the camp and now as we approached the bar.

'A table for two please,' said Jamie.

The plump woman who stood there looked him up and down in his British uniform and said nothing, her eyes porcine with feigned stupidity.

'Yes, yes, of course,' said a man I assumed was her husband, who bustled up and showed us to a table near the fire.

Jamie's German was good – there was no way she'd misunderstood.

The innkeeper obviously sensed my discomfort because he dumped a jug of beer on the table and announced, 'On the house.'

'Thank you, my friend,' said Jamie evenly.

I took a sip and wrinkled my nose. Rustic didn't cover it.

'Would you prefer wine?'

'Do you think it's safe?'

'And I had you down as the daring sort.'

I looked at him over the candle the innkeeper lit with some ceremony. 'Who me? I'm so boring.'

'Now that I doubt very much. But then, I hardly know anything about you.'

'It's probably best we keep it that way.'

'Why, Maggie? What's changed? You're suddenly so cold and distant.'

I gulped, my thin facade ripped apart by the honesty in his voice and eyes. Eyes which betrayed his confusion.

'I-I'm sorry,' I stumbled. 'I don't mean to be.'

'Don't you?' There was no escaping his gaze, frank now. 'You see, I think you do. I think you're trying to protect yourself and that's understandable. But it breaks my heart to see you pull away from something that could be wonderful.'

'I thought your heart was going to break when I leave here with Leah.'

'It will then too, which is why it's so important to me to enjoy what little time I can have with you. I thought you wanted that as well.'

His brutal honesty was breaking me down. I could feel my defences crumbling as I gazed at him over that damn candle, wishing I could simply bury my feelings deep within me and never let them out, knowing that was impossible. If Jamie was going to speak so candidly, then so was I. I wanted no secrets between us.

'I do. I did. I'm just... so afraid, Jamie. I knew another man, in Auschwitz, a fellow doctor and a friend. We were planning to blow our way out of the camp at the same time as they blew up the crematoria there, but they caught him and the others before they could do it. They hanged all of them, in front of us, just a week before the camp was liberated. I was made to watch.'

I could hear Aleks's voice in my head now, shouting out, 'Long live freedom.'

'What was that?'

Jamie was leaning across the table, cupping my chin with his hand. I must have spoken aloud.

'I said "long live freedom". It's what Aleks shouted before he died. He kicked the stool away rather than let the hangman do it. Even when he was facing death, he did it his way.'

'He sounds like a remarkable man.'

'He was. And a good friend.'

I bowed my head to try to hide my tears. I could feel Jamie's thumb gently wiping them away. A soft thumb for a soldier. But then, Jamie was no ordinary soldier, no ordinary man. He was remarkable too, in his own way.

'Don't you think he'd want you to be happy?'

'He would,' I whispered.

'So be happy, Maggie. I think we could be happy together. What do you think?'

I stared down at my hands, twisting them together over and over. I had no idea what to think. Maybe it was better, then, to go with what my heart told me.

I raised my head, staring back into Jamie's eyes, so patient, so tender.

'I think so too,' I whispered.

FIFTEEN

'They hanged those women this morning at roll call. The ones who smuggled out the gunpowder for the Sonderkommando.'

I stared at the nursery nurse. 'All of them?'

'All four. They've left them there of course, for everyone to see.'

Another grisly spectator sport the SS favoured, designed as ever to send a stark warning to us inmates.

I tried to quell the surge of fear that shot through me. It would be alright. We'd be alright. Now, the Nazis were under even more pressure, desperately aware that the Russians were drawing ever closer. That kind of pressure meant they'd be less careful. Or at least, that was what we hoped.

Hope was a strange thing. You couldn't survive in here without it, and yet it could also kill you, leading you into a false sense of security or the kind of wild optimism that had misled so many to their deaths.

'Better a tiger than a sheep,' I murmured.

'Sorry?'

'It's better to have lived one day as a tiger than a thousand years as a sheep. It's a proverb. Tibetan, I think. Anyway, it's what I believe.'

The nursery nurse's eyes had a new glint in them. 'I like that,' she said.

I looked at her, at this young woman who I so often saw from a distance as I hurried in to check on Leah, listening to her report on her condition but never really taking in anything other than the facts. 'What's your name?' I asked.

'Hanna.'

'Maggie. It's good to meet you, Hanna. I mean, properly.'

She blushed, her pretty face lighting up with a rare smile. Normally she looked so anxious, as if she was about to be caught out in a mistake. Come to think of it, that was how so many looked in a camp where the guards would make up a punishment on a whim to humiliate someone for an imaginary transgression.

'I watch you,' she said. 'You're so good with the babies. They sense that you want to help them and so they remain calm. I don't have much experience with them. Before I came in here, I was only a trainee nurse. I'm never sure I'm doing the right thing.'

'From what I see, you're an excellent nurse, and you're right – I do want to help them, very much. I want to help all of us in here.'

For half a second, I was tempted to tell her about our plans, to offer her the chance to join us in our escape bid. Then I thought better of it. We'd already agreed that no one was to know anything until the last moment, except those of us who were actively planning the breakout. Instead, I motioned to her to accompany me to the cot where the other, smaller baby lay, somehow clinging to life.

'See this little one? I thought she wouldn't be with us much longer, but she's still here, still fighting. I want you to cuddle her as often as you can, to make sure she feels your touch. It can work miracles, you know, a loving touch. Hold her as if she were your own.'

I picked her up out of the cot and placed her in Hanna's arms, then moved to Leah's and took her in mine.

'They need it,' I murmured, smiling down into Leah's face. 'No baby can thrive without being held and loved. It's the same with adults.'

I looked over to see Hanna rocking the other baby, relaxing into the rhythm. 'Talk to her,' I said. 'Does she have a name?'

Hanna shook her head. 'Her mother died before she could name her. She was Catholic, which is why they haven't tried to take her.'

They were also too distracted by the Soviet advance to bother right now about murdering one tiny baby.

'Has she been baptised?'

'I'm not sure.'

'We can do it anyway. Call in a priest. I know of a couple in the camp. Ask him to baptise her and give her a name. What was her mother's name?'

'I don't know.'

'Let's give her a variation of your name. We can call her Anna.'

'Anna. It's a nice name. Do you like that, Anna? Oh my goodness, did you see that? She smiled. I swear it. Look, she's smiling still.'

Hanna's face was alight with pride and not a little love. The timid girl who'd skulked in the corner whenever someone in authority came near now stood taller, confident that she could give something to the baby in her arms. Hope, life, health – it didn't matter. Hanna could help her in some way, and I could see that meant everything to this young woman.

Leah, too, was gurgling in delight, reaching up with her doll-sized fingers to try to grab hold of my hair, managing to get hold of a few strands in that surprisingly strong grip an infant has and tug at it.

'Ow,' I said softly. 'You don't know your own strength, little Leah.'

In truth, I hoped she did. She would need all of it to get out of here alive, let alone undamaged by Mengele and his deranged experiments.

Her eyes were wide open now, a definite, clear blue. I shuddered even as I took in her gaze and held it with mine. Any day now, he or Nurse Clara would decide it was time, even as time was running out for the Nazis. It didn't seem to stop Mengele. In fact, it drove him onwards. I had the feeling that nothing would stop him except, perhaps, a Russian bullet to his brain, and that wasn't going to happen. Josef Mengele would make sure everyone else died first.

SIXTEEN

22 FEBRUARY 1945, NEAR THE DISPLACED PERSONS CAMP, GERMANY

I sipped at the wine the innkeeper had brought. It wasn't too bad. It was hitting the spot at least, sending a welcome languor through my limbs and loosening my inhibitions.

'So what would you like to know about me?'

'Oh, the usual. Name, rank and serial number.'

I pulled up the sleeve that covered my left arm. 'Do you mean this?'

He looked at me and then at the tattooed numbers on my arm, the horror in his eyes fading to pity.

'That's the one thing I don't want you to do,' I said. 'Don't ever feel sorry for me. What's done is done. I survived when thousands upon thousands didn't. I know I said I was just a number back there in the forest, but I didn't mean it. They may have branded me for life, but they haven't taken away my name. They can never do that.'

Angrily, I brushed away another tear. I hadn't meant to cry again. I hated crying, but the brush of his fingers along my arm undid me. It was the tenderness of his touch, the infinite care with which he unrolled my sleeve again to cover it, leaving his hand to linger there a moment longer.

'Forgive me,' he said. 'I don't feel sorry for you, for what it's worth. I'm in awe of your courage and the way you've survived against the odds. It's truly my honour to know you.'

I looked at him stumbling over his words, trying not to say the wrong thing while reaching for the impossible. The truth was that there were no words for what had happened, for what thousands had suffered. Maybe millions. Those numbers on my arm were simply a record that I had stood among others there, had lived while those without tattoos had died, not worthy even of that on their way to the gas chambers. I could see the question in his eyes.

'It's an honour to know you too,' I said. 'You saved us. If it wasn't for you and the Soviets, I wouldn't be sitting here now. That took some guts, attacking those Nazi bastards like that. Especially as I know exactly what they're capable of.'

I was aware I was weeping openly once more, but I had to carry on, to get some of it out. 'I worry what happened to all the others on the march. Where did they take them? How many survived? But I also know that there's nothing to be gained by thinking like that. What's done is done. I can only hope and pray that they're alright. That someone saved them too.'

I glanced at the innkeeper placing a dish of sausage in front of us. He could have been one of the Auschwitz guards in another life. Except that he didn't seem to have the requisite sadistic streak. Just an ordinary man. Like all the other ordinary men this war had turned into monsters. I took another gulp of my wine and erupted in a fit of coughing.

'Deep breath, there you go,' said Jamie, patting me on my back then handing me a glass of water.

I looked at him through streaming eyes. 'I always seem to be crying when I see you.'

'I hope it isn't me.'

I smiled, grateful for his gentle humour. It was that which had got many of us through in Auschwitz and beyond – the ability to lighten the mood even in the most desperate of circumstances.

I took a deep breath. 'You said you had news?'

'I do.'

'And?'

He broke off a chunk of the bread which accompanied the sausages. It was dark and heavy, tastier than the black bread they'd given us in Auschwitz, probably because it wasn't thinned down with sawdust and other dubious ingredients, although it still stuck in my throat.

'I have a message for you.'

Hope flared in my heart. 'What? Where?'

He handed me a scrap of paper on which someone had written out the decoded message. It was the penultimate verse of 'Chanson d'automne', the poem I'd used in my last message from Lyon. At the end of it, a question mark. This had to be one from one of them, from my network. Possibly even Marianne. I felt that flare in my heart explode in a burst of joy.

'Can I send a message back?'

'Of course. Do you want to scribble it down?'

'No. I want to send it myself. I was a radio operator before, in France. I still know my codes.'

'Then by all means do. I can take you back to base with me now, if you like.'

I looked at the sausages still on the plate and the bread alongside them. 'If you don't mind. I'm taking these for Hanna and the others.'

He laughed and beckoned the innkeeper over. 'Be my guest.'

We left ten minutes later with a bag full of more sausages, bread and cheese, all purchased from the innkeeper, who looked delighted at his windfall although his wife still glowered from her corner of the bar. I gave her a cheery wave as we left.

'*Tschüss.*'

She didn't look as if the prospect of seeing either of us again brought her any pleasure.

Outside, the snow had stopped, the stars a glittering canopy in a cloudless sky.

'Thank you for a lovely evening,' I said.

'It may be about to get even lovelier.'

'Oh, how?'

'Well, you get to send your message and then there's this.'

His kiss was long, sweet and only the tiniest bit tentative. By the time we came up for air, I was intoxicated.

'You're right,' I murmured.

'About what?'

'It did get lovelier. Now take me to your barracks. I have a message to send.'

SEVENTEEN

8 JANUARY 1945, AUSCHWITZ-BIRKENAU

Two days later, I once again bumped into Aleks in the dispensary. Except that this was no accident. Dr Laba had suggested I go there to pick up my prescriptions. I didn't need to be told twice to understand that he was in on our plans too.

'I believe some of these are in the drug cupboard,' Aleks said, waving his chits at the pharmacist on duty. 'You'll probably find yours are as well. Don't worry, we can find them ourselves. We know you're busy.'

The orderly for whose benefit this was said picked up his packages and left. Aleks jerked his head towards the room that served as the drug cupboard.

'They announced they wanted volunteers at roll call this morning. Specifically anyone with experience handling explosives as well as civil engineers. It looks as if they're going to blow the crematoria any moment. We must be ready. I've already passed word to the farm crew that they should all volunteer.'

I looked at his eyes blazing with belief, heard the absolute certainty in his voice. 'Did you hear what else they did at roll call only the other morning?'

'Of course I did. It was bound to happen. But this is different, Maggie, as you know. You said it yourself. They're distracted now and running out of time, which makes this our time to act.'

I so wanted to match his fervour, but something in me held back. Maybe it was the way they'd hanged those women or perhaps it was something older, primeval, a sixth sense that told me this wasn't going to work.

'You're right. I did say that. But what if it all goes wrong? What if, instead of saving people, we're leading them to their deaths? You know what the Nazis are capable of, and they wouldn't hesitate to shoot anyone trying to escape. They shot every single one of the Sonderkommando and hundreds more besides. What's to stop them murdering us?'

A shadow flitted across his eyes. He seemed taken aback. Disappointed even. 'There's a risk, but there's always a risk in here. Outside those fences there are risks too. You know that and I know that, but the difference between us, it seems, is that I'm prepared to take that risk.'

'You misunderstand me. I'm willing to take the risk. Of course I am. But I'm not prepared to take a risk that won't pay off or that will end up in the unnecessary deaths of hundreds or even thousands more.'

He stared at me and then his face softened. 'Maggie, what's changed? What's frightening you?'

'I don't know. Nothing. Everything. I look at Leah and I'm terrified Mengele will take her and do awful things to her or her mother. I worry about reprisals. About them killing all of us so that none of us can ever tell what it was really like in here. I lie awake and I wonder how any of this could have happened and how no one would ever believe it did...'

My voice cracked and I gulped, unable to continue.

He looked at me for a second longer and then pulled me into his chest, stroking my hair, soothing me as you would a child. It felt so good to be in his arms, to be held. This camp might be overrun with thousands of people, but I had never felt so lonely, always watching my back, never really connecting with anyone because I might not be able to trust them or tomorrow they could be gone. I missed my family, my friends and comrades, the camaraderie of working as a team, fighting a common enemy. In here, the real enemy was your own mind. If it broke, you were gone.

'Ah, Maggie. That's it. You cry. It's good for you. Go on – let it out. I'm scared too. We all are.'

I wiped my hand across my eyes, aware that they must be pink, that my nose was streaming and I didn't care.

'I also want you to know that I don't expect you to do anything about the escape plan apart from being ready. It would be madness to ask you to help lay explosives when they would spot you at once. Everything is organised. I'll let you know precisely where and when. Until then, you don't need to know anything. For your own safety.'

Another low clutch of fear, gripping and twisting my guts. I forced a smile. 'I'll be waiting.'

'Good. I'm glad to hear it. Go carefully.'

'I always do, my friend.'

As we came out of the cupboard, I looked at the pharmacist, seeing his kindly eyes behind his spectacles, his expression of concern mingled with what appeared almost paternal affection.

'I hear Mengele's on the prowl. Greedy for new subjects while he can still get his hands on them.'

Another clutch at my guts, sharper this time. 'Do you know where he is?'

'Last I heard, he was heading for the women's ward.'

Oh God no. Eva.

I turned and started to run without so much as a goodbye.

EIGHTEEN

The wireless operator sat me in front of a set that was far bigger than any I'd ever seen. 'You press here and here. It's already set up to transmit.'

'Thank you.'

Nervously, I tapped in the first few letters, the machine encoding them as I did so. The last verse of Verlaine. The proof it was, indeed, me.

Et je m'en vais
Au vent mauvais
Qui m'emporte
Deçà, delà,
Pareil à la
Feuille morte.

And I go
Where the winds know,
Broken and brief,
To and fro,
As the winds blow

A dead leaf.

Except I was no dead leaf. I was alive and well and, somewhere out there, were my friends.

I felt a touch on my arm, guiding me out of the radio room, bringing me back to the here and now even as I imagined my message soaring across the Channel, the words written on the winds.

'I hope it works,' said Jamie.

I looked at him, at the generosity of his smile, at him standing there, the epitome of a gentleman. He was everything that word suggested – gentle yet strong, tough when he needed to be but so tender at his core.

'Thank you,' I whispered. 'You have no idea what this means to me.'

'I think I do.'

There was a note beneath his words, one of infinite sadness. We both knew this meant I might be leaving soon. At least, I hoped so. Then again, another part of me wished I could bring him with me or at least keep him close in some way.

No, Maggie. There's no way. Not with who you are and what you do. What you need to do now.

I thought of Leah. Of Antoine. Of Eva crying out for him.

'I'll never forget your kindness,' I said.

'I'll never forget you,' he murmured.

The wireless operator called us back into the room. There, he handed me a piece of paper with the message he'd decoded. Just five words but they sent a surge of joy through my heart.

We will bring you home.

'Can you send another message?' I asked the operator. 'Tell them I need to drop something off on the way.'

'I have a better idea,' said Jamie. 'Why don't we tell them

that I'll bring you back? Then we can drop that, ah, package off on the way.'

I stared at him, confused. 'But don't you have to stay here?'

'Actually, I've outstayed my posting. I was due to rejoin my original regiment three weeks ago.'

'Why didn't you?'

As soon as the words left my mouth, I knew the answer.

'There was an urgent situation I needed to resolve here.'

'I see.'

'I have a duty to ensure the safety of innocent civilians.'

I was hardly a civilian, but I bit my tongue. 'Does that include escorting those civilians wherever they might need to go?'

'Absolutely. It would be a dereliction of duty to do otherwise.'

'You're a fine soldier, Captain Maclean.'

'I like to live by my regiment's motto.'

'Which is?'

'Who dares wins.'

NINETEEN

Eva was gone, her bed empty. I looked at Dr Laba and he shook his head. Nurse Clara was standing there, reading her chart. I wanted to scream, to punch the space where she'd been lying. Instead, I walked over and held out my hand for the chart.

'I've just been to the dispensary to collect this patient's medication. I need to record it on there.'

She smiled, her rouged lips extending in what was more of a sneer. 'Don't bother. Dr Mengele has decided to change her medication.'

'What does that mean?'

'It means it's none of your business.'

She slammed the chart into my chest and strode out, sneer still firmly in place. I stayed where I was, too stunned to do more than stare at the chart as if I could somehow find a clue there.

Dr Laba walked over and gently took it from me. 'Come on. There's nothing you can do.'

'Oh but there is. There really is. I'm going to go right in there now, into that bastard's office, and explain to him what it means to take the Hippocratic oath.'

'You think that will stop him? It won't change anything. All you can do is wait and hope that he spares her.'

He was right.

Another thought smashed into me. 'Leah. I have to make sure he hasn't taken her too.'

I was off again, running back in the opposite direction towards the nursery, trying to block out the look I'd seen on Dr Laba's face. It was a look of infinite compassion, the kind you would give someone who couldn't accept that their loved one had died.

Don't die, please don't die, I chanted in my head as my feet pounded the floorboards, the noise resounding off them as I ran, uncaring who saw or demanded an explanation. I burst into the nursery, breathless, searching frantically for Leah in her cot.

She was there. Thank God. I sank to my knees, sobbing.

The nursery nurse came over to me. 'Is something wrong, Doctor?'

I raised my head. It wasn't Hanna but another prisoner nurse, older, more stolid. 'No. Nothing. I'm fine.'

An obvious lie but one she knew to ignore. 'Well then, can I help you in some way?'

'I just came to check on my patients.'

'They're doing well, both of them. Sound asleep as you can see.'

In spite of me bursting in. That, at least, was a blessing.

'Both of them? That's wonderful.'

I pulled myself together, standing tall as I dusted myself down, pretending that nothing had happened. In this godforsaken place where people lost their minds every day, one more was nothing unusual. At least I hadn't completely cracked and hurled myself at the electrified fence as many did to try to bring about a quick death, often perishing instead in a hail of the guards' bullets.

Composed now, I carried out my customary checks on both

babies, tucking Leah's blanket around her extra tight as she slumbered.

'Sleep well, little one,' I murmured. 'Everything's going to be alright.'

A lie I had to tell myself rather than her. Anything to try to alleviate the lead weight that was now weighing down my heart. It was a weight that dragged at my footsteps as I returned to the women's ward and one that I carried with me for the rest of the shift.

Towards the end of it, I heard the orderlies pushing a stretcher along the corridor. I hurried out, heart in mouth to meet them. Eva was lying on it, unconscious.

'Eva, no. What has he done to you? What has that evil bastard done?'

One of the orderlies gently took me by the elbow, steering me to follow the stretcher as the other one wheeled it back into the ward. 'Shhh,' he whispered. 'She came with us.'

He didn't need to say any more. At the far end of the corridor, I could just see Nurse Clara, watching to make sure they got their cargo back to the ward. Then she turned on her heel and was gone, no doubt to report back to Mengele that his latest experiment was ongoing.

The two orderlies lifted Eva and placed her back in her bed as carefully as they could while I hovered, wringing my hands, wanting to weep, to scream at the insanity of it, knowing that if I did, I could be putting both our lives at risk.

By the look of it, she had already lost a lot more blood, but she was still breathing. That gave me some hope, although very little. Dr Laba appeared to raise one eyelid and then the other, feeling for her pulse, positioning the IV so I could reinsert it without collapsing a vein, my hands shaking as I did so.

'We need to get her into surgery now,' I said. 'And get this into her so we can operate.'

'Here,' he said. 'Allow me.'

I watched his deft fingers slide in the needle, half-blinded by the tears that were threatening to spill. No point in crying. No point in anything but doing all I could to save Eva.

Near the insertion point for the IV, I noticed another needle mark, still livid. I had no idea what Mengele had done to her or what he'd given her. All we could do was watch and wait, hoping for the best, fearing the worst.

'Come on, Eva, you can do it,' I whispered as we wheeled her towards the operating theatre.

For once, I didn't even believe my own words.

TWENTY

22 FEBRUARY 1945, VOSGES MOUNTAINS, FRANCE

The converted inn they were using as a training base was hidden among the trees in the forest that bordered the village. Marianne surveyed the recruits sitting around the large oak table. At one end of the room was a board with photographs of the most well-known Nazi war criminals tacked to it.

'These are some of the people we most want to track down,' she said, pointing at each photograph in turn with her stick. 'We don't have pictures of all those we wish to apprehend, which is why we're relying on the intelligence you manage to gather on the ground. Then there are the names on the lists in front of you.'

The recruits duly studied those lists as well as the photographs. To her left, Jack rapidly translated, his German flawless, even more so since his recent insertion with hard-line Nazi POWs back in Wiltshire. She still shivered at the memory of what they'd tried to do to him. These POWs were less sinister, chosen from specific groups including Catholics, Austrians and political prisoners. They were all handpicked from the stockade at Sarrebourg near Lorraine. Marianne could only imagine that there were slim pickings.

Somewhere in the corridor beyond, a bell rang, signalling that it was time for a lesson change. This group would swap with those undertaking parachute training outside while yet another would rotate from learning basic espionage skills with Suzanne. To be honest, all their skills seemed basic. And these were the best they could find, creamed off after days of observation as they carried out work detail and interviews to determine why they were willing to betray their country.

Most seemed only too eager to become spies, worn down by the harsh German military regime or years of incarceration because of their beliefs. Those were the ones she observed most keenly, wondering which might turn out to be a traitor. There were three women among them she had yet to meet, the first to be selected. As with the Resistance, women found it easier to blend in on the ground.

She watched now as they filed in, grubby from their parachute training. Two kept their eyes down but the third flashed her a glance, taking her seat with a toss of her head. She'd have to watch that one.

'She was the mistress of a high-ranking SS officer,' said Suzanne as they debriefed later that evening. 'She's perfect for our purposes because she can identify many of those who carried out war crimes.'

'Very handy. And what are our orders above and beyond training them?' asked Marianne.

'They have to complete training with you, some more with OSS and, as soon as they're ready, we're sending you in with them. You'll drop in pairs.'

Marianne's eyes lit up. 'We're going to parachute behind German lines?'

Suzanne nodded. 'Absolutely. Easier than ground insertion. Hitler has already ordered his government be evacuated to the Alpine Redoubt in Bavaria. As you know, he's had a house there for many years. The Berghof. From what we know, his troops are expected to join them for one last stand, which means you conveniently have them gathered together in one place.'

'What are we supposed to do with them once we find them?'

'The war hasn't officially ended so you may not officially apprehend or kill them except in the course of combat.'

'I thought we were completely unofficial?'

'Exactly.'

Marianne looked at Jack. There was no need to say anything – they both understood what this entailed. Not that there was ever a need to say anything. They more or less read one another's minds. It had been that way since the beginning, minds and hearts working as one. She wouldn't have it any other way. He was her lodestone, the north star she'd looked to when they were apart and her anchor now that they were back together, as she was for him.

'Is Hitler going south with his government?'

'That we don't know.'

Another glance at Jack, his eyes alive with excitement at what lay ahead. They were going into the heart of Hitler's world, the centre of the Nazi universe. It was a suicidal plan on so many levels and yet they couldn't wait to get started. It was what they were here to do, to go places no other agents could. To defy the odds and keep on defying them until this war was over and peace reigned once more.

TWENTY-ONE

11 JANUARY 1945, AUSCHWITZ-BIRKENAU

Three days passed and still no news. The crematoria were still there, still standing, an affront to humanity. As I watched over Eva, I waited, half-expecting at any moment to get a message from Aleks or see him standing at my shoulder, but there was nothing, just an endless, agonising silence. All I could do was tend to my patients and hope, although even that was fading, along with Eva's strength. This time, she seemed unable to fight back in spite of the surgery.

We'd repaired Mengele's damage as best we could, all of us sickened by what we saw. A firing squad was too quick for him, too merciful. Come to that, so was hanging, but it was all we had. The worst thing was imagining him a free man and Germany the victors. From the news that filtered into camp, there was now no way they could win this war, but Mengele was devious. Even if they lost, I suspected he would find a way to save himself. I silently swore I would find a way to bring him to justice, no matter what it took.

I did so now while I carefully rearranged Eva's hair on the pillow as she lay, still unconscious. Just one short, tiny curl that was out of place, but she would be so proud to see it. All the women were as they saw their hair grow back, faster now that the Nazis were no longer concerned with shaving it. They had better things to do – like trying to save their own skins.

'There now, you look lovely,' I whispered as I smoothed it down.

'Doctor, I need to speak to you outside.'

A voice at my shoulder but not the one I was hoping to hear. I looked over it to see Dr Laba. The expression on his face sent a bolt of sheer terror through me. I heard the ward door click as he closed it. It sounded exactly like the click of a revolver.

I watched him compose his face, searching for the right words.

'Just tell me,' I whispered.

'Look out of the window,' he said.

I ran to the nearest one and stared out, seeing the guards marching a group of men along at gunpoint, running to the next one and the next to try to find out who they were, recognising Aleks among them, grabbing on to the wall to stop myself collapsing.

'Oh God no,' I whispered.

They'd caught them. And judging by the direction they were coming from, right by the crematoria. They must have been carrying out their reconnaissance, deciding where to place the explosives.

'But how?'

The guards were shoving at them with their guns, shouting out what they were going to do to them, their faces twisted in glee.

Just before he disappeared from view, I caught a glimpse of Aleks's face. He looked proud. Unbroken. Which meant they would try all the harder to break him and the others before they executed them. And there was nothing I could do to stop them. Or to save them.

I stumbled away from the windows while all my instincts

screamed at me to break through them and somehow rescue them from their fate.

There was an infinity of compassion in Dr Laba's eyes, a pool into which I wanted to hurl myself and drown. My lungs felt as if they were filling up now, as if I was suffocating.

'What will they do to them?'

Stupid question. I already knew the answer.

Dr Laba shook his head. 'That is anyone's guess. They're keeping them in Block 11. Officially we don't know any of this. I think we have to be prepared for the worst.'

Block 11 was the punishment block where prisoners were tortured and kept in the standing cells for days. It was also where people were shot against the Death Wall in the yard, standing naked until someone put a bullet in the back of their neck or a firing squad dispatched them. They would be executed, in one way or another. By hanging probably, to warn the rest of us, especially as they were about to march us out of here, although we had no real idea when that was going to happen either.

The pulse of the camp was quickening, the drumbeats of fear sounding louder and louder. It was a tattoo that reverberated through my head now, pounding against my skull in time with the beat of my broken heart. One way or another, Aleks would die along with all the others. It was inevitable, just as so many deaths in this war were inevitable. Except that I could have stopped this. I should have spoken out and told him of my fears.

'It's my fault,' I whispered.

Dr Laba took me by the shoulders, staring me in the face. 'Don't ever talk like that. It's not your fault. None of this is anyone's fault save that of the Nazis. Get those ideas out of your head right now.'

'You don't understand. I thought this might happen. I had this feeling, you see, deep in my gut.'

He sighed. 'We all have those feelings and we act anyway. That's what Aleks and the others did. They knew the risks.'

As I did and yet I hadn't taken them. I was in here, safe, while they were facing certain death.

'We will speak of this no more, Maggie. Aleks kept your name and mine out of it for a reason. He didn't want either of us involved because he knew this might happen. Don't betray him now by doing anything stupid. You must carry on as if nothing has happened, as we all must.'

I drew in a breath, one that rasped down my throat, rattling my bones. My soul. 'I won't. I promise.'

My words tasted bitter, poisoned by grief and regret. I should have stopped him. I knew that, no matter what Dr Laba said. And now there was nothing I could do except wait to see how Aleks died, much as I watched and waited each day to see if Eva lived. Somewhere deep in my heart, I knew I would probably lose them both.

TWENTY-TWO

25 FEBRUARY 1945, DISPLACED PERSONS CAMP, GERMANY

Hanna handed me a parcel she'd wrapped in paper from the schoolroom, decorated with the children's handprints in multi-coloured paint. 'Here, take this.'

I unwrapped it as carefully as I could, wanting to preserve those tiny palm prints, imagining the little ones giggling as they smeared them with paint and pressed them into the paper. Hanna had worked miracles with them, playing with them when she wasn't in the infirmary, giving them back some sense of joy. She'd also worked a miracle with what she'd created for me. It was a drawing of me holding Leah by the stove, my face bent to hers.

'For you to remember her by,' said Hanna. 'Once you've delivered her safely to her father.'

'Oh, Hanna.'

The sketch was beautiful, every line speaking of Leah, of me. You could see the exact expression she wore once she'd finished feeding, a sleepy-eyed contentment that brought a smile to my face. It was that smile Hanna had also captured, one I scarcely recognised. It had been so long since I'd gazed at myself in a mirror, let alone smiled into one. The washrooms here were utilitarian and basic, the bits of hammered tin that served as mirrors hardly worth peering into. Then again, I knew that they avoided using glass to help stave off the growing number of suicide attempts. I'd bandaged up too many arms of survivors not to know how many could no longer cope with their suffering. It was a suffering I was escaping.

'I wish I could take you with me,' I said.

Hanna threw her arms around me and pulled me close for a hug. 'Hush now. Don't cry. You have to do this. I know how much Leah means to you, and I know how much it also means to you to keep your promise. I'll miss you, Maggie. Don't you forget me either.'

'How could I? Not when I have this and all the memories of the time we've spent together. Yes, even here, in this place. And the other. I hope we meet again when the war is over.'

'I hope so too. Now go. Your Jamie is waiting.'

She was irrepressible was Hanna, the dimples by her mouth speaking volumes.

'He's not my Jamie.'

'Oh, I think he is.'

She laughed as I snapped my suitcase shut and hauled it off the bed. Another gift from the Red Cross, stuffed with nappies and baby clothes, along with my few possessions. The knapsack Dr Laba had given me would serve as a day bag, stuffed too with more nappies and bottles. Leah was growing fast and had a voracious appetite, no doubt because she'd almost starved on the way here, her stomach forever demanding food in case it ran out again.

She was all ready for the journey, bundled up in knitted layers, some of it produced by the ladies in the camp. Knitting was one way of filling the hours, and they loved to try out their creations on her. I could see from some of their faces that it also helped them just a bit to come to terms with the loss of their own children. Not that this baby could ever replace their own, but she represented something they thought they'd lost. Hope. Along with proof that life really could go on. Eva would have liked that, knowing that her daughter brought solace to those who needed it most.

Jamie was waiting for us inside Major Nicholson's office. The forms were ready for my signature and, in return, he presented me with papers for me and for Leah.

'These should get you through all the borders between here and England,' he said, walrus moustache accentuating a smile that was as clipped as his accent.

I looked at them. They bore our names and nationalities according to the camp registers – we were both described as French. Leah had been given my surname. I was about to protest when I realised that to do so would mean I would have to leave her here. Far better to keep up the fiction she was my child and sort it out later.

'Thank you.'

'Good luck, Dr Dubois.'

Major Nicholson rose and saluted me.

'Thank you, Major.'

Without another word, I followed Jamie out to the waiting car, settling Leah carefully in a bassinet on the back seat before climbing into the front passenger seat. It was only once we were driving away from the camp that I let out a long, slow breath.

'He knew, didn't he? Nicholson.'

Jamie flicked me a glance. 'Knew what? That you saved Leah's life and that you're going to give her a better one? He might be a stiff old stick, but he recognises right when he sees it. It doesn't matter that you're not technically her mother. You might as well be now.'

I stared out at the desolate countryside, empty fields stretching for miles on either side of the road, the earth yet to spring to life with new crops. Within a few hours we would be in Paris and from there to Lyon. I could hardly believe I was going to see my homeland after what felt like forever. But I was one of the lucky ones. Some people had been away from their homes for years. Some never returned. And some now had no homes to go to, their towns and villages decimated by war. Then there were those like Eva, who would forever lie in a foreign land, one that had treated her so cruelly.

I looked over my shoulder at Leah, fast asleep thanks to the motion of the car. She had a home with Antoine, wherever he was. At least, I hoped she did.

I turned to Jamie. 'You said I could call my people once we're in Paris?'

'You can,' he said. 'It's all arranged. A secure line to London courtesy of Supreme Headquarters Allied Expeditionary Force. You'll be able to speak to your people, and they can help you find Leah's father.'

'I don't even know if he's alive.'

'Chances are that he is if he's been in France all this time. The war is over there. You say he's with the Resistance?'

'He worked with them and SOE.'

'They're a resourceful lot. Have faith, Maggie. It will turn out just fine.'

'I know. You're right. I just worry for Leah. She's so little, and she's all alone apart from Antoine.'

I could see the airfield up ahead. Then we were slowing, turning into its gates, presenting our papers, the guard saluting, carrying on through.

'Leah's not alone,' said Jamie as we drew to a halt beside a building. 'She has you as well as Antoine. Which means she's a very lucky little girl.'

I looked at him. 'I'm lucky too, to have met you.'

'Not as lucky as I am, although, unlike Leah, I fear I'm about to lose you.'

I reached out then and stroked his face, feeling the roughness of his chin under my fingers, the sharp planes of his cheek-bones. 'I don't believe you're afraid of anything.'

'I'm afraid of that.'

'You're not going to lose me. You're coming with me all the way to Lyon and then on to London, unless you've changed your mind.'

'I haven't, and I'll be by your side all the way, but after that, you'll be with your people, and I'll be with mine.'

'So? We can arrange to meet.'

I saw something then in his eyes, a shadow that slid behind them. As quickly as it appeared, it was gone. 'We can.'

I swallowed down the past, the fear, the anger and desperation as I leaned forward and brushed my lips against his. 'I'll hold you to that.'

TWENTY-THREE

They marched them out of Block 11 in time for evening roll call. Mengele appeared at the hospital shortly before, along with Nurse Clara, instructing me to accompany him back to his office. He barely glanced at Eva, grunting in that way he had, a sound that both dismissed and denigrated. Unless she lived, he had no further use for her. Even then, his interest was purely academic. She would be added to his precious notes that detailed every experiment.

He wanted to show me those notes now, or so he said as we walked back towards the main camp.

'I would be interested to get your opinion, Doctor,' he announced as he strode along, boots as shiny as ever, uniform immaculate. He wasn't a particularly tall man but some considered him good-looking. Certainly, he had a revolving parade of female companions, Nurse Clara and the Beast among them. His wife had visited once but fell ill and now kept her distance. I couldn't imagine him as a normal family man, although apparently he also had a son. It beggared belief that this monster could be a father and still treat the children in here as human guinea pigs for his inhuman experiments.

He slowed as we neared the square where the gibbet stood and where the prisoners were taking their places for roll call. The Beast was there among them, her arms folded as she gossiped and laughed with one of the guards. She had no business being here. Her domain was the women's camp. I had no doubt she'd turned up purely for the entertainment.

'Let's watch,' he said, more to Nurse Clara on the other side of him than to me.

I glanced at him and then at the gibbet in panic. He knew something was about to happen.

Sure enough, I could hear shouts and then see the SS guards marching the prisoners into the square, the dogs nipping and growling at their heels. I counted eight of them. That was their mistake – they should have kept it tighter. On SOE sabotage missions, we stuck to two or three at most, laying the charges as fast and efficiently as we could, although who was I to talk? I was in here because I'd been caught doing exactly that on the railway line at Lyon.

All I wanted to do was tear my eyes away, but I had to keep looking. I could feel Mengele watching me, and I wondered if he knew. It was unlike him to suddenly want a chat and a stroll through the camp, even if it was to his office. If he knew, that meant I was in danger too. He loved his cat-and-mouse games. There was nothing for it but to feign indifference as I watched the men line up, listening as the charges were read out, although, as hard as I tried, I couldn't help but gaze at Aleks, his head erect, shoulders back in spite of the terrible injuries they'd inflicted on him.

His face was black and blue where they'd beaten him, blood congealed around the contusions. One shoulder looked to be dislocated, and his hands, too, bore signs of violence, the knuckles so raw I could see even from this distance that they barely had any flesh covering them.

Maybe he felt my eyes on him or perhaps it was coincidence

but, at that moment, he looked straight at me, our eyes locked and I felt my knees give way. He flashed me the briefest of smiles, so brief that not even Mengele could have noticed. That was Aleks. Brave to the last. Which meant I had to be brave too or I would let him down again. I sucked in a great gulp of air, pulling back my shoulders, keeping my eyes fixed on them all.

They placed a noose around each of their necks and made them stand on individual stools, kicking them one by one from under them. Some called out shouts of defiance or prayers before their deaths while others remained silent. When it came to Aleks's turn, I forced myself to watch. To witness.

'Long live freedom!' he cried, and then he kicked away his stool before the hangman had a chance, jerking and twitching once or twice before, finally, he was still.

I could feel tears streaming down my face, and I didn't care. Let Mengele think what he liked. I stood, ramrod straight and then I lifted my arm, touching my hand to my temple as I saluted them all.

'Go well,' I whispered under my breath.

Mengele let out a bark of laughter. 'Very good, very good,' he said as if we'd just been watching a circus trick performed. I almost thought he might burst into applause.

Nurse Clara inspected her nails, bored.

I had to keep taking long, slow breaths to stop myself trying to snatch his pistol so I could shoot them both on the spot.

The gathered prisoners were silent. Few even knew why these men had been hanged except those near enough to hear the charges. Word would soon spread, whispers passed along with the bowls of thin soup that served as sustenance. By the time they reached the far corners of the camp, the story would be grotesquely exaggerated.

I could see snow starting to swirl, drifting down on the heads of the prisoners standing to attention in the square, dancing through the gallows, icy sprites tickling the faces of those who could no longer feel their featherlight touch but were already turning as cold as the flakes. One or two settled in Aleks's hair, barely visible among the pale strands. His hair, like his eyes, fitted their damn Aryan ideal. Too bad they'd decided instead to murder him.

There was a hollow now where my heart had been, a void that resounded with the beats of something else. I wanted to fill it back up with his touch, to run over and cut him down, take him in my arms and tend to him. But there was no comforting Aleks now. He was gone, and the sooner I accepted that, the better. *Farewell, my friend,* I whispered in my heart.

Mengele was looking at me with scarcely concealed impatience. 'Come along. We have work to do.'

'Show's over then?' I muttered, turning my face away so he wouldn't hear. As I did so, I caught sight of Dr Laba at the edge of the crowd, staring at the men swinging from the gibbet. He bowed his head for a moment and then glanced at me. The look we exchanged said everything.

There was no time to linger as I turned to follow in Mengele's wake, my mind racing with a thousand thoughts, my heart shattered into a million pieces.

As he strode towards his office, Mengele hummed that damn tune. The same one he hummed on the platform when he carried out selections.

Mengele's office was stacked high with files and folders. There were more boxes filled with paperwork on the floor and piled against the walls. It looked as if he was packing up, readying himself for the evacuation that was now inevitable.

He indicated a chair in front of his desk. 'Sit.'

I picked a file from it and placed it on his desk before obeying.

'Coffee,' he snapped as Nurse Clara hovered. She scowled but went off to do his bidding.

'I want you to look at this,' he said, digging out a folder from under a pile on his desk and extracting a document from it. It was closely covered in his handwriting, accompanied by diagrams I guessed he'd drawn, the whole neat, precise and horrifying. I wouldn't give him the satisfaction of looking at it or of praising his ghastly efforts. I handed the report back to him without saying a word.

He looked at me, perplexed. 'I thought you were a scientist, Doctor, with a keen interest in research. At least, that's what your former professor told me.'

'I am interested in scientific research.'

'I see.'

Had I gone too far? I could sense his indignance and, beyond that, a rising anger. There was no use angering him. It would only lead to yet more pain, not just for me but for those he took it out on.

I took a breath and then leaned forward slightly, acquiescing to his apparently superior intellect.

'Of course, Dr Mengele, you're the expert. You've been carrying out your research for so long now and in such difficult conditions. I must confess, I'm somewhat intimidated by what you've discovered. I'm not sure what to say except that I admire your diligence and the wealth of knowledge you've acquired.'

He took in this little speech and then permitted me a nod of agreement. 'There is so much I have discovered.'

'I'm sure, Doctor, and I know that the world will be amazed by your discoveries. The thing is, I'm just a junior doctor, barely out of medical school. I worry that I won't be able to live up to your achievements and superior intellect.'

'Oh come, come, Doctor. You are very able. I realise that my work is complex, but I'm sure you can grasp the intricacies of it.'

'I try, Dr Mengele. I try.'

It was the closest I would ever come to a simper.

I heard a barely concealed snort from behind me. Nurse Clara advanced bearing a tray on which two coffee cups were perched along with a plate of cookies. I almost laughed aloud at the incongruousness of it. Here we were in a prison camp and she was serving up coffee and cookies to a psychopathic despot. There was no other word for it. Josef Mengele simply didn't care what he said or did as long as it served him and his grisly experiments.

He waved at his papers again. 'If you're interested in scientific research, you'll understand why I need constant fresh specimens. That baby in the hospital, for example. The one with blue eyes.'

I felt as if ice were seeping through my veins, freezing my heart so it stopped. 'I'm concerned the child may have caught something. She has the beginnings of a rash.'

Mengele leaned back as if I also was carrying some kind of disease. If there was one thing he hated, it was a rash. 'The beginnings?'

'Yes. I observed that her skin was raised and pink this morning. Of course, I'll keep a close eye on her.'

No use claiming she had a high temperature too. For some reason, Mengele dismissed those as faked when it was actually the rashes we faked to protect our patients.

'Do that,' he snapped. 'I'll send the nurse to check too. My research is urgent. There must be no delays.'

Not when the Soviets were getting closer each day.

I glanced at the files on his desk again and the boxes piled high beside it. These notes were the evidence of all the crimes against humanity Mengele had committed, and he obviously intended taking them with him, wherever he was going from here. I had no idea where we prisoners were going from here, but I suspected it wouldn't be to a better place. All I could hope for was to survive this and live to tell of what Mengele had done. What they had all done. I swore to myself I would as I sat there, waiting for his dismissal.

I hadn't touched the coffee in front of me. I was unable to

stomach it when I was surrounded by his trophies, the body parts and even heads that had once belonged to a living, breathing person. Or a child.

He took a long gulp of his, smacked his lips in satisfaction and then waved his hand once more. 'You may go. I want a full report on that baby.'

'Yes, of course, Dr Mengele. Thank you for our discussion. It was most enlightening.'

I was barely through the door of his office when I once again broke into a run. Leah. I had to get to Leah before they did.

It felt as if a horde of demons were on my tail as I ran, snapping at me, trying to tear me down and rip out my throat. In my imagination, every single one of them looked like Mengele.

I ran faster, slowing as I passed guards, speeding up again as soon as they were out of sight, all the while praying that I wouldn't be too late. That I would get there first.

TWENTY-FOUR

26 FEBRUARY 1945, PARIS, FRANCE

Paris looked much as I remembered it and yet so very different. The streets appeared greyer, the people sapped of the joie de vivre for which they'd been famous. Even the birds seemed to sing a more muted song. It was as if the years of Nazi occupation had sucked the soul out of the city. I stared up at the Faculty of Medicine building, thinking of Dr Durand who had taught me here and who had also ended up in Auschwitz, working for Mengele. Strange how things turned out.

'It looks the same,' I said, 'and yet so different. Last time I was here it was during the student protests against the occupation. The Nazis cracked down on us hard. Some were killed, others arrested. It was awful.'

'Did you protest?'

'Of course, even though I was at the teaching hospital by then. The Pitié-Salpêtrière. It's just up the road. They arrested me along with some of my friends. It was shortly after that I decided to go to London and ended up applying to SOE. I could see the way things were going here and I wanted to fight them as best I could.'

'That you've certainly done. What about your family? Weren't they worried about you?'

'My parents left for the south not long after the Germans invaded. Our house in Normandy is very large. It's been in the family for generations. The Germans requisitioned it along with our farmland, so my mother and father decided to go and stay with my aunt in Marseilles. My younger sisters went with them while my two brothers joined up. I have no idea where any of them are right now.'

A flash of a memory, only half-formed. All five of us running through the fields, we girls chasing after our brothers, who'd taken all the bonbons my aunt had brought us as a treat. Them laughing as they outran us, us shrieking in fury. We caught up with them by the stream, where I dunked my oldest brother's head in the water in retaliation, holding it under until he begged for mercy. Papa simply laughed when he told on me. 'Serves you right for stealing from your sisters.'

I ran my hand through my hair as if to brush away the memory. It was so painful to think of them that I tried not to, and yet it was all I had. Memories. My brothers were somewhere out there even now, still fighting. Or perhaps they weren't. Maybe one or both of them was already captured. Or dead, like Aleks. He was my brother too. A brother in arms. I blew them all a silent kiss from my heart.

'I've not heard from my parents since before I was sent to Auschwitz. I wrote to my aunt's address from the camp in Germany, but I had no address of my own to give them. I have no idea if they're still there, but I wrote to our old home too, just in case.'

I took the carriage from him and began to push it along, as much to give me something to do as anything. Even speaking about my family hurt, although it had been so long since I'd seen them. Perhaps more so because of that. At least there was Leah to focus on, safe in her shiny new baby carriage. It had been waiting for us at the airfield when we landed, along with blankets and napkins. Whoever Jamie's contacts were, they were good.

I hadn't breathed a word about Leah to London. It felt only right that Antoine should be the first to know he had a daughter. As for the circumstances of her birth and what had happened to the rest of his family, that was something I was dreading telling him. But tell him I must. Although so far there had been no word on his whereabouts.

'And what about you?' I said. 'How did you come to join up?'

He smiled. 'Ah, now there's a story.'

'Tell it to me.'

'My father was in the army and, when the war broke out, I volunteered for the new commando unit. I'd already been commissioned into the Scots Guards from the officer training corps at my school, so it wasn't a big leap.'

'How did you end up in the SAS? I hear they do things very differently.'

He tapped his nose and dropped a wink. 'Afraid I can't tell you that. It's all hush hush, but let's just say it involved a few too many drams of whisky at a villa in Cairo.'

'Sounds intriguing. And how did you come to be in France?'

'I've been all over the place – North Africa, Greece, Germany. Poland, as you know; France before that. We're sent wherever we're needed, the idea being that we go in, act swiftly and get out even faster.'

'So I've seen.'

He caught the teasing note in my voice and chuckled. 'Yes, well, when I see something I want, I tend to go for it.'

'Something or someone?'

We were blocking the pavement now, facing one another across the carriage. An old man tutted as he squeezed past us, but I didn't care. All at once, I found it hard to breathe, pinned down as I was by the expression on his face.

'Someone of course. Someone very special, Maggie. You've become so dear to me. Half the time I want to look after you, the other half ravish you.'

I felt myself beginning to blush, the colour staining my cheeks with perceptible heat. 'Should we be talking like this in front of Leah?'

'I don't think she's too interested.'

She was fast asleep, lulled once more by the carriage bumping over the broken pavements of this once proud city. It would be proud again, in time, but the ravages of war were everywhere to see.

'So many people,' I breathed, indicating the queue outside a grocery shop, waiting patiently for their rations. I glimpsed feet shod in wooden shoes and faces worn down by subjugation. I also saw women defiantly dressed in their best, hair coiffed and lips scarlet with defiance. Yes, they seemed to say, our city might be broken, but we can rebuild. We will live and laugh again.

A sudden thought occurred to me. 'Why don't we have a drink at the bar I used to visit after lectures? You'd love it. It's only a few minutes from here, in the Hotel Lutetia.'

'Sounds wonderful,' said Jamie. 'We still have some time to kill before we have to be in Versailles. I could murder a drink.'

His words landed like a knife in my heart. 'Don't say that,' I whispered. 'Don't ever say that.'

'Oh my God, I'm so sorry, Maggie. I didn't mean it like that. It's just an expression.'

'I know. Forgive me. I don't know what came over me. When you said it, I was back there instantly. Hearing those guards shout. Watching them send people to their deaths. To the right, to the left. It could happen in minutes. One moment you were standing in a line or on that square, the next on your way to the showers.'

'I can't imagine what it was like.'

'I don't think anyone can. Not unless you were there. That's why I want to fill every moment of the time I've been given rather than waste it. I was fortunate, you see. I lived while so many died. I saw so much killing.'

Including Aleks's execution. And here I was. Sometimes the guilt crushed me so I couldn't breathe. I made myself take a deep breath now, unknotting the cords around my heart.

At that moment, Leah squawked, aware that the rocking and jolting had stopped again.

'Come on,' said Jamie, seizing hold of her carriage. 'Let's do some of that living.'

We picked up pace, striding along the Rue des Écoles, left into Rue Racine and then across the Place de l'Odéon. Six years melted away and I was a medical student once more, heading off to have a well-earned drink with my compatriots, instead of a war-torn woman pushing a baby that didn't belong to her, accompanied by a man she'd borrowed temporarily. At least, that was what it felt like. This war made everything seem temporary. One minute you were alive, laughing and kissing. The next, gone. In a heartbeat. Or the blast of an ill-timed bomb. Perhaps Jamie was right. I should just seize the day. Get on with living.

'Here we are,' I announced, gazing up at the facade of the Hotel Lutetia. It was still magnificent in its faded glory, a melange of art nouveau and art deco.

I pushed through the revolving door and stopped dead, Jamie almost cannoning into me with the carriage. There were people everywhere, wandering aimlessly across the lobby or huddled in armchairs, their hollowed faces and sunken eyes bringing it all rushing back like a recurring nightmare.

'My God,' I whispered. 'Just look at them.'

Beneath a chandelier, a group of them were sitting around a table, some still dressed in their striped camp uniforms,

others in a mishmash of donated clothes. What they all wore
was the expression I'd seen so many times – one of blank disbelief. Their haunted eyes stared out from faces that were still
grimed from the hell they'd escaped. All men, their hair was
shaved close to their skulls. They'd obviously just arrived from
their long journey across Poland and Germany to freedom. In
front of each sat a silver cup and a plate of bread, butter
and jam.

'This place must have been requisitioned,' said Jamie. 'Let's
ask this woman.'

The same woman who was serving them with a smile and a
kind word for each.

'Excuse me, madame, but has the hotel been taken over?'

She embraced us, too, with her smile. 'It's been requisitioned on General de Gaulle's orders. It's now a reception
centre for the displaced and those returning from the camps.
The general felt the Lutetia was the right place for them as it's
not too grand or imposing.'

'I see,' I murmured.

She caught sight of Leah in her carriage. 'What a beautiful
baby. How old?'

'She's nearly two months old. She was born in one of those
camps.'

I hadn't meant to say it, but somehow it had slipped out. It
seemed important that she and the men felt that we understood
– that we knew what they'd gone through.

'*Mon Dieu.*' The woman crossed herself. Then she leaned
towards Leah and stroked her cheek with such tenderness it
made my heart contract.

'And you,' she said, looking at me, 'how are you?'

'I'm fine, thank you, madame. I'm glad to be home.'

At that, one of the men at the table started to weep, the tears
rolling down his cheeks unchecked, no sound coming from his
open mouth save the odd gulping sob.

One of his companions patted his arm. 'There, there, my friend. It's alright.'

But it wasn't alright. And for many, it would never be alright again. They had seen too much. Suffered too terribly.

'Here,' I said, walking over to him and lifting his silver cup to his lips. 'Take a sip of this. Just a sip and then another. Now a deep breath. That's it. Look at me. I'm a doctor. You're safe now.'

Slowly, the tears stopped and he blinked, his gaze returning to the here and now instead of staring down the last months and years. His mouth formed the word, '*Merci*,' although he still couldn't utter it. Time would help, although it might not fully heal.

'It doesn't feel right to be here,' I said to Jamie. 'I'm sorry.'

'Don't be sorry. It seems to me we came at exactly the right time. Or rather, you did.'

The woman looked at us both. She reminded me of Maman with her hair twisted into neat waves, a few silver strands interspersed among her caramel locks. She had the same expression too, a little reserved but anxious to help in any way she could. 'You're welcome to stay. Everyone is welcome here. My name is Sophie. I'm one of the volunteers.'

'I'm Maggie and this is Jamie. Are there many of you?'

'Plenty, although we could always do with more. We're determined, you see, to look after our own. Many of them were in forced labour camps in Germany, sent by the Vichy government. These here have only just arrived, the first we've seen from the other camps. The death camps. We had no idea such horrors existed.'

'Believe me, madame, they do and you will see more and more of these people. There are many thousands of them, some yet to be freed.'

'But you got out?'

'I did, along with Leah here. They were marching us from

one camp to another when Jamie helped save me.'

She beamed, her smile encompassing us. 'That's wonderful. And now you're here.'

I could feel the men looking at me. To my immense shame, I could no longer look at them. I just wanted to get out of there. To breathe the fresh air and forget. 'Yes, but we're not staying long. We have to travel on to Lyon.'

'Surely you have time for something to eat before you go?'

Jamie glanced at his watch. 'That's very kind of you, but I fear not. We have an appointment in Versailles this afternoon, and we need to leave for that shortly.'

It was only when we were out through the revolving door once more that I could feel my heartbeat returning to normal.

'Thank you,' I said. 'I feel terrible but I couldn't bear to be in there another second. It brought it all back. I don't know what's wrong with me.'

'Nothing's wrong with you, Maggie. You've been through hell. That leaves a mark on the strongest person. Believe me, I've seen the toughest of men cry like babies over what they've seen and done. Let's go somewhere else and get that drink. You look as if you could do with one.'

'How about the Café de Flore? It's not too far from here.'

He looped his arm through mine, and we walked back up the boulevard, pushing the carriage, looking for all the world like a normal family out for a stroll. Except there was nothing normal about us or about the world right now. Everything had been upended, although the war was staggering to a close. The Soviets were breathing down Hitler's neck from one side while we were poised to take him from the other, the Allies sweeping across western Germany, aiming to cross the Rhine and invade the rest. Then, maybe, we could make a new normal. Although I had no idea what normal looked like anymore.

I glanced at Jamie – perhaps he was part of it. Time would tell.

TWENTY-FIVE

11 JANUARY 1945, AUSCHWITZ-BIRKENAU

I slowed again as I reached the nursery, aware that I could frighten the babies with my thundering footsteps and my gasps for breath. Inside, all was calm. Hanna was filling in her notes. A far cry from Mengele's.

'Quick,' I gasped. 'Tear up some of the paper bandages.'

Hanna didn't need to ask why as together we stuck them at irregular intervals to Leah's skin.

'They'll take a couple of days to work,' I said. 'I need to do something in the meantime. Stick some of these on Anna too so it looks as if they're both infected.'

While Hanna got to work, I rubbed and pinched Leah's skin while she howled, her face screwed up in indignation.

'I'm so sorry,' I murmured. 'There's nothing else I can do.'

Her delicate skin turned pink and mottled under my fingers and not a moment too soon.

'Let me see the baby,' snapped Nurse Clara as she swept in, darting me a look that said she hadn't forgotten or forgiven the coffee she'd been forced to bring me. How or why these women vied for Mengele's attention was a mystery to me. I would rather die than sacrifice my principles over such a man, but then again, I doubted she had any.

She stood a foot or so from Leah's cot, clearly unwilling to get any closer for fear of catching something.

I pulled the blanket back down where I'd tugged it up just seconds before and indicated the pink, blotchy patches on her skin as well as the bandages stuck to it. 'We've covered the worst of it as you can see to try to avoid any pustules bursting. The other one has it too.'

Nurse Clara grimaced, not even looking at Anna. 'I'll inform Dr Mengele. You will provide me with reports until the rash has disappeared.'

'Please do. You can tell him I think we may be over the worst in a few days. With any luck, the child will make a full recovery.'

She sniffed, adjusting her white cap so it sat perfectly straight before marching off to relay this information to Mengele. I let out a long, slow sigh of relief.

'We have to keep him thinking this isn't as bad as it looks, otherwise he might just decide to euthanise them both.'

Hanna's brow puckered in concern. 'I know. Hopefully he won't come anywhere near and nor will she until we tell them the rash has gone.'

'By that time, I hope we'll be close to getting out of here.'

'Is there any more news on that?'

'I'll go and visit the dispensary. Find out if they know anything.'

I couldn't bear to tell her of Aleks's death and those of all the others they'd hanged. She knew nothing of the escape plan anyway. It was better not to crush what little hope she had. Instead, I would find out if there was anything I could tell her that would raise it.

My footsteps dragged as I approached the pharmacy, and I started to shiver. Delayed shock, no doubt, along with having to revisit the last place I'd seen him alive. And right there I vowed to keep fighting in his memory.

The pharmacist looked at me over his spectacles in that way of his, sorrow and exhaustion creased beneath his eyes although his gaze was, as ever, warm. 'It's good to see you, Doctor,' he said. 'What can I do for you?'

Bring him back, I wanted to howl. *Take that noose off his neck and let him live again.*

'I have some chits,' I mumbled, handing over a wad of blank ones I pulled from my pocket.

He looked at them, then at me. 'Why don't you have a seat, Doctor? These will take me a little time.'

I sank into the one, hard chair that was set by the dispensing counter and stared into space. All I could see was Aleks's face. His smile, so like my brothers'. That last, brave smile.

'Here you go,' said the pharmacist, handing me a small bottle. 'It's for you to take. For medicinal purposes.'

I took it, a whiff of the contents immediately conjuring another memory. It was the same brandy Aleks had given me – local hooch, potent and strong. I gulped it down in one, erupting in a fit of coughing that had the pharmacist patting me on the back. He continued to do so even after the coughs turned into sobs.

'That's it,' he murmured. 'Let it out.'

At last, I lifted my head and wiped my eyes on my sleeve. His colleagues were tactfully averting their eyes and going about their work.

'Is there any more news of the Soviets?' I whispered.

The pharmacist glanced around the room and at the doorway before murmuring, 'Less than a week away.'

Hope surged through me once more. Less than a week. Six days. Maybe five. I could keep going for that long. Keep Leah out of Mengele's clutches. For Eva it was too late, but I could try to save her baby, although I had no idea what the Nazis would do with us. None of us did. All I knew was that if there was a glimmer of a chance, I would make sure Leah got out of here alive. That we all did. A bold thought but, when everything else was lost, it was the only way to think. Long live freedom – Aleks's last words. I wouldn't let him down.

TWENTY-SIX

26 FEBRUARY 1945, PARIS, FRANCE

Sophie was staring at the revolving door, shaking her head.

'Something wrong?' asked Antoine.

'No. Not really. Is there something I can do for you?'

'I need to go and help sort out the new consignment of clothing. Can you get someone to take over here?'

'Of course. Have they all had something to eat?'

'They have, although they might need some more coffee.'

They both jumped as one of the men suddenly shouted out, 'Doctor!'

'You need a doctor?' said Antoine.

Sophie drew him aside. 'There was a doctor here – a young woman. She calmed him down. He was crying.'

'I see,' said Antoine. 'A doctor? What was she doing here?'

'They came to have a drink at the bar, she and her husband, along with their baby. They didn't know the hotel had been requisitioned. I said they were welcome to stay, but the young woman, well, she'd been in one of the camps too. Such a pretty young thing although she had that haunted look in her eyes. The one they all have. I think it was too much for her.'

'Poor thing. There are so many like that. And we'll be seeing more and more.'

Antoine glanced at the man again, the one who'd shouted out. He hadn't uttered a word since his arrival a couple of days before. Others spoke but struggled to know what to say, unable or unwilling to convey the horror of what had happened to them. The few things they did say returned to jolt Antoine awake in the night.

Was this what Eva had suffered too? And the children? *Were* suffering. He must never give up hope. Look at the people who'd found their way to the Lutetia. If they'd managed it, Eva and the children could as well. Then there was Maggie, transported on the last train to Auschwitz from Lyon, caught sabotaging the railway line the day they'd freed Jack and the others. Maybe they'd somehow found each other in there, she and Eva. Anything was possible.

That was if they hadn't been moved on to other camps. Auschwitz may have been liberated, but there was still no news of his family, although he'd badgered SHAEF to send their descriptions to the displaced persons camps they were in charge of organising. The problem was that chaos reigned everywhere, in spite of SHAEF's best efforts. People were registered under the wrong names and nationalities. It was going to take months or maybe even years to reunite some with their families. If they could be reunited. Antoine didn't even want to contemplate the alternative.

She was strong, his Eva. She would survive. As for Maggie, he had no doubt she would have made it too. Or perhaps it was all wishful thinking. He dabbed at his cheek with his handkerchief, feeling stubble graze his fingertips. He'd barely grabbed four hours' sleep last night, so busy was he settling in the new arrivals. They'd piled out of the trucks just before midnight, exhausted from their journey, standing in silent rows, staring at him with empty eyes as he tried to process them.

Each had to be carefully entered in the register before they could go on to receive some hot soup and be allocated a room. Antoine was determined that no mistakes would be made at his end. Every name was checked to make doubly sure it was spelled correctly and hometowns or villages painstakingly logged. Then, of course, he had to keep an eye out for infiltrators or collaborators hoping to escape justice. It was an arduous task, but at least it kept his mind occupied. Each time another lorry arrived from the train station or further afield, hope ignited once more, only to be extinguished as he scanned the faces and realised that they were all strangers, probably even to themselves.

Alone in his room later, he would weep, his face buried in his pillow. Sometimes he thought he could smell her there, the faint whiff of lavender reminding him of the linen sheets at home and the way she'd always scented them with lavender water. It reminded him, too, of the fields near Lyon, great purple swathes that filled the country air with their scent or helped disguise the airfield high on the ridge behind the chateau they'd used as a hideout and HQ. He could hear Maggie now, bicycle wheels rattling as she sped off on an assignment, to send a message or to bring news. She was always dashing around, copper curls flying. That was how he'd last seen her, feet pumping the pedals as she cycled as fast as she could, determined to sabotage the Germans. She had succeeded, but at what price?

The same price his wife and children had paid – incarceration in Auschwitz.

Every single night, as he dried his tears on the pillowcase, he prayed for their safe return, but so far God was deaf. Or maybe he'd simply stopped listening.

TWENTY-SEVEN

26 FEBRUARY 1945, SHAEF HEADQUARTERS, VERSAILLES, FRANCE

'Lieutenant Colonel Steed will see you now.'

I gently removed the bottle from Leah's mouth and wiped it. She smiled beatifically and burped.

'Well, that saves me a job,' said Jamie, laughing as he scooped her up.

We entered a room where a basalt-eyed American sat surrounded by packing boxes.

'Gordon Steed,' he said, offering his hand to each of us in turn as we introduced ourselves. 'Forgive the chaos but we're moving to Reims. Your call is all set up. I just wanted to get a few details from you first.'

He looked at Leah and his eyes softened. 'And who is this?'

'This is Leah,' I said. 'We're on our way to Lyon, to meet her father there. That's why I need to speak to my people in London. Find out where he is.'

Not the exact truth but close enough. Antoine might have no idea Leah even existed, but I was sure he would meet us as soon as he knew that she did. In the meantime, Lieutenant Colonel Steed could simply assume I was her mother. It

avoided too many awkward questions or even Steed insisting he
hand her over to the French authorities.

'There may be a problem with that.'

'Oh?'

I waited him out. Beside me, I could feel Jamie sitting very
still, listening hard although he appeared completely at ease.

'I already spoke with London,' said Steed. 'They told me
that most of your people are elsewhere, on a top-secret mission.
But there is one person you can speak to. Name of Edward.
Apparently he can point you in the right direction.'

I tried to conceal my surprise. Surely not Marianne's
brother Edward? I thought he'd been executed by Klaus Barbie
back in Lyon when we were on our mission there. It was a
common enough name but still a strange coincidence.

'I see.'

Steed sighed and spread his hands. 'I'm sorry. I know you've
come a long way. That you've been through a lot. London didn't
mention anything about a baby to me.'

'That's because I didn't tell them.'

'I'm sure you have your reasons.'

'I do.'

'Understood. Before I take you through, I just want to get
some more information. You were liberated from Auschwitz, is
that correct?'

'From a death march. By Captain Maclean here.'

He turned the full force of his attention on Jamie. 'And
what were you doing there?'

'I was with the Red Army, sir.'

This time, Steed's eyebrows nearly shot through his scalp.
'In what capacity?'

'I'm afraid that's top secret, sir.'

'Captain Maclean, do you know where you're sitting?'

'Indeed I do. In the Supreme Headquarters Allied Expeditionary Force, sir.'

'And do you know who I am?'

'The head of US counterintelligence here, sir.'

'So I assume you understand that I need to know what you were doing with the Red Army in Poland.'

'I would love to help you, sir, but I'm sure you understand that when I say that's top secret, I mean it.'

Steed sighed and steepled his fingers. 'What regiment are you with?'

'The Second Highlanders, sir.'

'No, I mean your real regiment. The one with which you regularly serve.'

'I think you can guess, sir.'

'I think I can. You're one of Stirling's boys. Or is it Mayne's now? Anyway, God only knows what you were getting up to with the Soviets. I guess I should commend you for rescuing Maggie here.'

'Thank you, sir. I'm here to make sure she and Leah get safely to their destination.'

I could feel Leah fussing and fidgeting, no doubt picking up on the atmosphere. Although Jamie sounded and looked completely relaxed, I could feel the tension coming off him in waves. He evidently hated Steed's attitude. I wasn't too keen on it either.

'Do you have any more questions for me?' I asked. 'Because if not, I'd really like to make that call.'

'Just one. Is Leah your daughter?'

I looked him straight in the eye. 'She is.'

'You were sent to Auschwitz in August 1944?'

'I was.'

'You were already pregnant when you got there?'

I felt Jamie twitch beside me. 'Is this really necessary?' he demanded. 'These are indelicate questions, and Maggie has been through quite an ordeal.'

'This is an indelicate war, Captain Maclean. I'm sure

Maggie has been asked a lot worse.'

'For God's sake,' I snapped. 'I am here. And I can answer for myself. Yes, I've been asked worse. I'm sure, Lieutenant Colonel Steed, that you can count. As for the rest, that really is none of your business.'

He had the grace to look slightly ashamed but only slightly. 'I apologise, ma'am, if I offended you, but I have a job to do.'

'So do I,' I said, rising from my seat. 'And I would like to do it by speaking with my colleague in London now. You said Edward is available to talk to me?'

'I did.'

'Then what are we waiting for? The last train to Lyon is at six o'clock, and I intend to be on it.'

A fractional pause as pugnacity battled diplomacy and then Steed, too, rose. 'Very well. Right this way.'

He led us into a room where a telephone sat waiting, an operator beside it. 'This is a SIGSALY phone. Completely secure. Corporal Johnson here will set you up and he will then withdraw so you can carry on your conversation.'

'Thank you.'

Jamie looked at me. 'Want me to stay?'

'Yes I do. You can rock Leah if she starts grizzling.'

The expression on Steed's face was priceless. I suspected that, if he had children, he'd never once rocked them. Well, too bad. It was about time men like him started learning. We women had taken on so much during this war, doing things we'd never have dreamed of before. If we could strap on parachutes or learn how to lay explosives on railway lines, then men like Steed could rock babies. It was as simple as that.

'You're connected, ma'am,' said the corporal, saluting as he exited.

I put the receiver to my ear. 'Edward?'

'Is this Maggie?' He had a cultured voice with a hint of warmth to it.

'It is.'

'Just to be absolutely sure, perhaps you could tell me your favourite poem.'

Now, that was easy. '"Chanson d'automne" by Verlaine.'

He exhaled softly. 'That was what I wanted to hear. It's so good to know that you're alive.'

'I could say the same, I think.'

He chuckled. 'You think correctly but that's a story for another time. I understand you want to get to Lyon. Any particular reason?'

'I need to find Antoine. I have something for him.'

'But Antoine is in Paris. Did no one tell you?'

'Paris? No. No one told me. Us. I'm here with a Captain Maclean.'

'So I understand. It was his people who got hold of me. Antoine is keeping up our end of things in Paris, looking after displaced persons while making sure none of them are collaborators or Nazis who've slipped through the net.'

I felt a faint dawning in the back of my brain. 'Where exactly is he in Paris? And where is everyone else?'

'They're on a mission in the Vosges mountains, but you can find Antoine at the Hotel Lutetia.'

I gasped. Jamie threw me a questioning glance while I could hear Edward again down the line.

'Is something wrong?'

'No. Nothing. It's just... we were there only this morning. At the Lutetia.'

'Quite a day for happy coincidences.'

'It is,' I said softly, looking at Leah. 'It really is.'

TWENTY-EIGHT

26 FEBRUARY 1945, PARIS, FRANCE

The Hotel Lutetia was no less busy late at night, the public areas still teeming with hollow-eyed people, wandering like restless ghosts.

'Can I help you?'

Another smiling woman; Sophie was nowhere to be seen.

'I'm looking for Antoine,' I said. 'Antoine Melville.'

'You just missed him. He left about ten minutes ago.'

'Do you know where he went?'

'To his apartment, I assume.'

'I don't suppose you can give me the address? It's very urgent, madame.'

She hesitated, eyeing us up, taking in Leah fast asleep in her carriage. 'Just one moment. I'll try and find out for you.'

I watched as she bustled off. Leah chose that moment to open her eyes and let out an almighty howl.

One of the men still dressed in his striped camp uniform approached. 'May I hold the baby, just for a moment?'

I hesitated, taking in his sunken cheeks that appeared to be ingrained with the kind of dirt that would never wash off. Then

I looked in his eyes, seeing in them a glimmer of something I recognised.

Of course,' I said, lifting Leah from her carriage and handing her to him, swaddled in her blankets.

'Thank you. My name is Joseph.'

'I'm Maggie, and this is Leah.'

'It's good to meet you, Leah.'

He cradled her tenderly, rocking her to and fro in the age-old motion known to parents and grandparents everywhere, making little soothing sounds as he did so. Within seconds she was calm, staring at him in fascination.

'You're beautiful,' he crooned. 'So beautiful.'

At that, Leah began to laugh.

'She's never done that before,' I said. 'Jamie, look, she's laughing.'

The man pulled a couple of faces before he handed her back, still laughing. 'Mine do that too,' he said. 'Heaven knows, I should have been a clown. But that was before Sachsenhausen.'

And then his face crumpled, collapsing in a paroxysm of sobs. He was still standing there, sobbing, when the woman returned.

She handed me a folded piece of paper. 'There you go,' she said. 'It's not too far from here. A few minutes' walk.'

I looked at her in surprise. 'Thank you, madame.'

She patted my arm. 'You have an honest face, my dear. You're such a lovely family. Now please excuse me but I must tend to my charges here. Who would like some more champagne?'

I glanced at the address written on the piece of paper, recognising the name of the street. 'It's just a few roads away,' I said to Jamie. 'Let's go.'

'Look at them,' he murmured, 'drinking champagne out of silver cups. They must think they've died and gone to heaven. It's surreal.'

I followed his gaze, taking in the men waiting patiently for their cups to be filled, drinking the champagne as if it was water. 'They deserve it after all they've been through. You invited us to a dance, remember, and then plied us with wine.'

'I did no such thing,' retorted Jamie. 'I merely offered you the best the village had to offer which, admittedly, wasn't much.'

All at once, he grew very still, his eyes fixed on one of the men waiting to be served. He looked ordinary enough, if you could call any of them ordinary – a tall, thin man dressed in ill-fitting donated clothes rather than camp uniform, his black hair close-cropped, eyes lowered.

'What is it?' I murmured.

'I – nothing.'

'You look like you've seen a ghost.'

'I thought he was someone else. That's all.'

Something in me didn't quite believe him.

He took me by the arm and turned towards the revolving door. 'Come on. Let's find your friend Antoine.'

I stopped under the street light outside, looking up at him, at his face illuminated by its glow and by something else – that inner light he always seemed to possess. He was that rare thing – a good person. Not saccharine sweet or holier than thou but simply possessed of a deep sense of what was right.

'I was teasing you,' I said. 'It was a wonderful evening. One I'll remember for the rest of my life for so many reasons.'

'I hope there'll be many more,' he said, his voice thick with an emotion I didn't recognise. Not then, at any rate.

'Of course there will. Now we'd better hurry before Antoine goes to bed. It's going to be enough of a shock for him. I don't want to have to rouse him from sleep as well.'

Although the Antoine I knew would be instantly awake, alert to any danger. He slept like a cat with one eye half-open. I'd seen him do it many times in the barns and farmhouses where we'd hidden out, constantly aware we could be caught at any moment by the Germans.

But it was me who hesitated as we drew close to his building. I stopped dead a few metres from it, unable to go on.

'What's the matter?'

'I... I don't know. Yes, I do. I'm scared, Jamie. What if he doesn't even want to see Leah? Or me? I have to tell him about Eva and the twins. How's he going to react to that?'

'You don't know and I don't know either. What I do know is that any man in his situation would want to meet his daughter. He would also want to know what happened to the rest of his family. It's the not knowing that kills people.'

'I realise that, but I can't tell him everything. If he knows what Mengele did to his little boys before they died, he'll lose his mind.'

'Does he need to know that?'

'No. I think it better he doesn't. Just look at her, Jamie. She's so very young. Now she has to grow up without a mother. I don't want him to resent her because she's alive while Eva is dead.'

Jamie took me by the shoulders, looking me straight in the face. 'What are you really afraid of, Maggie? That you'll lose her? She was never yours in the first place, although she's become such a big part of you. If Antoine is the friend you say he is, he'll want you in her life.'

He was right. I was being selfish. It wasn't my place to decide what happened now. That was up to Antoine. And fate.

'I know. I just love her so much, and I want to do what's best for her.'

'I know you do, and the best thing for Leah is to be with her own.'

It felt as if a score of knives were twisting deep in my belly, but I pushed the carriage forward, step by step, until finally we were standing in front of the entrance to the apartment building. A concierge opened the door and eyed us up and down.

'We're here to see Monsieur Melville – Antoine Melville.'

She peered at Leah and then at me before addressing Jamie as if we two didn't exist. 'Apartment seven.'

'Thank you, madame.'

I could sense her eyes on us as we squeezed the carriage into the tiny lift, pulling the gate across so that the doors closed, thankfully obliterating her from view.

The doors clanged open on Antoine's floor and we emerged, my heart plummeting into my stomach, nausea washing over me, sending my head spinning.

'It's this one,' said Jamie, indicating the apartment door to the left of the lift.

I stared at it. An ordinary wooden door. That was all. But the moment I knocked on it, the world would change forever. Or at least, my world would, along with Leah's and Antoine's.

He answered the door almost as soon as I knocked, peering out and then flinging it wide as he realised who I was.

'Maggie! Is it you? Is it really you?'

'It's me,' I said, half-laughing, half-crying.

'My God, Maggie. How did you get here? How did you find me?'

I looked over my shoulder, sensing the concierge standing in the lobby a couple of floors below the open stairwell, ears no doubt sharpened almost as much as her tongue.

'Come in, come in.' He ushered us in, closing the door behind us. 'This will keep the concierge gossiping for weeks. Mind you, she already thinks I'm a very suspicious character.'

'How so?'

I looked around the apartment, taking in the small but tidy salon, the pictures on the walls of flowers and countryside scenes. This wasn't a home. It was a stopping place like so many we'd occupied over the past few years. Although perhaps Leah would change all that. Maybe Antoine would once again create a home.

He glanced at her now, looking from her to me with curiosity.

I lifted her out and took a breath. 'This is Leah.'

He looked again, his expression changing. 'Leah?'

Had he guessed? I thought I saw realisation dawning across his face, although that could have been my imagination.

'Yes. She's yours. Yours and Eva's. This is Leah, your daughter.'

He gaped at me in disbelief, barely able to take in what I was saying, stumbling back and then righting himself as he grabbed hold of a side table.

'Where do you keep your drink?' asked Jamie.

Antoine waved towards the kitchen. I heard Jamie rifling through the cupboards, uncorking a bottle.

Finally, Antoine managed to speak. 'Mine? How can she be mine?'

I struggled to find the words, to know what to say first.

'Drink this.' Jamie handed him a glass he'd filled with cognac. 'Why don't we all sit down?'

Antoine stayed where he was, swaying slightly.

'Sit down,' I ordered. 'And drink up.'

He sank into a chair and took a swig from the glass, his eyes never leaving Leah.

'Here,' I said. 'Would you like to hold her?'

He shook his head.

I glanced at Jamie. 'She was born in Auschwitz,' I said. 'I delivered her. Eva was very brave. She did everything she could to make sure Leah survived.'

My voice cracked. I took in another gulp of air. This was so hard, but I had to tell him, for his own sake.

'I'm afraid your other children didn't make it and nor did

Eva. She lost a lot of blood giving birth, but she held on as long as she could so that she could nurse Leah.'

No mention of Mengele or his ghastly experiments. There was no need. Let Antoine have his memories of them unsullied.

His face turned ashen, and he swallowed, fighting to control himself. I could see his fists clenching and unclenching. A single tear spilled from one eye and coursed down his face.

'They're all gone?' he whispered. 'All of them?'

'Not all. You still have Leah. Why don't you hold her, Antoine?'

He was still staring into space, refusing to look at her. He was in shock – that was understandable. Then, all at once, he bent over, clutching at his stomach, rocking backward and forward as he cried silently, lost in the kind of pain I could never imagine. Yes, I had lost people too or seen them die. Many of them, including Aleks. But nothing like this, nothing like knowing your entire family had been wiped out. All except for one, an innocent child who needed a father.

I tried again, lifting Leah to my shoulder, her cinnamon baby smell filling my nostrils and, I hoped, Antoine's.

At last, he straightened, looking now at the infant in my arms, the agony in his eyes giving way to that thing I'd seen before in the eyes of the man who'd held her at the hotel, Joseph. Pure, protective love.

'Give her to me,' he said.

I placed her gently in his arms.

'Hello, Leah,' he murmured. 'You have your mother's eyes.'

She stared at him in the way that babies do, with complete fascination, and then she reached up one tiny hand as if to try and touch his face. He dropped a kiss on her forehead, a mere brush of a butterfly's wing, careful not to startle her, keeping his voice low.

'And look, you have so much hair already. Blonde, just like

my Eva. I bet you're going to be as strong and intelligent as she was. As kind and loving too.'

I swallowed, my throat closing over the words I so desperately wanted to utter. How she had loved him to the last. The way she'd tried so hard to live for their daughter. Her insistence I bring her here, to Antoine, to her father, even while she knew she would never see either of them again.

But those words could wait. What mattered now was that Antoine was falling in love with his daughter, right here in front of our eyes. I'd been so afraid he might reject her. Worried that she would remind him too much of his other children and Eva. But I needn't have worried – he had enough love in him for all of them, for those he'd lost and the daughter he'd found.

TWENTY-NINE

27 FEBRUARY 1945, PARIS, FRANCE

Dawn was painting the sky shades of pale gold and pink when I stirred, sitting bolt upright in bed as I remembered what had happened the night before. I could see Leah in her crib, arms flung wide, bent at the elbow in the way only babies can sleep. Beside her, Antoine lay curled up on a camp bed, one of his arms stretched towards his daughter as he, too, slept. He'd insisted I take the bedroom while we tucked Leah into a drawer we lined with blankets from her carriage and set on the floor.

She'd only squawked twice as we talked through the night after Jamie tactfully withdrew. Each time Antoine insisted on giving her the bottle, cradling her against him as she filled her stomach while I spoke of the time I'd spent with Eva and then, later, with Leah in the displaced person's camp, filling him in on every detail I could remember. Now he was finally getting some sleep too, I didn't want to disturb him.

I eased my legs from under the covers and tiptoed to the bathroom.

'Good morning.'

As I emerged from the bathroom, I found Antoine sitting on the edge of his camp bed, staring in wonder at Leah.

'They're amazing, aren't they, babies? They eat, they sleep, all they want is food, a clean nappy and love.'

'I'm sure you can supply all of that.'

'I'm not sure I can.'

I looked at him, seeing the fear in his eyes. 'Of course you can, Antoine. It may take time to adjust, but you'll be just fine. You'll see.'

'I don't know, Maggie. What am I supposed to do when I'm working? How can I look after her then? She's barely two months old and already so much has happened to her. Now I must be Papa and Maman too. What if I get it wrong?'

'Listen to me, Antoine. You'll work it out. We met the ladies at the Lutetia. I'm sure they'll help. They'll be delighted to have a baby to fuss over, as will many of the displaced people there.'

He visibly recoiled. 'I'm not taking my daughter there.'

'Why not? She was born among people like them. I could have been one of those people. I'm just fortunate that Jamie and the Red Army rescued me.'

He dropped his gaze. 'I'm sorry. You're right. I just so want to protect her, to look after her now that everyone else is gone.'

His words ended on a small, strangled sob. My heart ached for him.

'Antoine, Leah is strong, like her mother. She wouldn't have survived this long otherwise. We marched through the snow with those Nazi pigs shouting at us, their dogs barking all the time, and she never once complained. It was as if she knew she had to keep quiet in order to stay alive. I think she gets that strength from you as well as from her mother.'

As if to prove my point, Leah's eyes flew open. She saw Antoine and immediately opened her mouth and roared, her fist flailing as if to demand breakfast there and then. I smiled as Antoine jumped to his feet and reached for her bottle. She had him well trained already. I suspected it would stay that way for the rest of their lives together.

'I promised to meet Jamie at the hotel for breakfast. The nappies are in that drawer.'

Might as well get him in training for that too, although, by the look of things, Antoine was a hands-on father. He barely looked up as I let myself out, far too busy tending to his daughter to give me more than a nod. And that was the way it should be. It lifted my heart to see it.

Not as much as my heart lifted at the thought of seeing Jamie though. He'd secured us rooms at the George V, pulling in favours from an old pal. It seemed he knew everyone, or at least everyone worth knowing. There was so much more to Jamie than I'd first thought, more perhaps than I would ever know. He was full of surprises while remaining remarkably tight-lipped.

He was already in the hotel dining room when I got there, an envelope sitting by his plate.

'This is for you,' he said. 'Delivered directly from SHAEF.'

I opened it and scanned the few lines on the message inside.

Return to London immediately for medical evaluation and rest. We will organise transport.

Jamie was watching my face as I read it through twice, my heart sinking. 'What do your orders say?'

'That I'm to return to London for rest and medical evaluation.'

'Sounds sensible to me.'

'Jamie, I'm a doctor. I know whether I need medical evaluation or not. I don't want to rest. I want to be with my colleagues, who are also my friends.'

He looked at me and I could see the concern in his eyes. It made me want to scream.

'Maggie, you've been through a huge ordeal. You're bound to have some after-effects from that. I can see them.'

'What do you mean you can see them?'

All at once, I was icy cold with fury and something else, something I didn't even want to name.

'I saw the way those displaced people in the Lutetia affected you. I also saw you back at the camp when you were a displaced person yourself. You were doing your best, Maggie. You always do, from what I can see. But it was costing you. I think some rest and recuperation would be a very good thing.'

'Does that mean you think I should go to London?'

'Those are your orders.'

My voice thickened with unshed tears, and I hated myself for it. 'You want me to go?'

'Of course I don't want you to go, but I do want what's best for you.'

I stared at my plate, at my brioche with the butter still melting into it. I took a bite. Sawdust. Still I forced it into my mouth, chewing and swallowing. It felt like shards of glass scraping the back of my throat. But I had to eat. Whatever it was, I had to eat it. My stomach growled at me, remembering the months of starvation. That voice in my head, shouting at me. *Eat. Stay alive.* Another, quieter voice murmuring, *You don't deserve to live.*

I remembered that voice from Auschwitz. From the DP camp. It followed me everywhere, sly and insidious, whispering at me that I wasn't worthy. Who was I to live while so many had died? Why did I get to eat when I'd worked alongside the Nazis, tending my patients?

But you had to do that, the voice of reason cried. *You had to or they would have killed you.*

Still, I hated myself for it. Hated the fact I was here, in a luxury hotel in Paris, while people like Eva were no more, their bodies slung into mass pits before the Nazis set fire to them, watching them burn, what body fat they had left acting as fuel.

I caught sight of my arm, plump in comparison to theirs, although I was thinner than I'd ever been.

I pushed my chair back from the table. 'Excuse me.'

Safe in the toilet cubicle, I retched until there was nothing left in my stomach, the few crumbs I had swallowed brought up in bile. Only then, when I was sure there was nothing left, did I sit back on my haunches, satisfied.

'My God, Maggie, what have they done to you?' I whispered.

I hardly dared look in the mirror as I washed my hands and then my face, splashing away the sour smell of vomit. When I did, I saw a phantom staring back at me, someone I scarcely recognised, as if I'd known her long ago.

I tugged my fingers through my hair as best I could and then stumbled back to the table.

Jamie took one look at me and poured me a glass of water. 'Here, drink this. Slowly now.'

I sipped at it, my eyes lowered, feeling a deep sense of shame washing through and over me. I couldn't look at him. Couldn't look at anyone. I had no idea what I'd become, but I knew that I had to keep it from him, from them.

'Thank you,' I said.

'Are you alright? You look terrible.'

I smiled. Or at least I tried to. 'I'm fine. Just a funny turn. I didn't get much sleep what with Leah and Antoine in the next room. A nap this afternoon and I'll be right as rain.'

'It'll take more than a nap, Maggie.'

'Oh for God's sake,' I snapped. 'Who's the doctor here?'

'It doesn't take a doctor to know that you need help.'

'I don't need any help. Least of all yours.'

I hated myself as soon as the words left my mouth, hated the way they landed on him. And then he smiled.

'That's good,' he said. 'They haven't broken your spirit. But let me tell you the one thing I've learned through this war and that's to take help when it's offered. Go back to London, Maggie. Take some time for yourself. Your friends will still be here when you return and so will I.'

'Will you?' I whispered. 'What if you disappear too?'

He leaned forward and took my hand in his, curling his fingers round it so he held it safe. 'I won't be disappearing anywhere. I have this girl, you see. One that I'm mad about.'

I smiled. 'You do?'

'Well, I hope so anyway. If she'll have me.'

I placed my other hand on top of our clasped ones, pressing them tighter together. There was nothing more I could say.

THIRTY

I hugged Antoine tight. 'Look after Leah.' I stroked her petal-soft baby cheek. 'Look after your daddy.'

She beamed with the toothless grin that was becoming ever more frequent.

'We'll be here waiting,' said Antoine. 'Whenever you're ready to return. And if you want to write to your family and give them my address, I will take great care of any replies. I can even forward them to you in London.'

I looked from him to Jamie. Had they been talking about me? Or was it so obvious to everyone?

'Thank you,' I said. 'But I'll be back before you know it. On my way to join the others, wherever they are.'

Antoine dropped a kiss on each of my cheeks. '*Sois sage.*' *Be a good girl.*

I patted his cheek in return. 'I've never been a good girl in my entire life, Antoine. I'm not about to start now.'

I had to force myself to turn then and walk away from him and Leah. It had only been three days since they'd met one another but already I could see the bond that had formed between them. They would be fine.

'I thought we could walk back to the hotel,' said Jamie as soon as we were outside Antoine's building. 'We have time.'

'That's the one thing I wish we had.'

'Oh, Maggie.' He brushed a wisp of hair back from my face and looked at me, his eyes sombre. 'We'll have all the time in the world once this war is over. And it's almost over.'

'Almost but not quite. A lot can happen and so fast. Just think, only a few years ago I was walking this same street as a student, carefree. Now look at me.'

We'd paused by a small city park, its trees just beginning to show signs of life, the benches arrayed around it empty.

'Come,' he said. 'Let's sit here a moment.'

The air, too, was springlike, chilly but full of promise. We sat beside one another, not quite touching, on a bench opposite a statue. He dropped his arm across my shoulders and pulled me in closer.

'There now,' he said. 'That's better.'

I laughed. 'Do you always arrange things the way you like them?'

'Pretty much. I like you, for instance.'

'Explain to me how you arranged me.'

'I didn't. You just happened, like a dream coming true or, how do you say it in French, *un coup de foudre*?'

Love at first sight.

'What rubbish. I looked terrible the first time you saw me. I was running through those trees in that forest, filthy and terrified.'

'That's not what I saw. I saw a woman who was determined to survive. Not just that – a woman who wanted to save the lives of others too. You were leading your friend, protecting Leah. That's how I still see you, Maggie. As someone strong and brave.'

'I'm not as strong or brave as I used to be.'

'That's hardly surprising. It's also not true. You're stronger

and braver because of what you've been through. You might not
see it, but simply carrying on takes courage. A quieter courage
maybe, but it's still there.'

I turned and looked at him, maybe really looked at him for
the first time. I could see the compassion in his eyes along with
something I thought no one could ever show me again – real
understanding.

'You know what it's like, don't you? The bad dreams. The
flashbacks. Thinking you'll never be yourself again.'

'All of that, Maggie, and more. But you will be yourself
again. Just a different self. I won't say a better one because I
wouldn't wish what you've been through on anyone. And
anyway, I don't think you can be improved.'

His smile lightened the moment, bringing an answering one
to my face.

He cupped my chin with his hand. 'I'll miss you,' he
murmured.

The kiss we shared was so sweet and yet so sad. It felt as if
something was ending just as it was beginning.

'I'm coming back,' I said. 'I still have work to do here.'

'And I'll be waiting for you.'

'What if they send you somewhere far away?'

'Then I'll return from there. Trust me, Maggie. I will find
you, wherever they send me.'

'I'll hold you to that,' I said. 'Now we'd better be getting
back.'

His hand tightened on mine. 'Do you hear that? Music.'

I listened. There it was. The sweet, sultry notes of a saxophone playing a waltz, drifting across to us from goodness only
knows where.

Jamie tugged at my hand. 'Shall we?'

As we rose from the bench, I caught a glimpse of the man
playing the saxophone on a street corner opposite, eyes closed
and body swaying as he moved with his music. We began to

move too, our feet matched in perfect rhythm, our bodies inches apart and yet feeling as if we were melded together, whirling around in that tiny park as if it were a ballroom. Or a village hall in Germany.

We drew to a halt by our bench again as the last notes died away, our silence mirroring his. And then he started to play again, this time a tune I didn't recognise at first until Jamie began to hum it – 'The Way You Look Tonight'.

'Or even the way you look right now.' He smiled, kissing my hand before once more taking it in his as we strolled back to the hotel.

The moment we stepped through the doors, I knew something was wrong. I could feel it in my bones as we approached the reception desk.

'Captain Maclean, a message for you.'

Don't open it, the voice in my head screamed.

'Thank you.' A heartbeat as he read it. Then: 'Do you have a telephone I could use? One somewhere private?'

'Of course, sir. This way.'

Jamie looked at me. 'You go on up and finish your packing. I won't be a moment.'

'Is everything alright?'

'Absolutely fine. I just need to clarify a couple of things. Won't be long.'

My stomach lurched. I knew what that meant. Nothing was clear in this war except for orders, and I had no doubt Jamie was receiving his now.

Sure enough, when he tapped on my door and I opened it, his expression was guarded.

'You have orders, don't you?' I said.

'Maggie, I...'

'It's fine. Really. Does this mean I'm going to London on my own?'

He looked pained. 'It does.'

I felt something splinter, possibly my heart. 'Then we should say goodbye here and now. No sense in dragging it out.'

'Maggie, you know I would come with you to London if I could, but my orders are to join my regiment immediately.'

'Which regiment?' He didn't need to tell me. My heart plummeted. 'Be careful out there,' I whispered.

He stepped forward, pushing me gently into my room and closing the door behind him. 'Do I have to be careful in here too?'

The blood was thudding in my ears now, louder than any drum. 'No.'

'Good.'

We were kissing as if there was no tomorrow, no time but the here and now, his hands exploring, tentatively at first and then emboldened as I arched my back, pressing into him. I could feel my nerve ends thrilling even as I fought down the fear. I might be a virgin, but I was also a doctor. I knew about all of this.

Jamie must have sensed my nervousness because he paused, drawing back to drop featherlight kisses all over my face.

'You're so beautiful, Maggie. So strong. Have I ever told you how proud I am of you?'

His words thudded true into my heart like arrows finding their target. Of all the things he could have said, those hit home, opening up a wound I'd thought was healed.

'I'm not strong. I'm just someone who survived and feels guilty for doing so. Like all those people at the Lutetia.'

'You are strong, my love. All of you are for surviving it. Don't ever feel guilty. To me, you are perfect.'

He dropped a kiss on my lips, reaching round to undo the buttons on my dress, gently peeling it from one shoulder and then the other, all the while murmuring words of love. My dress slithered down over me, and I stepped out of it as it dropped to the floor, keeping my eyes firmly locked on Jamie's, feeling all of a sudden shy and exposed.

'So beautiful,' he said, caressing me, running his hand over my front, down my sides, then reaching up to cup one of my breasts.

I let out a tiny moan of pleasure, tendrils of it shooting through me at his touch.

At that, he let out a groan as if he could hold back no more, kissing me deeply, his tongue melding with mine, white heat engulfing us both. I have no idea how we sank onto the bed or how the rest of my clothes came off. All I could see was his face; all I could hear was his voice murmuring to me, reassuring me, while his hands roamed, trailing fire wherever they went.

'Are you sure you want to do this?'

'I've never been more sure of anything in my life.'

'Me too,' he muttered, lowering his body onto mine.

There was a moment of sharp pain as he thrust into me, a slice like that of a dagger. He hesitated. 'Are you alright?'

'Yes, yes. Go on.'

Then we were moving together in a rhythm that built as we listened to the music of one another's bodies, hearing the songs of our hearts and souls, crying out in our passion, reaching a crescendo as he shouted out my name.

Afterwards we lay together, his hands now soothing.

'It gets better,' he said.

'That seemed pretty good to me,' I gasped, completely spent, my limbs so heavy I couldn't move them. Above all, there was that sense of deep peace for which I longed, a feeling that this was right, that we were now as one, a team like no other.

But there was no escaping time and, beneath the drumbeats of my heart, I could hear the ticking of the clock.

'Jamie, I have to go. I have a plane to catch.'

He groaned. 'I know, I know. So do I.'

He scrabbled for his clothes, pulling a scrap of paper from

his pocket. 'This is for you. I got it from one of the Red Army chaps. Many of them carry it into battle. It's a poem.'

I unfurled the paper and read:

Wait for me and I'll come back
Wait with all your might
Wait when dreary yellow rains
Tell you nothing's right...

I glanced at him and carried on, reading the last lines aloud: 'Only you and I will know / How you got me through / Simply – you knew how to wait / No one else but you.

'That's lovely,' I said, carefully folding the piece of paper and tucking it in my purse. 'I'll carry it with me too. Come with me to the airfield?'

'I can't. I have to report for duty in an hour.'

'I see. That urgent?'

'Unfortunately, yes. My car will be here in ten minutes. What I would love to do with you now will take far longer than that. A lifetime hopefully. I think that's worth waiting for.'

'I agree.' I pressed my hand to his lips. 'Don't say any more. Just promise me you'll find me.'

'Wherever you are and whatever it takes.'

'Then that's enough.'

THIRTY-ONE

Antoine was looking at me as if I'd lost my mind. 'Even if I knew where they are in the Vosges, I wouldn't tell you, Maggie.'

'Antoine, please. You have to. I can't go back to London on my own. All I would do is think, and I don't want to be alone with my thoughts. I want to be with the others, doing something useful.'

'Maggie, you're disobeying orders. What time is your flight due to leave?'

I looked at the clock on his mantelpiece. Leah caught the movement of my head and cooed. 'Half an hour ago.'

'*Merde.*'

'In any case, Antoine, I'm not officially disobeying orders because I haven't yet officially agreed to join whatever it is you're a part of now.'

'True, but of course you are a part of it, Maggie. That's if you want to be. It's not as if any of us signed anything. We just accepted what they offered.'

'Which is?'

He sighed. 'That I can't tell you. I assume that's what they would have explained to you in London. At least, Edward would have done. But you are still here, which makes things a little messy, to say the least.'

'I'm sorry if you feel I've compromised you. It's just...' My voice cracked as I stumbled over my thoughts, my words. 'It's just that I couldn't do it. I didn't want to leave France, not now that I'm back here. I thought that if the others were in the Vosges, maybe I could just go there.'

'Maggie, you're not thinking straight. You need to take some time out, to recover from Auschwitz and all that has happened.'

'But that's just the point, Antoine. I can't take time out. If I do, I'll start thinking about it all, and then I'm afraid it will engulf me. I don't want time to think. I want to be busy, to be doing something to help.'

I looked down at the hands I was twisting together, at my fingers, the same fingers that had eased Leah into this world, that had smoothed the hair back from Eva's brow. That had stroked Jamie's cheek just a few hours before.

Jamie. Goodness knows where he was now. As far as he was concerned, I was on a plane back to England. Another reason not to go. He could find me easier here.

'You can help by getting your strength back.'

'You really think a few weeks in England will make any difference? I can't erase the past. I can't wipe Auschwitz from my memory and nor would I want to. Don't you see? I have to remember. We all have to remember. So we can tell the world what it was really like and make sure we get justice for all those who died. I just can't remember right now.'

His eyes glistened as he raised them to meet mine and I knew he was thinking of Eva and his other children, the family he would never see again. 'It's a noble thought, but what if we never get justice for them? What then?'

'We will. I swear on my life and all that is sacred to me that we will. Otherwise it was all for nothing. The suffering, the pain, the inhuman acts they inflicted on people. I saw it,

Antoine, with my own eyes. Things I can never unsee. It has to mean something. It just has to.'

I could hear myself sobbing now, gulping out my words, but no tears ran down my cheeks. Perhaps there were none left to weep. Or maybe I was afraid to let them flow. And yet I was so exhausted, so tired of holding it back, except I had nothing more to give. I was utterly spent.

'Come, Maggie, sit here and hold Leah for me. She needs her feed.'

And I probably needed her.

I held out my arms, feeling the warm weight of her fill them, trying to smile down into her baby face so she wouldn't be alarmed.

She gazed back at me with that ancient wisdom some babies seemed to possess, her eyes staring into what felt like my very soul. If there was one person I couldn't lie to, it was Leah; as she broke into her gummy smile, I finally began to cry.

I could hear Antoine making coffee and then smell it as he placed it by me, felt him take her from me and saw through the blur of tears him expertly feeding her from her bottle.

Finally, when I was all cried out, I took a sip of the coffee. It tasted sharp and bitter on my tongue, warming me through, seeping into the corners of my brain.

'Now,' he said, 'I've had an idea. You can stay here, with me. With us. Help look after Leah and, when you feel ready, with the displaced people at the hotel. Many of them need medical help.'

I shook my head. 'I can't do that, Antoine. Besides, I want to be out there, at the front, with the others.'

'It will take time to make contact with them without alerting London. In any case, London will soon start asking questions when you don't arrive. We can send a message to say that you suspect you may have caught something infectious and don't want to travel yet.'

'That's not going to hold them off forever.'

'No, but it buys you time. Time we can use to contact Suzanne by other means.'

'Is she really in charge? How on earth did that happen?'

He winked at me and smiled. 'She can tell you that when you see her. In the meantime, you can be a great help here. Remember how you were with that poor man who can't speak? You might not think you can do it, but I think you're wrong.'

There was a challenge in his voice, and I could never resist a challenge. Then there was Leah. I looked at her happily staring at the dust motes that floated past her as if she was seeing fairies or some other kind of magic. To be able to spend more time with her would be equally magical. It might even make up for the absence of Jamie.

'I'll do it,' I said. 'I'll stay.'

Antoine beamed. 'Excellent. Let's get moving then. No time like the present.'

I stared at him and then laughed. This was the old Antoine – clever, smart and kind. I knew what he was doing.

'Roger that,' I said. 'Give me five minutes.'

Ten minutes later, we were leaving the apartment, Leah bundled cosily against the breeze which had sharpened, losing its springlike feel. As we walked, Antoine filled me in on some of the more mundane duties at the Lutetia.

'Then, of course,' he added, 'there's the covert aspect to cover too.'

My ears pricked. 'What covert aspect?'

'We check every newcomer against known Nazi sympathisers and other possible war criminals. Some have disguised themselves as displaced persons in the hope they will escape justice. Then there are others who are still actively spying, still hoping that Germany might win.'

'You think there might be spies among the people at the Lutetia?'

'It's possible. Not just Nazis either. There may be communists as well. They would dearly love to be running this country too, if not the whole world.'

'But why here? Surely they'd be better off spying at the front or behind enemy lines as we are.'

'The important decisions are made here in Paris and in London as well as Washington. The Americans are here along with the world's press. There's no point spying on frontline troops. They want to find out our plans, not what they can already see. What better cover than as a refugee from war? That way, they can access all kinds of departments while pretending to try to find their loved ones or get papers.'

'How many have you caught?'

'So far, none.'

All at once I felt it kick in, that need to get in there, to change things. 'Then we must do something about that.'

I felt rather than saw him smile. 'We must.'

THIRTY-TWO

10 MARCH 1945, PARIS, FRANCE

'London is sending someone to get you. A car is on its way even now from the airfield. I'm afraid they've lost patience, Maggie.'

I stared at Antoine across the desk. 'I'm not going. They can't make me.'

Antoine sighed. 'They can. Maggie, you're not even talking about SOE here. They're bad enough, but this new outfit are a law unto themselves. They will claim that it's for your own good as well as that of the Allies, that they need to debrief you, that you may be holding vital information that will help win this war.'

'I'm not.'

'That's as maybe. They will say and do anything they like. You know that – you worked with them.'

'Yes and they're my friends. Or at least I thought they were.'

'They still are, but your friends are not the ones based in London. From what I understand, this has gone above Edward's head. The fact that you have refused to return has sent alarm bells ringing in other departments.'

'Then I'll go and find my friends. My real ones.'

'You're mad.'

'I'm not. Think about it. What would you do? Sit here and wait for a big car to turn up along with several soldiers to force me on to a plane? Or go where they least expect – to join the others?'

I could tell by the look on his face that he really did think I'd lost my mind. Perhaps I had. All I knew was that I couldn't put the English Channel between me and those I loved best. Or what I loved best. The more I thought about it, the more I realised that the only answer was to get back in the thick of it while I still had a chance. Far better to go out fighting than with a whimper in some office in Whitehall.

'If they take me to London, I won't get back here before the end of the war. I can't do that, Antoine. I need to help end this. It will make some sense of it all, of Auschwitz. Of all the evil that happened. Not just to me but all the others. So many millions dead. Someone has to strike back for them.'

I gestured to the hotel beyond the confines of the room in which we were huddled, Antoine's makeshift office. Every day more and more people were turning up here from the camps. Families had started to come too, looking for their loved ones, putting up pictures in the lobby of those they'd lost in case they should turn up at the Lutetia. Those photographs were as heart-breaking as the lost souls who roamed the corridors, endlessly searching for peace where there was none. Their eyes stared out from faces that looked nothing like those in the pictures, unrecognisable thanks to the horrors they'd witnessed.

'Many of these people will never go home, Antoine. Their people are dead. Or they're dead to them. Whatever the others are doing, I need to be a part of that. Then, once we've ended this damn war, I'll be back to help you here.'

His eyes held mine, searching for something, although I had no idea what.

'I'll tell them you've already left when they get here. That I don't know where you've gone.'

'Thank you,' I whispered.

'In the meantime, we'd better hide you. Or at least get rid of you for the next few hours until they've been and gone.'

'I'll take Leah for a walk.'

'Good idea.'

'And, Antoine?'

'Yes?'

'Thank you for everything.'

'No, Maggie. It is I who should thank you.'

THIRTY-THREE

18 MARCH 1945, PARIS, FRANCE

I stared at the man sitting in front of me, looked down at the ledger Antoine had given me and then back up at him. 'You say you're from Limoges?'

'Yes, madame.'

'And you were in Sachsenhausen for three years?'

I looked him over once more. He seemed suspiciously healthy, his cheeks smooth and padded, unlike the others whose skin was stretched tight over muscle and bone.

'Your name again?'

'Pierre François Badeau.'

Sure enough, his name was on the list. But I would bet my life this wasn't the real Pierre François Badeau. He'd probably perished in the same camp this man claimed to have come from, where he was more likely a guard or gangmaster working for the Nazis than the prisoner he claimed to be. Then I remembered.

'Wait here one moment,' I said.

I left him sitting in the side room used for processing new arrivals and hurried to the lobby, where I'd seen Joseph only a half hour or so before. Sure enough, he was still there, once more cooing at Leah as Sophie fussed over her.

I placed my hand on his shoulder. 'You were in Sachsenhausen?'

'I was.'

'How did you escape?'

'They were marching us to another camp so I and my friends...'

I could see it in his eyes – the torment. 'You ran?'

'We hid in a ditch. I'm too old to run. Somehow, we managed to get away without the guards noticing.'

'Would you remember those guards? The ones at Sachsenhausen?'

Something flared in his eyes. 'I will never forget them.'

I took him by the arm. 'Could you come with me?'

The man calling himself Pierre François Badeau was still sitting in the chair where I'd left him. It was that kind of dumb obedience the Nazis prized. I remained standing, my arm still looped through the other man's.

'Stand up,' I commanded. 'Turn around.'

He may have had an inkling of what was coming. His shoulders sagged a fraction as he turned slowly, a smirk on his face. I felt the air leave Joseph's body as if he'd been punched in the chest.

'Do you recognise this man?' I asked.

Joseph nodded.

'Was he a guard at Sachsenhausen?'

Another nod.

'Did he abuse you and others?'

A pause. Then the quiet sobs started, growing louder as he simply stood there and wept. All the while, the fake Pierre François stood too, the contempt on his face slowly giving way to fear as he realised the game was up.

Finally, Joseph raised a shaking hand and pointed an accusing finger.

'You,' he gasped. 'You were the one who kicked my friends

to death. Who watched and laughed as the commandant shot them in cold blood. Your own countrymen. You traitor. Murderer.'

This last was spat straight into his face.

From behind me came Antoine's calm voice. 'I'll take over here. Thank you.'

I ushered Joseph out, closing the door behind us. I wished we could dole out the same punishment he'd given Joseph and all the others in the camp, but we had to abide by the rules even when they hadn't.

'An eye for an eye,' I muttered.

Joseph squeezed my arm. 'It's not the way.'

I looked at him, startled.

'We must forgive,' he said. 'Not for them but for our own sakes.'

I heard the infinite wisdom in his words, the understanding. He saw me. He knew what I'd been through too. At that, I started to weep.

THIRTY-FOUR

Darkness had fallen by the time Antoine emerged from the room, shutting the door firmly behind him. I threw him a questioning look, but he walked straight past me, heading for the bar. I was torn between following him and making sure the fake Pierre François wasn't going anywhere. I had my hand on the door handle when I heard a soft voice in my ear.

'Leave it.'

Joseph was looking at me with such a burning intensity that I felt compelled to take a step back, away from the door.

'Leave it,' he said again. 'Remember the camp. What they did. How they took us and interrogated us. Tortured us.'

I looked back at him, mute, remembering. I could see her now, Eva, calling out for Antoine, the life ebbing from her as she demanded I save their child. The child now cradled, safe in Joseph's arms.

Leah smiled at me sleepily, a tiny pearl of milk still clinging to her lower lip from her feed. Her china-blue eyes were so innocent. What lay beyond that door was not.

I took another step back and then turned, following

Antoine's route into the bar, where I found him sitting, hunched over a tumbler that was full of a tawny liquid.

I walked up to him. 'Cognac?'

'Whisky.'

'Mind if I join you?'

He waved a hand at the chair opposite.

I raised my hand to the solitary barman on duty. 'Another one for him and one for me. Make it a double.'

I took a sip and felt the welcome burn at the back of my throat. Macallan – Jamie's favourite. Then I noticed Antoine's knuckles as he clutched his glass – cut and bruised with one open wound still oozing blood.

'What happened?'

'Nothing.'

'Come on, Antoine. Your fists didn't end up like that through nothing. Did you use them on him? Was that what happened?'

'I don't want to talk about it.'

'Why? Because he wouldn't talk?'

'Because he did.'

I stared at him, hearing the rasp of pain in his voice, the agony that comes with knowing things you can never unknow.

'What did he say?'

'Nothing I didn't already know. But all the time he was talking, I imagined Leah there, with Eva. An innocent baby in the kind of camp where that scum was a guard. I pictured him doing to them what he confessed doing to others. You know what affected me the most? He didn't sound sorry. He sounded bored.'

His voice caught on that last sentence, cracking, and he hastily threw back his whisky.

I matched him gulp for gulp, in silent empathy. There was nothing either of us could say. Some things were beyond words.

'Another?' The barman removed our glasses, replacing them with freshly filled ones. He, too, had seen and heard enough to know that all you could do sometimes was blunt the sharpness of the pain with whatever it took.

Finally, Antoine set down his glass, sat back and looked at me with such a penetrating gaze that I had to look away.

'You're scarred, Maggie,' he said. 'But those scars only make you all the more lovely.'

I raised my eyes. His were frank and full of nothing other than friendship.

'You think so?'

'I do. I also think that Jamie is a very lucky man.'

'That's if I ever see him again.'

'You will. Trust me.'

'Did you think you would see her again? Eva?'

The words were out of my mouth before I could stop them. I wanted to bite them back, to swallow them whole, but there was no going back. I watched the tears well in his eyes and then he took a long, slow breath.

'I see her all the time. When I'm asleep. When I'm awake. Most often in my dreams. She's always smiling. Always beautiful.'

'She was beautiful when I last saw her.' It was true. Even in her agony, Eva had a grace that shone through, illuminating those perfect bones, the eyes that had once gleamed with love as she'd smiled at Antoine.

He placed his hand over mine. 'Thank you for saying that.'

'Excuse me.'

A tall, wiry man was standing beside our table, dressed in an assortment of donated clothes. One of the guests, as we called them. It took me a moment but then I remembered who he was – the same man Jamie thought he'd recognised. Then, as now, my hackles rose.

'May I join you?'

His accent was odd, not French and not anything else either. It was as if he was putting it on. I glanced at his close-cropped hair. Black. The kind of flat black that looked dyed. His eyes darted from my face to Antoine's, assessing us – a conman's eyes if ever I saw them.

'Yes of course.'

I heard the hesitation in Antoine's voice even as he indicated the spare seat at our table. It was unlike Antoine to be needlessly courteous. I wondered if he detected in this man the same thing I did.

'Thank you. My name is Victor. I've seen you both around the place so I thought I would introduce myself and get to know you a bit better.'

Very smooth. Too smooth for the broken shell of a man I'd seen him pretending to be. The guests were friendly and grateful, but few were as confident as this. Mostly they were still trying to get used to life beyond the confines of the camps, which was why they wandered the public areas, unable to stand being alone after months and years spent in cramped blocks with hundreds of others.

Antoine regarded him with a steady gaze. 'I see. Well, it's good to meet you, Victor. Tell me, where are you from?'

'Oh here and there. You know.'

'No, I don't. Where is here and there exactly?'

Antoine's tone had hardened so slightly it would be detectable only if you knew him well. Or if you had made an art of reading people, which this Victor evidently had.

I watched him consciously soften his posture, baring his teeth in what was intended as an open, easy smile.

'Forgive me,' he said, 'I've grown used to keeping secrets. I worked with the Resistance, you see. That was why they sent me to the camp.'

'Ah yes. Of course. And which camp was that?'

A fractional flicker before he answered. 'Auschwitz.'

I automatically glanced at his arm. His sleeves were buttoned at the cuffs. Although he was thin, it wasn't in the same way as the others – I could see the muscles under his shirt, wiry but strong. Those of us who'd survived the camps all exhibited some degree of muscle wastage, but this man appeared to be in excellent shape under those baggy clothes.

He saw me looking and crossed his arms, almost immediately uncrossing them as he realised how that must look.

'Really?' I said. 'That must have been awful.'

'You have no idea.'

I wanted to scream, to shout in his face that I had every idea while he had none. Instead, I murmured something noncommittal, waiting for him to fill the silence that fell.

'I still have nightmares,' he added.

'Of course you do.'

God forgive me if I was wrong, but my gut told me I wasn't. I knew a fake and a liar when I saw one, and my time in Auschwitz had only honed those instincts. What interested me now was what he really wanted from us.

Antoine was obviously of the same mind. 'So how can we assist you?'

'Assist? You've already done so much for me, for all of us. I just wanted to come and make your acquaintance.'

'But surely you have some specific request? Most of our guests, for example, are desperate to be reunited with their loved ones and to return to their homes, if they still exist. I hope we're doing everything we can to help you in that regard?'

Victor didn't even blink. 'You are, and I'm very grateful for all your assistance. Of course I miss my family terribly. But I'm sure that with all the help you kind souls are providing, we'll be reunited very soon.'

His eyes shone with what looked like tears glistening at the edge of his eyelashes. Pale lashes. At odds with his black hair.

'Let's hope so. And now, if you will excuse us, we need to discuss some confidential matters.'

Antoine's smile was pleasant, his tone final.

Victor got the message, bestowing a little bow on us as he stood.

'It's been a pleasure,' he said, keeping his gaze fixed on us as he backed away from our table before he turned and sauntered off with all the ease of a free man.

'That man has never seen the inside of a camp,' I breathed.

'I agree,' murmured Antoine. 'We need to keep an eye on him for sure. Find out what his game is. He could be trying to escape retribution like that bastard claiming to be Badeau. Or worse.'

'Did you see his eyelashes? They were kind of blonde even though his hair is black. It's obviously dyed but why? Do you think he's trying to disguise himself?'

'Probably. His accent is strange, although his French is perfect. He strikes me as a chameleon, able to step into another skin whenever it suits him.'

'A spy in other words?'

'Could be. Or someone who used to be a spy and is now on the run.'

'You mean for the Germans? There were so many who not only worked for the Germans in Auschwitz, they tried to outdo them.'

'Exactly. Alternatively, he could have worked for the SS or the Abwehr. I will check against all the names and descriptions of known fugitives that we have, bearing in mind he's obviously tried to change his appearance.'

I felt a shadow pass over me, sending a chill deep into my bones. There was something about this Victor that spoke of evil, the same kind of evil I'd encountered far too many times. Only his was an evil he tried to conceal, another hallmark of someone who was used to dealing in secrets and lies.

'Jamie spotted it,' I said, half to myself. 'He looked at him as if he recognised him. Or as if he'd seen a ghost.'

'There is no such thing as a ghost.'

'There is such a thing as a living ghost. Someone who haunts others. Who stalks them for their own ends. I don't know what he wants from us, but I don't trust him at all, Antoine.'

Neither had Jamie. I could see him now, staring at Victor, as still as a hound that scents its prey.

'Nor do I,' said Antoine. 'But I don't think we should move in on him just yet. He's up to something. Let's watch him as it plays out. Then perhaps we can catch bigger fish apart from him. I don't think it's a coincidence that more of them are turning up. Maybe this Victor has something to do with that bastard from Sachsenhausen.'

'I agree. It could be they're all working together, and there's never just one rat or even two. There are bound to be even more of them.'

'It's going to take more than you and I to handle this. There are so many now arriving here, and there will be others like him. I'm going to try to get that message to Suzanne and ask her for assistance with this. We need it, Maggie.'

I paled at the thought. We needed help, but I was now officially missing. Possibly even AWOL. Part of me was terrified of anyone turning up to help. Another, bigger part of me longed to see my comrades again. 'Are you sure that's a good idea?'

'Absolutely. Our job is to identify anyone who had a connection to the Nazis or worked for them. We need to catch them now, while they're afraid and on the run. That's why they come here, hoping to get away with what they've done by slipping in among the other displaced people. Except that we won't let them. Don't worry – I'll square it with her about you.'

His voice trembled with all the pent-up fury and pain he felt over Eva and his twins, over everything the Nazis had done.

He raised his glass to me. '*À votre santé*, Maggie. *Et pour les absents.*'

To your health and for those who are missing. It was a fitting toast.

I clinked my glass against his. 'We'll find them, Antoine. Every last one. And we'll make them pay.'

THIRTY-FIVE

19 MARCH 1945, THE VOSGES, FRANCE

Suzanne burst into the room, waving a piece of paper. 'Change of plan. We're going to Paris.'

They looked up from the map they'd been poring over. Suzanne was out of breath, hair in disarray. This had to be important.

'Why?' asked Marianne.

'Because Maggie is there with Antoine. They need our help.'

Marianne was on her feet in a flash, reaching for the piece of paper in Suzanne's hand, reading the message there.

Maggie in Paris with me. Safe and well. Request your urgent assistance.

Antoine

'Oh my God. Maggie. She's alive.' Marianne flung her arms around Suzanne, squeezing her tight. 'How the hell did you get this message? No one is supposed to know we're here.'

'I have my ways. And so does Antoine.'

'Let me see that.' Jack read it through, punching the air in delight. 'But what's this about assistance? It must be serious if Antoine is asking for help.'

'I agree,' said Marianne. 'We have to get there as soon as we can and see Maggie. I still can't believe it.' Eyes shining, she whirled around the room, throwing her arms around Jack too, laughing at the sheer joy of it all. Maggie. Her friend as well as her comrade. She couldn't wait to hug her too, to hold her.

'We need to sort out the logistics,' said Suzanne. 'We're in the middle of a mission here.'

'The recruits are ready for the next phase,' said Jack. 'We can pass them on to OSS for that while we head for Paris. Catch up with them when they're ready for the drop.'

Suzanne nodded slowly. 'That could work. Very well. I'll get a message to OSS HQ. Ask them to send transport ASAP.'

'Today. Tell them to send it today. The recruits can ship out at the same time we do.'

Marianne's face was pink with excitement. Jack ruffled her hair. 'Steady now.' It was an unaccustomed display of affection in front of their boss, but this was an extraordinary day.

Suzanne chose to ignore it. 'I'll do what I can. In the meantime, I suggest you go and pack so that you're ready to move at a moment's notice.'

It was only when they had both left the room to follow her orders that Suzanne pressed the piece of paper to her lips, gazing at it as if reading it one more time would make it even more real. Maggie was alive. It was almost too good to be true, and yet that was exactly what it was.

A single tear slid down to the corner of her mouth, mingling with the smile that was as rare as it was heartfelt. Maggie was alive and that was all that mattered. For once, the rest could wait. She and Antoine needed help. So that was exactly what they were going to get. The Network looked after its own, especially when it seemed they'd been lost. Now that she was found, Maggie was as much a part of them as she'd ever been – if that was what she wanted. And Suzanne hoped very much that it was. She might not have known Maggie for long, but from what she'd seen, the young doctor was one of the best.

THIRTY-SIX

20 MARCH 1945, PARIS, FRANCE

He was back – Victor, the man with the dyed hair. I hadn't seen him since he'd accosted us in the bar, but there he was, in the lobby, playing cards with a group of men while Sophie served them coffee.

'Do you know him?' I asked her as she walked away to refill her pot.

She followed my gaze. 'He's one of the newer ones. I think he arrived a few weeks ago.'

'Who processed him?'

'I'm not sure. Why? Is there a problem?'

'No problem. Just keep an eye on him. Let me know if you see him doing anything unusual.'

She looked bewildered, as well she might. Sophie was such a good soul – she could never imagine one of these people might not be what they seemed.

'Yes, of course,' she murmured.

I went to find Antoine, who was in his office, bent over his paperwork as usual.

'He's back,' I said. 'That man who spoke to us in the bar.

Victor. I asked Sophie when he first arrived and she thinks it was a few weeks ago. She has no idea who processed him.'

'That's just what I've been looking for,' said Antoine. 'His name. No Victor registered as an arrival within the last month. In fact, no Victor at all.'

'So he's somehow sneaked in?'

'Looks like it.'

I ran my hand through my hair. 'I don't like it, Antoine. Any response from Suzanne?'

'Not yet.'

'We need tighter security. We have to keep tabs on who's coming and going. Post guards at the entrances and exits if necessary.'

'We don't have enough people to do that.'

'Well, you've got three more now,' said a familiar voice.

I whirled round, blinking once, twice, not trusting my eyes. There they were – Marianne, Jack, Suzanne. I let out a cry of pure delight and felt myself engulfed in Marianne's embrace.

'Maggie, Maggie, Maggie.' She was murmuring in my ear, her voice choked with emotion, her arms holding me as if she would never let go.

I clung to her too. It had been so long. All those months thinking I would never see her again, see any of them again.'

'Is it you? Is it really you?' she asked.

I raised my head so I could look at her. She hadn't changed – same huge eyes that glowed like amber when she was fired up with emotion. They were glowing now, behind the tears.

'Yes, it's really me.'

A different me, maybe. One who'd experienced things they could never imagine. Who would never be the same because of that. I was no longer the Maggie who'd raced around the countryside on her bicycle to send and receive messages for SOE, charming German sentries into letting me through when necessary. The Maggie who'd tried to blow up the railway line outside of Lyon to distract the Gestapo and had been caught in the act. That Maggie was gone, and a new one stood in her place. I didn't need to say a word. I knew Marianne could sense all of it. She could see it too.

She had her hands on my arms, her gaze fixed on my face, travelling across it as she took in whatever it was she saw. I wanted to look away but forced myself not to. Let her look. Yes, I'd changed. I wasn't the Maggie she'd known. I could see that in her eyes, in the set of her mouth that pressed together a little tighter, as if she was trying to hold back words she might regret.

'Say it,' I whispered. 'Tell me I look different. That I'm not the same person anymore.'

'No I won't. Yes, you look a little different. That's inevitable after your ordeal. There are shadows and hollows that weren't there before. Perhaps the biggest is in your heart. But you are you, still one of us.'

'Am I?'

'Of course. I think of you like a sister. We all do.'

I could see Jack behind her, his eyes damp, his handsome face crumpled. He reached out and stroked my still-growing hair as if he needed to touch it, to feel it, to know that I was real and not some spectre risen from the dead.

'It's good to see you,' he said.

I gave them both a watery smile. It was good to see that they were still together. I could tell by the glances they shared, the invisible electricity that flowed between them. Marianne might be a professional to her fingertips, but there were some things you couldn't hide.

Suzanne stepped forward and held out her arms. 'May I greet you too?'

I stared at her. 'I understand you're in charge now.'

'Yes, I am.'

'In charge of what exactly?'

She hesitated. 'Of the new unit we've formed. All of us. Including you, Maggie.'

'Is that so?'

Anger boiled up, bursting over me, startling me with its intensity. I had so longed to see them all, and yet I was furious. I could feel pain surging through my veins along with the anger.

'You barely know me,' I said. 'You don't know what I've gone through. You say I'm one of you, yet you tried to have me dragged back to London when I wanted to be with you all, with my colleagues. You think I'm too broken, don't you? That I can no longer do anything useful to help.'

Antoine cleared his throat, obviously uncomfortable. Marianne looked stricken, but Suzanne remained imperturbable.

'You're right,' she said. 'I don't really know you, but I know what I've heard about you from your colleagues. I know that you're incredibly courageous and that you risked your life many times. It's the same courage I saw you display in Lyon. I may only have met you that one time, but I've never forgotten it. Or you.'

'And yet you wanted me out of the way. In London. To rest and get well supposedly.'

I couldn't help the bitterness that seeped through my words. I hated myself for it.

'Not at all. That was nothing to do with me. I didn't even know you were here until I got Antoine's message, although there's nothing wrong with wanting you to rest and get well.'

'Get well? I'm not sick. It's the Nazis who are sick. I know. I saw the worst of what they can do, and believe me, it's beyond your imagination.'

'I'm sure it is, and I know I can never begin to imagine what you've suffered. If I could erase that from your memory, I would, Maggie. But I can't and neither can you. I simply don't want to make things worse for you. None of us do. Especially not those of us in London.'

'Well, you have.'

To my horror, I felt the tears gathering at the back of my throat, stoppering it up so that my words trailed off in a whisper.

An uncomfortable silence fell. This wasn't how it was supposed to be. Our reunion was meant to be joyful. Ecstatic even. And yet here we were, steel strands of tension stretching between us, tangling around my heart. I so wanted to let it all go. To simply be one of them again. But it was impossible – I knew that now. I probably was too broken.

Distant shouts crashed through my thoughts. I looked at Antoine. 'That's Sophie's voice.'

The shouts turned to a scream. Together, we raced back to the lobby where Sophie was cowering while a man stood over her, pointing a gun at her head. It was him – Victor.

'Hold it right there,' snapped Jack, pulling a gun from his belt and levelling it at him.

Victor leaped out of the line of fire and I gasped.

There was a woman behind him – a woman I recognised immediately.

The Beast.

I must have said it out loud because the next second Victor aimed his gun at me and fired.

THIRTY-SEVEN

I threw myself sideways. The bullet missed, slamming into the wall behind me. With a roar of rage, Victor lunged, grabbing me by the throat, wrapping his arm around it as he pulled me against him, my back to his chest.

'Nobody move,' he growled. 'I'm walking out that door, and I'm taking her with me.'

My eyes slid to the Beast. There was a grin on her face I knew of old. It was the one she wore when a prisoner was dragged to their knees to be kicked and punched or hauled to the showers, where at least the end was swifter.

Victor waved his gun towards the main door of the hotel then pressed it against my temple.

'Let her go,' snarled Suzanne.

'Not a chance.'

I weighed up my options. There weren't many. The lobby was crowded with people waiting to be processed so even if I managed to get the gun away from my head, it could go off, killing or injuring someone.

He was dragging me towards the main door, walking backward with the barrel digging into my skull. God knows what he was going to do to me once we were outside. *Can't let him do that. Think, Maggie, think.*

A sudden shout; a cracking noise. His grip on me slackened.

I grabbed his gun hand by the wrist, twisting it upwards just in time to feel it as he fired, seeing the bullet miss the chandelier by inches, hearing it clatter to the ground as he let go, throwing myself to the floor to scrabble for it.

A shot. And then another. Voices shouting. Looking at the gun in my hand then up at Marianne blocking the doorway.

'It's alright, Maggie. He's gone. Everyone else stay right here.'

Standing beside her was a man clutching a table lamp, the base of which was covered in blood. I squinted at him, remembering. It was the man who'd been unable to speak when I first met him. Now, though, he'd found his voice.

'Good riddance,' he muttered. 'I only wish I'd killed the bastard. At least I've given him one hell of a headache.'

'Thank you,' I said.

'He had it coming. I knew there was something about him that was wrong.'

The light had returned behind his eyes, shining with righteousness. In striking Victor down, he'd also been striking back at all the people who'd degraded and hurt him, who'd taken the life he'd once had and destroyed it, destroying many of those he loved in the process.

Behind him, I could see the shock on some faces. Others were blank, so numbed were they to violence that one more act failed even to register. I wondered if I was like that, if I'd seen and undergone too much to even know how to really feel anymore. I hoped not. I could feel where Leah was concerned. And Jamie. For my friends and those who needed my help, but not for a man like Victor. Or someone like the Beast.

There were those here, though, who'd lost all sense of what it was to love or to hope or even to hurt. They were adrift in the grey mists of shell shock or combat stress reaction, call it what you would. I saw it simply as trauma. And I knew I suffered from it too.

'He got away?'

'I'm afraid so,' said Antoine. 'But we've rumbled him now, so I don't think he'll be back.'

'Let's get everyone out of here and into another room. They're already traumatised. This will have been deeply upsetting for most of them. Everyone except her.'

I could see the Beast sidling towards the doorway where Marianne was standing, looking round for a way to escape, her eyes darting around like a creature that had been cornered. Which is exactly what she was.

'Seize her,' I said, pointing at her. 'Get her into Antoine's office. She's one of the guards from Auschwitz. One of the worst.'

A hush fell over the room, a rumble running through the crowd beyond. Before the place could erupt, Marianne grabbed her by one arm and Jack the other, frogmarching her into Antoine's office, where I slammed the door behind her, turning the key in the lock.

'This woman,' I said, 'was known as the Beast in Auschwitz. I think you can guess why. I don't want to be anywhere near her for longer than I have to or I'll tear her limb from limb, so help me God. But I do want her to answer just one question.'

She stared up at me sullenly from the chair into which she'd been deposited, Marianne tying her arms behind her and then to the chair itself. 'I have no idea what you're talking about,' she said. 'My name is Yvonna. I'm a Polish refugee fleeing the Soviets.'

'Rubbish,' I snapped. 'You're a paid-up member of the SS and you were one of the chief wardens at Auschwitz. You raped, brutalised and murdered prisoners as well as sending others to their deaths thanks to your selections. Worst of all, you were Dr Mengele's sidekick as well as his mistress.'

'I have never been to Auschwitz.'

'Yes, you have. I saw you there. Remember me, the prisoner doctor whose face you once battered with your rifle butt?'

At that, her eyes flickered again, but her mouth stayed firmly shut. She glared at me in dumb defiance, the ghost of a smile playing around her mouth.

'What are you smiling at?' I snarled. 'I'm going to wipe that smile from your face if it's the last thing I do.'

As I moved towards her, Antoine blocked my path. 'Leave her to me, Maggie.'

'Maggie?' She echoed my name, sounding amused. 'The one Mengele liked so much? Did you fuck him too?'

I heard a roaring in my ears. It could have been my own voice yelling as I leaped or her laughter as Antoine dragged me off, depositing me in Marianne's arms.

'Maggie,' she said. 'Out.'

I could still hear the Beast laughing as I stumbled down the corridor and sank gratefully into the armchair Marianne found for me in a quiet corner, my chest heaving with sobs, my heart splintering into dozens of tiny, sharp shards. I could feel them ripping through me in turn, tearing me open from top to bottom.

As I heaved and gasped, Marianne stood patiently, patting me tenderly on the back.

At last, the sobs subsided enough for me to speak. 'I want to kill her,' I gulped.

'I know you do, but we need her alive, Maggie. At least for now so she can tell us everything she knows.'

At that moment, Suzanne appeared. 'I brought you a glass of water.'

I took it and sipped at it gratefully. 'Has she said anything about how she got here?'

'It seems Victor has been helping to run a ratline for Nazis, getting them over the border into DP camps and places like this and then on to Spain. They're running from the Soviets as well as from us. They know the game is up and that, if we catch them, they'll be tried for war crimes. He had quite a nice racket going there. Until now.'

'Do we know where he is?'

'No, but we will. Antoine told me to find out what it was you wanted to ask her.'

Antoine. He'd get the answer out of her. In a way, it would be poetic justice if he did, for Eva and his twins. She of all people would know. She was obsessed with Mengele, wildly jealous of any other woman he so much as looked at. If there was anyone in the world who could lead us to him, it was her.

'Tell him to ask her where Mengele is.'

'Mengele.'

'Yes. Dr Josef Mengele.'

The man who'd killed Antoine's family, among so many. I wanted to see his face as he died.

THIRTY-EIGHT

'She says he's hiding out near Gross-Rosen. That's the camp where he went after Auschwitz, according to her, on the border of Germany and Poland. He wants to get his papers back apparently. He left them in there when the Red Army arrived.'

Antoine looked exhausted but oddly elated, as did Jack. Suzanne was still in there, no doubt working her own special magic on the Beast.

'Does she know exactly where?'

Antoine shook his head. 'No. And I believe her. If she knew, she'd have told us. You can trust me on that. But she did say he kept trying to break back into the camp to retrieve them. When she last saw him, which was only a few days ago, he said he'd found a way.'

I could scarcely believe my ears. Of course. His beloved notes along with his specimens – the evidence of all his crimes – and now we knew where it was.

'How does she know all this?'

'She was with him until some nurse she referred to as "that bitch" showed up. It seems they left it too late to escape the Red Army so they had to flee the camp and hide out. Mengele apparently headed east to Czechoslovakia but quickly realised that was a mistake and turned around. She hooked up with him again when he showed up at a house where a few of them were staying in a nearby town. That's when she found out about him trying to get back into Gross-Rosen and blackmailed him into paying for her to escape via the ratline.'

'The Soviets are in charge at Gross-Rosen, aren't they?'

'Yes,' said Suzanne, emerging from Antoine's office. She tucked a stray strand of hair behind her ear with a hand that looked bruised, streaks of blood smeared across it. Her hands were as delicate as the rest of her and no doubt equally made of steel. Part of me almost pitied the Beast. Almost.

'Do you think they'd help us catch him?'

I thought of Jamie, running through that forest with the Red Army. It wasn't beyond the bounds of possibility. We'd collaborated with them before.

'The danger in that is they'll want to arrest him if they catch him,' said Suzanne. 'That's why we've been running the mission in the Vosges along with the Americans. To try to get to the Nazi war criminals before the Soviets do.'

'Then we need to go there ourselves as soon as we can. Find him. And find his papers if he hasn't already, so that we have all the evidence to convict him. The man did unspeakable things to children. To the elderly and the disabled. To pregnant women and their babies.'

Antoine shot me a look and I stopped dead, wishing the ground would swallow me whole. I'd said too much. I had to learn to be more careful, especially around Antoine.

'You told us our mission was to track down war criminals,' said Marianne. 'Now we know exactly where one is. An important one. I vote we carry out an urgent drop near Gross-Rosen, infiltrate the camp and try to find him and his papers. Hopefully he hasn't managed to retrieve them already. Of course, we have to make sure we don't tip off the Soviets, otherwise they'll want to get their hands on him and the evidence. Then we'll never bring him to trial.'

'I'll have to talk to OSS,' said Suzanne. 'See if they can cover us in the Alps.'

'You will ask?'

'I'll get a call patched through now.'

I looked at them all, at their faces white with fatigue but still determined, fists and fingers bruised and bloody. All except Marianne's which were gripping my arm.

'You know what Mengele looks like, don't you?'

How could I ever forget? I could see him now, humming under his breath as he flicked his finger left and right, boots polished to a mirror-like shine, uniform perfectly pressed. It was almost as if he'd put on his Sunday best for the selections. He'd certainly enjoyed them, smiling broadly as he'd played God.

'Yes, I do,' I whispered. 'I certainly do.'

'Then we have to take Maggie with us.'

Suzanne's face darkened and then Jack chimed in. 'Absolutely. She's the only one of us who can identify him.'

I looked at Suzanne. 'You think I'm not up to this, don't you?'

'I didn't say that.'

'No, but I can see it on your face. Tell you what, give me five minutes alone with the Beast.'

'That won't be necessary.'

'Trust me, it is.'

Before anyone could stop me, I pushed past them and into Antoine's office, shutting the door behind me before I locked it with an emphatic click. The Beast was still in the chair, blood dripping from her nose and chin, head dangling at an odd angle. She managed to raise it as I entered and attempted a sneer.

'Mengele's hiding out near Gross-Rosen?'

She spat out a tooth along with a bloodied gobbet of matter. 'What's it to you? Want to go find lover boy?'

I stared her down. 'You're pathetic. As if I would let a man like Mengele lay a finger on me. That's for the likes of you.'

She glared at me through narrowed eyes. 'You weren't so high and mighty in Auschwitz. Back there, you were just a filthy prisoner like all the rest.'

'I might not have had the finest washing facilities, but my soul was clean, unlike yours. You'll go to hell for what you've done, in one way or another.'

I saw that hit home for some reason. Perhaps she was Catholic. Many of them were. I reached forward and wrenched open her blouse. There it was, dangling around her neck. A small gold cross, probably stolen from one of the inmates. She blanched, and I smiled.

'What would your family think of you? Your mother? Not to mention the courts. Even if you repent before they hang you, they'll never forgive you and nor will your god. You'll burn forever while those people you beat and tortured and killed will be in a far better place for eternity. Just think about that when you're sitting in your prison cell.'

She wouldn't look at me, but I could see her thinking that one over. She might not care too much about the church or her family, but the hangman's noose was a very real prospect.

'You won't find him,' she muttered.

'I'll give him your love when I do.'

I left her there lying in a pool of her own blood, unlocked the door and walked out.

'Don't worry. I didn't kill her. I didn't even touch her.'

But something inside me had died. I knew then there was no going back. We had to go on. To find Mengele. To bring peace to all those he'd harmed as well as to me.

THIRTY-NINE

We just about managed to squash around the table in Antoine's apartment. It was a safer choice than any of the hotels. If anyone got wind of what we were up to, especially OSS, there would be hell to pay.

'We have four days,' said Suzanne, 'before we need to join those recruits and carry out our original mission in the Alps. That gives you no more than forty-eight hours to get in there, find him and get out. Think you can do it in that time?'

Marianne spread out the map on the low coffee table. 'We have to.'

Along with the map of the area on the border between Germany and Poland was another one, hand-drawn, of the Gross-Rosen camp itself with the gas chamber and crematorium clearly marked. Pinned to it was an old photograph of Mengele, grinning in that ghastly way of his, the gap clearly showing between his front teeth.

'Is that him?' asked Marianne.

'Yes, although he looks different in the flesh. He's not as tall as you would expect or as impressive, but some people considered him good-looking. At least, some of the nurses and guards did. He was always immaculately dressed. And he hums under his breath all the time – Wagner mainly. He used to do it at selections.'

Marianne shuddered. 'He sounds like a madman.'

'He is. A very cunning psychopath.'

'This is the main camp at Gross-Rosen,' said Suzanne. 'It was liberated by the Red Army on the thirteenth of February, but before that, there were many sub and satellite camps as well. A former prisoner drew this map and smuggled it out. I understand he was an architect so it's probably accurate.'

I bent over it, taking in the blocks, the execution site with its gas chamber set conveniently close to the transport reception area, the hospital blocks situated right behind that, to the left of the main gate.

'He took his papers to Gross-Rosen when Auschwitz was evacuated. He used to keep them all in his office at Auschwitz so I'm sure he'll have done the same there. His office will have been somewhere in here,' I said, jabbing at the hospital blocks with my finger. 'That way he had easy access to the patients as well as to the execution site for a ready supply of fresh specimens.'

Marianne stared at me. 'What do you mean?'

I glanced around even though I knew Antoine was still at the Lutetia. He wasn't coming with us on this mission but, even so, I felt awful uttering this within his walls. 'I mean, he wanted the subjects for his experiments either still alive or freshly killed. Often he would kill one twin when the other died so he could compare them immediately.'

'Compare them for what?'

'He'd take all kinds of samples and measurements, but ultimately there was nothing scientific about what he was doing. It was all about eugenics. Mengele believed he was discovering how to repopulate Germany fast with as many perfect sets of twins as possible, among his other insane ideas. The problem for him was that he simply couldn't make it work.'

Marianne's face was white. 'Dear God.'

'Shall we continue?' Suzanne pointed to an area next to the camp. 'This is the stone quarry the prisoners were forced to work. As you can see, it's surrounded by trees, as is the rear area of the camp. I suggest you drop in here, a couple of kilometres from that quarry and make your way to the camp from there.'

'Are those fences still electrified?' I asked. They surrounded the entire camp, as they had at Auschwitz.

'That we don't know. They might still be electrified to protect the camp rather than keep people prisoner now.'

'We need to find out. I saw far too many people die against the fences in Auschwitz, mostly because they threw themselves against them rather than take any more.'

'You'll only be able to find that out once you're there. As I'm sure you'll understand, any intelligence we have on the camp now is patchy at best. We know that many of the Nazis who ran Auschwitz went to Gross-Rosen fleeing the Red Army and then left some prisoners behind when they evacuated Gross-Rosen. The Red Army may have set up a field hospital in Gross-Rosen, as they have at Auschwitz. The Polish Red Cross are helping them care for the prisoners left behind at Auschwitz along with local volunteers, but Gross-Rosen is on the German side of the border so they can't help there.'

Memories flooded back of the hospital, the Polish doctors and nurses who'd done so much to save their fellow prisoners from Mengele and his like. 'That's it. That's our way in. We can pretend to be International Red Cross, visiting to see what help they need.'

'That's a brilliant idea,' said Marianne.

'No need to worry about fences. We can just walk right in. I speak perfect German now. We all speak French. I have some Polish and Russian as well that I picked up in Auschwitz. All we need are the right uniforms and credentials and then we can access the infirmary as well as any field hospital they've set up, keeping an eye out for Mengele.'

'Sounds good to me,' said Jack. 'Let's do it. What about comms? We're going to have to transmit over German territory. They're bound to pick up the signal. We don't want anything getting out that will warn them.'

Suzanne smiled. 'I'm glad you asked. OSS have been trialling a new system. It's called Joan-Eleanor, after the wives of the men who invented it. A plane flies in fast and low and then circles over agents on the ground. They talk to another agent on-board via a VHF radio transceiver. The Germans can't intercept it so there's no need for code. It's so quick that the Germans don't even realise they've been in their air space.'

'Won't OSS wonder why we're using it if we're supposed to be here, in Paris?'

'I told them we needed their help for agents we already have in the field. They were only too happy to oblige. I'll be the point of contact in the plane so there won't be any problems.'

'Then it sounds like we're all set,' said Marianne with that irrepressible smile of hers.

'When do we leave?' I asked, scarcely able to conceal my impatience. Now that we knew where he was, all my hunting instincts were focused on one thing: Mengele.

'Tomorrow night. We'll be able to get you Red Cross uniforms and false papers by then.'

Tomorrow. Just one more day then until I had him in my sights. Until I was back out there, with my comrades. Could I do it? Of course I could.

I'm coming for you, Mengele. We're all coming for you. Then we can do to you what you did to so many. To Eva and her twins. How I longed to hear him beg for mercy. To plead as all those people had while he'd smiled and sent them to their deaths, humming that stupid tune. He wouldn't be humming when we found him, although he might sing out his secrets like a canary. And that would be music to my ears as well as a balm to my soul.

FORTY

The plane was even noisier than the ones I was used to. Bundled into a tiny bomb bay at the back of it, I wondered if they would simply unload us over Germany. I crouched alongside Marianne, teeth rattling, one hand clutching the pouch strapped to my waist that contained my silk map, a few basic medical supplies, a shovel and our handheld transceiver.

'We'll check in with you at 6 p.m. precisely tomorrow evening,' said Suzanne. 'Good luck.'

I smiled at her, looking braver than I felt. 'Don't you worry. We'll find them.'

'I know you will.'

She reached inside her purse and handed me her own pistol. 'For you. It's served me well.'

A brief hug for us all and we were clambering into the plane, the flight sergeant shouting at us to lie down.

'When I give the signal, you hook up your line and assume a crouching position.'

I looked at Marianne; she gave me a thumbs up, then the floor fell away and I was dropped like a bomb.

I flicked the quick-release catch and floated down through

the inky darkness, not a single light below to greet me, just the ground rushing up. Then I was rolling, disentangling myself from my parachute, stepping out of my flying suit as fast as I could, looking round for somewhere to bury them both. We were under strict orders to leave no trace, the mission totally deniable and non-official. No one must ever know we'd been here.

We'd landed in a field, a clump of trees at the edge of it looming out of the darkness. I spotted Marianne further up the field, signalling that I should make for those trees. Jack was already there, having landed right by them.

I pulled my shovel from my pouch as I ran to join them, giving Marianne a brief hug before starting to dig.

I worked as fast as I could, using my shovel to dig along with my bare hands, the soil still semi-frozen and hard, my breath coming in pants, forming clouds in the night air.

At last, we were all done, huddling round Jack's map as we got our bearings.

'The quarry's a couple of kilometres across the fields as the crow flies. That's a lot safer than taking the road and risking a Red Army patrol.'

'Agreed.' Marianne checked her watch. 'It's a good four hours until dawn. Why don't we set off now and then we can recce the camp before the Soviets wake up?'

'If it's anything like Auschwitz, the searchlights will be on day and night. They might not be the Nazis, but I suspect they'll just leave them on too.'

As it turned out, I was right. Gross-Rosen camp was clearly visible as we skirted the quarry, its ring of searchlights blazing out across the night sky. From the shelter of the trees behind the camp, we surveyed the scene.

'The main gate is on that side. They'll have other gates as well, especially near the crematorium so they can dump the ashes somewhere.'

My words escaped on a cloud of vapour that reminded me
of the clouds that used to belch out of those crematoria chim-
neys. It was cold out here. It was always cold in Auschwitz too,
and, I suspected, all of these camps even in summer. Evil cast a
long shadow.

'That fence looks electrified to me,' murmured Jack.

The lights on top of the fence blared at us, penetrating the
dense forest, dazzling everything in their path. It was why the
birds sang at the wrong times, confused by what appeared to be
daylight in the middle of the night.

'If we tried to break in, we'd be spotted immediately,' I said.
'That's no doubt why Mengele has failed so far, although he's
too smart to try anything so crude. He'll be trying to slip in
somehow, just as we are.'

Marianne patted her Red Cross uniform. 'Yes, but he
doesn't have one of these.'

'Maybe not, but he'll be disguised in some way. He's not
going to be roaming around in his SS uniform.'

'I'm sure he won't, but we'll find him. We've got you,
Maggie.'

'We've also got at least a couple more hours until daylight,'
said Jack. 'Why don't we recce the perimeter and the main gate?
Get a rough idea of how many guards are on duty as well as a
look at how many buildings seem occupied? Might be useful if
we have to get out of there fast.'

'Maggie and I will go this way. You circle the other way, and
we'll meet back here.'

Marianne and I set off, careful to keep out of the range of
the searchlights, hugging the edge of the shadows instead,
which gave us a good-enough view of the camp through the
fence. It looked much the same as Auschwitz, with row after
row of blocks. There were no lights on in any of them and the
place looked eerily deserted, but as we came to the execution
site, I could see lights on in the buildings behind it.

'I think those are hospital blocks,' I whispered. 'I remember them from the map.'

My eyes slid past the crematorium chimney and the gallows. I couldn't bear to look at them.

We carried on, peering at the square where they'd once held their wretched roll calls, seeing the transport arrival platforms and the main gate, opposite which was what had been the SS camp along with the administration blocks. It was there that more lights shone from the odd window, and we could hear the sounds of people moving inside and between the huts. This must be where the Red Army were billeted now that they'd liberated the camp. I wondered how many prisoners had been left behind by the Nazis when they'd marched them out of here too. However many there were, they would be the weakest and sickest. There was no sign of a Red Cross flag or a field hospital other than the blocks. There was, however, a guard at each gate and, in the distance, the sound of dogs barking.

'Let's go back the way we came,' I muttered. 'Otherwise we'll wake the whole place up.'

'That's probably what Jack did, setting the dogs off,' whispered Marianne as we retraced our steps, ending up back in the woods where Jack was already crouched.

'Bloody dogs,' he said. 'I had to turn around and come back.'

'So did we, but I think we've seen enough,' I said. 'The hospital blocks are obviously in use, and the Red Army have taken over the SS camp. From the look of things, they're occupying around half the huts, so there are quite a number of them. No sign of the Red Cross. I think we should march up to the gate once it's daylight and demand to inspect the place. Tell them we understand that there are still ex-inmates here and we need to make sure they're treating them properly.'

'You think that will work better?'

'I do. The Red Army soldiers I've come across respect a tougher approach. And that's putting it mildly. The tales I've heard are hair-raising. They're as capable of torture, rape and murder as any Nazi. We can only hope their commander has instilled discipline.'

A commander like the one who'd raced out of the forest with Jamie to rescue us. The Soviets were brave too. But not as courageous as my Jamie.

I gazed up at the moon now sitting low in the sky, waiting for the sun to pass it as it rose. Soon it would be dawn. Maybe even the dawn of the day we caught Mengele. There was a star glittering just above the moon. I stared at it, wishing with all my might. *Keep him safe, wherever he is. Keep us all safe. Deliver up Mengele to me.*

The star carried on twinkling, diamond bright with promise. Nothing more than a promise. But it was enough.

FORTY-ONE

22 MARCH 1945, GROSS-ROSEN CAMP, GERMANY

There it was, above the main gate. The same sign. They hadn't taken it down.

Arbeit macht frei. Work sets you free.

I couldn't tear my eyes away from it. Couldn't take another step.

'Are you alright, Maggie?'

Marianne's hand on my arm, steadying me. 'Yes, yes, I'm fine.'

I had to keep moving. The mission – always the mission. If I cracked now, there would never be another. Maybe they were right; maybe I wasn't up to it.

Damn it, yes, I was. I could do this. Air tore down my lungs as I took the deepest breath I could, one foot in front of the other.

The guard at the main gate glared at us.

Jack brandished his credentials. 'We're from the International Red Cross. We wish to inspect the camp.'

He turned and conferred with the other guard, speaking in rapid Russian, the gist of which was that there was no way he was letting these foreigners in.

'You have an appointment?'

Jack glared back at him. 'We don't need an appointment. We're here on official business. You are obliged to let us inspect this camp. We understand you still have former inmates here. We need to see that you're treating them properly.'

'You don't have an appointment.'

His buddy stood there, silent beside him, picking his teeth as he listened, occasionally shifting his weight so that his Kalashnikov clattered against the side of the guard hut.

'Tell the camp commandant that we're here from the International Red Cross,' Jack patiently repeated.

The guard stared him down. It might be time for a different approach.

Quietly, I began to recite, almost as if I were doing it without thinking. 'Wait for me and I'll come back / Wait with all your might / Wait when dreary yellow rains / Tell you nothing's right...'

The guard stopped picking his teeth; the other one did a double take. 'You know this poem?' he cried. 'This is by Simonov. A great poem.'

'It is indeed,' I said.

He and his buddy conferred some more.

'Wait here,' he said.

Ten minutes later we were in the commandant's office, where an exhausted-looking officer greeted us, barely glancing at the credentials Jack presented.

'The commandant is busy, but he asked me to show you the hospital and anything else you need to see.'

We trailed behind him through the hospital blocks, taking in the rows of patients lying in cots, some asleep or unconscious, others staring sightlessly at the ceiling. Between them, Red Army nurses and orderlies moved, their faces almost as grey as their patients'. Everywhere there was the stench of diarrhoea and of vomit, as well as another smell I knew only too well.

Typhus. The place was in chaos. There must have been at least five hundred patients crammed into those wards.

'How many were here when you arrived?' I asked.

'Nearly two thousand. At least a quarter of those died. We sent the healthier ones to some of the subcamps we liberated and kept the weaker ones here, but, as you can see, we're over-stretched.'

We carried on, looking at the hospital kitchen with its harassed cooks trying to make the best out of meagre rations, inspecting the squalid washing facilities and taking note of the broken-down equipment along with the dilapidated state of the buildings. The Nazis had made a good job of running this place down before they evacuated, although they'd left their execution site intact, a sign perhaps of the haste with which they'd departed.

In the final hospital block, our guide led us up to another officer wearing a medic's armband.

'This is Dr Petrovsky. He's in charge here. He will be able to answer any questions you might have. I'll leave you with him.'

I looked at Petrovsky, taking in his lugubrious face, bright eyes looking back at me, belying his hangdog expression. Beside me, Marianne pretended to make notes while Jack scrutinised every inch of the place. If Mengele was here, we would find him. And if there was anywhere he would be in this camp, it had to be in this hospital because that was where his papers would be too. The next step was to find his old office, but all in good time.

'Are these people able to digest the food you're giving them?' I asked, looking at one particularly emaciated patient.

'They have great difficulty, as you can observe,' Petrovsky replied. 'Many of them have not eaten solid food for so long. By the time we got here, they were down to soup, if you could call it that, and that was all. The Nazis tried to starve them to death by leaving hardly any food.'

'Are you aware of refeeding syndrome?'

'Of course. We saw it with the people who'd been besieged in Leningrad. We're trying to refeed these people as carefully as we can, but we don't have much good food to give them ourselves. Supplies are running low for the troops, never mind these poor people. What can we do?'

He seemed sincere as well as dog-tired. I knew just how he felt. We'd felt the same all those long months in the Auschwitz hospital, battling impossible odds. The difference here was that the Nazis were gone. Other than that, medicines and basic equipment seemed to be in short supply, along with food.

'We'll see what we can do to help,' I said, surveying the grim scene. Many of these people wouldn't last another week, no matter what we tried to do for them. I made a mental note to ask Suzanne to organise a real Red Cross team as soon as possible. At least the sheets they were lying on seemed clean.

'You have a laundry here?'

Petrovsky shook his head. 'We send them out every day to the local town. We make the Germans wash them. We think it's the least they can do considering they knew about this camp all the time it was here.'

I could feel myself warming to Petrovsky. 'Absolutely.'

'Tell me,' said Marianne, 'were any of these patients treated by a Dr Mengele as far as you know? I believe he came here when Auschwitz was evacuated.'

He looked blankly at her and then recollection dawned. 'I don't know, but there is a room at the end of this block with that name on the door. We use it to store supplies. I have no time to sit in an office.'

I avoided looking at the other two, concentrating instead on Petrovsky. 'Could you show me where that room is, please? I'd like to check what supplies you have so we can try to supplement them.'

'Certainly. This way.'

As we passed one of the cots, the patient in it tried to speak, his words coming out as a croak. I went closer and saw a man who must have only been in his thirties but looked considerably older, his cheeks sunk so low that they formed caverns in what had once been a handsome face.

'Did you say something?'

He gazed at me with eyes that were filmy and grey, the whites shot through with bloodied filaments. 'Mengele. Dr Mengele.'

'Yes?'

'He did this.'

He lifted his arm out from under the sheet. Half of it was no longer there. From the bandaged stump, there emitted the unmistakable smell of gangrene.

'I'm so sorry,' I whispered.

That smell of rot stayed with me as Petrovsky led us to Mengele's office, using several keys in turn to unlock the solid-looking door.

'We lock it not so much because of the patients but because of the men,' he said. 'Many of them have been fighting so long they're reliant on chemicals to get them through. They'll do anything to get at the drugs.'

This place was pressing in on me, suffocating me with all that was too horribly familiar. The moment I saw Mengele's name still on the door, I wanted to run, to vomit myself until there was nothing left in me. Instead, I nodded in what I hoped was an understanding way. 'Of course. May we go in?'

Petrovsky stood in the doorway as we looked around.

'I see you have sulfa powder. No antibiotics?' No wonder that poor man had gangrene. Sulfa only worked so far. What they really needed was penicillin.

'It was hard enough to get hold of that.'

'I understand. We'll take an inventory of everything here so we can see what we need to provide.'

Still he hovered. It was going to be tough to get rid of him.

'Do you keep your records in here?' I asked as I wrenched open a drawer in the desk. Nothing.

He looked a little startled. 'What records do you mean?'

'Stock records. Deliveries. I assume you have your supplies delivered?'

I was looking round wildly now, my eyes scanning every box stacked on the shelves, searching for one that looked as if it might have belonged to Mengele.

'I need to see your charts,' snapped Jack.

'My charts?'

'Yes. Are those back in the wards?'

'Well, yes, of course.'

'Could you show me?' Jack was ushering him away from the door and back down the corridor. I could still hear him talking as they went, distracting a now confused Dr Petrovsky still further with a stream of questions.

I liked Petrovsky, and I wished we could tell him why we were really here, but it was simply too dangerous. Already, we Western Allies were competing with the Russians to apprehend Nazi war criminals. Mengele was too important a prize to let them take.

'Quick,' I said to Marianne.

We pulled open each drawer in turn – just a few discarded papers of no interest. The boxes on the shelves yielded nothing either. Petrovsky would be back any minute.

Then I spotted it, what looked like a safe door behind a shelf. 'Give me a hand,' I said as I shoved it to one side.

'Let me,' said Marianne, crouching to deploy the skills she'd learned from Gentleman Johnny, the Glaswegian safe-cracker turned SOE instructor, back at Beaulieu.

I held my breath as she patiently turned the dial this way and that, letting out a little whoop of triumph as the door swung open. Inside, notebooks, files and papers were neatly stacked.

'Eureka,' I breathed, pulling out a pile and dumping them on the desk.

'Now how the hell are we going to get these out of here?'

'You're not,' said a voice from the doorway.

I turned. Saw a man standing there, dressed in overalls with the name of a laundry embroidered on one pocket, pushing what looked like a linen cart. Only this was no laundry worker. I recognised him at once, in spite of the cap pulled low over his forehead and the overalls he wore.

'Mengele,' I gasped.

FORTY-TWO

He smiled with that same cocksure arrogance I knew far too well and stepped into the room, closing the door behind him.

'Thank you.' He smirked. 'You saved me a job. I've been trying to get into my office for days now.'

So that was it. He was coming in here on the pretext of collecting the laundry while hoping to get hold of the keys to his old office somehow. The keys I was holding.

'Give me those,' he said.

'No.'

He sighed and pulled out a gun. I recognised it at once – the same Mauser he'd used when a new arrival on the platform at Auschwitz had displeased him. I'd seen him fire it at a distraught mother who was desperate not to be separated from her daughter, shooting both of them dead.

I stared down its barrel now and smiled. 'Pull that trigger and you'll have half the Red Army in here, Josef.'

He blinked. I think it was the first time I'd ever seen him rattled. Then that gap-toothed smile was back in place.

'Well, well. If it isn't the little doctor. I didn't expect to see you here.'

'Evidently. Except I'm not just a doctor, Josef.'

I was getting to him. He blinked again, rapidly. The smile had disappeared as he worked out the odds.

'You stupid woman,' he snapped. 'Give me those now or you'll suffer for it.'

'Really? I've already suffered, Josef. I watched you make people suffer. Hundreds of people. Some of them babies and children. You think you can hurt me now? You see two women in here and you think you can do what you like. What you don't know is that we didn't come alone. You do anything to us and they'll get you, along with the Red Army. You won't get out of here alive.'

He laughed, a short bark that was devoid of mirth. 'Nice try.'

'You think? Try this.'

With that, Marianne whipped out her pistol and shot at his wrist. The bullet missed as he flinched, tearing at his sleeve, but it was enough for him to jerk his arm away, sending his Mauser flying so it landed by my feet.

I picked it up and trained it on his chest, the gun Suzanne had given me in my other hand. 'You think this is nice, too, huh, Josef?' I spat his name at him.

He looked from Marianne to me, weighing up whether he could try and grab either of us – I could see it in the way he stood, in those opaque eyes. And then he lunged, reaching not for us but for the pile of his papers I'd dumped on the desk.

I threw myself at them, snatching them back just in time, sending half of them flying in the air, slamming back against the shelves as I clutched the rest to me, out of his reach.

He let out a roar of rage, grabbing at them, but I kicked out, my foot catching him in the small of his back as Marianne brought the butt of her pistol down on his head. He stumbled, managed to right himself, turned and pulled bags of sulfa powder from the shelf, hurling them at us so they exploded against the walls and floor, showering us in clouds of yellow powder that filled our eyes, noses and throats, half-blinding us both.

I gasped and yelled out as I swiped the back of my hand across my streaming eyes, trying to see through the yellow fog, to take a shot at him. But he wasn't there.

'He's gone,' I croaked.

The door was swinging open, letting in fresher air. We stumbled out into the corridor, guns raised, but there was no sign of him.

'Go that way,' I murmured, locking the door after us and pocketing the key. 'I'll take the ward.'

I ran, brushing the sulfa powder from me as I went. Even so, there were one or two startled looks as I entered the ward, spotting Jack at the far end of it, keeping Dr Petrovsky engaged in what looked like deep conversation.

'Excuse me,' I said, striding up and taking Jack by the arm. 'May I have a word?'

Petrovsky looked at me, alarmed. 'Is everything alright?'

'Everything is perfectly fine, Doctor. I just need to speak to my colleague.'

The moment we were out of his earshot, I murmured in Jack's ear. 'He's gone. Mengele. He was here, at his old office, disguised as a laundry man. Did he come through here?'

'No. No one has.'

'We have to stop him.'

'I see,' said Jack for Petrovsky's benefit.

The last thing we wanted was for the Soviets to realise that a Nazi like Mengele was here, right under their noses.

'Thank you, Doctor. Dr Petrovsky, if you would give me a moment? I need to help my colleagues with something.'

'Yes, yes of course.'

We were already striding out of the ward, breaking into a

run as soon as we were in the corridor, heading in the direction Marianne had taken.

The door at the far end of the block was swinging open. We burst through it, seeing another hospital block in front of us and, beyond that, the old inmates' blocks, which were empty. There were no Soviet soldiers in sight.

Good. We zigzagged through it, catching sight of Marianne ahead.

'No sign,' she called out, waving her gun to indicate she was taking the left-hand side of the blocks, so we sprinted towards the right, seeing the execution site in front of us, the crematorium tower looming above it. I caught a glimpse of the guards on the main gate and a couple of soldiers by the administration block, but otherwise the place was deserted, everyone in their blocks or barracks. Everyone except Mengele. He was there, beneath the tower, heading towards the gallows and the gate beyond.

'Mengele,' I shouted in desperation.

He hesitated, half-turned, seeing us coming after him with weapons raised, then turned back towards the gate, reaching it in a couple more strides and wrenching it open. I could see a van beyond, emblazoned with the name of a local laundry. If we took a shot now, the Red Army would hear us and come running, realising something was up. Or rather, someone. Then they would get their hands on Mengele before we had a chance. We couldn't risk it. Besides, he was almost out of range.

He leaped into the van, started it up and roared off just as we reached the gate.

Too late. A few minutes more and we'd have had him. He was gone, and I'd never forgive myself. But at least we had his papers.

I stared after him, watching the dust trail left by his van, cursing the gods and anything else I could think of, my heart shrivelling in pain as it slowly sank in that he'd got away.

'Bastard must have got hold of a key to that gate,' I said.

Behind us, I could hear the guards at the main gate shouting.

'I'll go and pacify them,' said Jack. 'Make up some story.'

'And I'll get those papers. I made sure to lock the door so he couldn't go back and get them.'

He looked at the key I held in my hand. 'Bloody well done, Maggie.'

Back at the office, I piled the papers into the laundry trolley Mengele had left behind. Might as well make use of it. Wheeling it outside, I bumped into a breathless Marianne.

'Get this through the side gate,' I said. 'The one by the gallows. It's open. That's how Mengele got away. I'll go and distract Petrovsky.'

Marianne took it all in within half a second. 'See you back at the ward.'

She made it in a few minutes, strolling up as I mollified Petrovsky with words of praise. 'You're doing an excellent job here with very limited resources. We'll be more than happy to see what we can do to help.'

'I'm sure you will,' said Petrovsky.

I got the impression he wasn't fooled for an instant. I could also see that he was a pragmatist. You had to be, to survive this war.

'Thank you for your cooperation,' said Marianne, shaking his hand, as did Jack, who skidded up just in time, somewhat breathless but exuding charm.

'Yes, thank you, Doctor,' he said. 'We'll write up our report and send you a copy.'

Petrovsky waved a weary hand and turned back to his patients. It was our cue to leave, and so we did, striding back to the main gate, nodding at the guards with the requisite air of importance and then carrying on, out under that hateful sign, past the former SS quarters. Not once did I falter. There was no looking back.

'Where did you hide them?' I murmured once we were at a safe distance. Those papers were all we had now, but they were everything, the evidence of everything Mengele had done, of the atrocities the Nazis had carried out on so many innocent people. It was the evidence we could use to prove their crimes to the world. If it fell into the hands of the Soviets, there was no knowing what they would do with it.

'Among the trees, wrapped in one of the dirty sheets.'

'Appropriate. I just wish we had him too.'

'We'll get him, Maggie. One day, you'll testify against him in a court of law. Then you can prove to the whole world what he did. You have the evidence.'

Indeed I did, and there it was, hidden in the hollow of a tree. And yet my heart felt just as hollow. I had the evidence but not the man. It was Mengele I wanted to see hang, just as he'd watched Aleks and the others go to the gallows, although hanging was too good for him.

Retribution. Revenge. Call it what you like. For now, Mengele had got away scot-free, and that seared my soul.

FORTY-THREE

We trekked across the fields, putting as much distance as we could between us and the camp, stopping only to munch some of our rations before moving on again. The Red Army might have taken this part of Germany but that didn't make it any safer for us. Mengele's papers and notebooks were stuffed into my knapsack as well as the ones Marianne and Jack carried, weighing us down.

'How much longer until they send that plane over?' said Marianne. The shadows were growing longer, but it was still broad daylight.

'Six o'clock sharp. That's what Suzanne said. We have another hour and a half to go.'

'Let's try and get to some flatter ground. See if they can exfiltrate us at the same time.'

'Good thinking. Let's just check the transceiver as well. Make sure it's working properly.'

I pulled it from my pouch and stared at it in dismay. The aerial dangled from it uselessly, while the case was smashed. 'I must have landed on it when we were fighting Mengele. I don't think we can even try and mend it.'

'It looks too far gone to me. Now what are we going to do?'

Jack pulled out his silk map. 'By my reckoning, we're heading towards German-held territory. There's no way we can get a message to anyone until we get through that and reach the Allied lines. We need to try and steal some sort of vehicle, which means we have to head towards the nearest town or village.'

'Are there any farms on the way?'

'We just passed one. Look, here, this looks like a better bet. There's a large village over the next hill. Let's head for that. We're in Red Cross uniform so hopefully we can blag our way through. It's the only thing we can do.'

We looked at one another. If they even suspected for one moment we were Allied spies, they would arrest us. Or worse. The Germans were so desperate, pinned down as they were by the Soviets advancing from the east and our troops in the west, it was highly likely they would simply shoot us on the spot, especially as we were back in enemy territory here, the ever-changing Red Army lines behind us. All we could do was carry on and hope for the best.

'What about Suzanne? Won't she worry when we don't respond to her?'

Marianne's mouth was set in a grim line. 'She will, and there's always a chance she'll send in someone to find us. But it's a slim chance. Those planes fly low but not low enough to spot us out here unless we get extremely lucky. For the time being, I think we're on our own.'

'Well,' I said, 'I'd rather be on my own with you two right now than with almost anyone else on this earth.'

Except, perhaps, Jamie. God, I wished he was here. But I had no idea where he was. He could be anywhere doing goodness knows what.

We spotted the field hospital tents as we rounded the bend

at the top of the hill, to one side of a vast army encampment. We
stopped dead, gazing down.

'Christ alive, the Wehrmacht in all its glory,' said Jack.

'What do we do now?'

'Do? We get down there and steal a vehicle, of course.'

We made our way down the hill towards the field hospital,
trying to look as convincing as possible, dusting any remnants of
sulfa powder or forest twigs off as we went. As we neared the
hospital tents, we could see the ambulances parked next to
them.

'I can distract them while you hotwire one of the ambulances,' I said. 'I'll keep them talking. I'll pretend we're working
with the German Red Cross, if anyone asks.'

Inside the tent, the cots were laid out in regimented lines,
wounded men lying, some silent, some groaning in agony. I
snatched up a chart and pretended to study it, trying to get the
lay of the land. No one seemed to be paying me too much attention. I might not even need to distract them.

'Nurse.'

Damn. I turned to see a doctor beckoning to me.

'Nurse, give me a hand here.'

He was trying to examine a patient who was delirious,
thrashing around and trying to pull the drip from his arm.

'Of course.'

I got a firm grip on the patient, holding him so the doctor
could administer a sedative, watching as his face relaxed and he
slipped into unconsciousness. He was young, probably still a
teenager. Where his legs had once been, a bandaged stump now
protruded from the blankets. Poor kid. He might be the enemy,
but he was still just a boy and one who probably didn't even
want to go to war.

'Thank you, Nurse.'

The doctor's voice was cultured, his tone respectful. Not all doctors were so well-mannered, at least not the ones I'd encountered in Auschwitz.

I glanced at him. Froze. Felt his steady, widening gaze. It was him – the same SS doctor who'd given me his overcoat before the death march.

I opened my mouth. Closed it again. What could I say? Thank you for helping to save my life. Please don't give me away. So many thoughts scattering and regathering like a kaleidoscope, but I had no words to express them. He recognised me – I knew he did. But then he gave me a little nod and a half-smile, already turning away to go about his work.

I heard the distant hoot of a horn. Made my way back out of the tent as fast as I respectably could, seeing an ambulance pull up in front of me, the passenger door open.

'Get in,' called Marianne, reaching out a hand to pull me up.

'Now where the hell is the siren?' said Jack, steering the ambulance at speed as we careered down the road, the wail of the siren ringing out as his finger hit the right button.

'Where are we going?'

'Towards Frankfurt and then the Rhine. The Allies are poised to cross at any moment. With a bit of luck, we'll bump into them.'

I wanted to laugh aloud at the audacity of it, but it was too soon to count our chickens. 'Won't they spot that one of their ambulances is missing?'

Marianne grinned. 'Not this one. Its driver went off to answer a call of nature, so we thought we'd take the opportunity to relieve him of the keys as well. Possibly his life too. In any case, they won't find him.'

I didn't need to know any more. Didn't want to. It was enough that we were heading west into the setting sun, towards the Allied lines and freedom. All we had to do was get through hundreds of kilometres of enemy territory unscathed.

FORTY-FOUR

The moon shone bright and full, illuminating the road ahead, a silvered ribbon that stretched across the landscape, leading us west towards the Rhine crossing points and the Allied lines – or at least that was what we hoped. We'd pulled in for a few moments to study our maps and try to work out where the Allies would cross first.

'They're bound to cross near Mainz,' Jack insisted. 'It's the most logical place. If they aim lower, they have to cross two rivers instead of one.'

'Agreed, but that means the German commanders will think the same,' I said. 'So they'll be sending their troops into the area.'

'Are you suggesting we take a less direct route?'

'Absolutely not. There's nothing we can do but bluff it out. We're driving a German ambulance. If they stop us, one of you can pretend to be wounded. Then it will look as if we're on our way from a skirmish.'

'Good idea. Mainz it is. Let's get going.'

'Wait.' Marianne was pointing down the road ahead, along which lights were now approaching. 'What are those?'

'Looks like a convoy and it's headed this way.'

'Damn.'

Jack started up the siren as we shot out of the layby and raced down the road, heading straight for the convoy. I could see Marianne hanging on for dear life as we lurched and jolted. The ambulance was swinging from side to side, Jack trying to weave our way through.

All of a sudden, we came to an abrupt halt, my arms almost pulled from their sockets as I grabbed hold of the dashboard, pushing back to stop myself going through the windscreen.

I could hear shouting from outside the ambulance, and I braced myself, waiting for the doors to be flung open and to be faced with German troops.

'Drive, Jack,' Marianne muttered. 'They're not shouting at us.'

'You're right. There's a sheep in the road. They're trying to shoo it away.'

He revved the engine and we were off, moving more slowly now, passing what sounded like heavy trucks and tanks until at last there was nothing save the sound of the road beneath our wheels.

Just as I was beginning to believe we would make it, there was a loud bang, and the ambulance careered across the road, grinding to a halt at a forty-five-degree angle. We were still gasping for breath as Jack shouted, 'All out.'

'What's happened? A blowout?'

'Rear tyre. We'll just have to try and change it, although I don't know if there's a spare.'

I scrambled down after Marianne, looking around at the fields stretching, empty, on either side, falling away from the ditch in which we now appeared to be stuck and where Jack was getting to work on the tyre change.

'Look. More lights,' said Marianne.

Sure enough, there were pinpricks coming our way, just one

pair this time – a German jeep containing an SS officer, along with a driver and two soldiers riding shotgun. It looked as if it might drive right by us, but then I heard the officer rap out an order and it screeched to a halt. One of the soldiers jumped down and strode over to us.

'Leave this to me,' I muttered.

'The Sturmbannführer wants to know what has happened.'

Sturmbannführer – the equivalent of a major and an assault unit leader. That meant his unit was either the one we'd just passed through or had yet to appear.

'A tyre blew out,' I said, smiling coyly at him. 'He's useless at mending it.' I waved a dismissive hand at Jack, bending over the tyre in the ditch. 'Can you help us?'

The soldier glanced back at the jeep. 'We're already too far behind our unit. These damn roads. We had a blowout too.'

So the convoy was theirs. At least it was behind us now.

'How many do you have in there?' asked the soldier, jerking his head towards the ambulance. Any minute now, he might go and look.

I thought fast. 'We're on our way to pick up some casualties. We got a call.'

'Ah yes. The next town was hit pretty bad. It's a mess.'

'Is it far?'

'Maybe three kilometres from here. Those Allied bastards bombed it to bits. They're sending planes over day and night. We think they're trying to clear the way before they cross the Rhine.'

There was a shout from the jeep. '*Schutze!*' The major was obviously growing impatient.

'You go,' said Marianne. 'Don't worry about us.'

'You need a real man to help,' leered the soldier.

I sighed. 'I know, but what can we do? Thank goodness we have men like you out there.'

Suddenly, I heard a shot. Then another followed by the

sound of the jeep's horn blasting. I pulled out my pistol as the soldier whirled, his rifle raised. The driver's head was jammed against the horn where he lay, blood spreading across the back of his jacket. The other soldier in the rear of the jeep was hanging off the back of it, presumably as dead as the driver looked. The major had ducked low in his seat, his gun raised, shouting furiously.

Then I saw them, a squad of four men dressed in commando gear, firing at the Germans from a copse on the other side of the road. Jack, too, was firing at them from under the ambulance where he'd crawled.

Another volley of return fire from the Germans as the remaining soldier realised what was happening. In slow motion, I watched him turn and aim his gun at Marianne. In that same moment, I fired, hitting him square in the chest, then fired again, seeing blood spurt from his temple, his gun dropping from his hand as he fell, lifeless, to the ground.

The major was crouched behind the jeep, retuning fire, when all at once it burst into flames. A bullet must have hit the petrol tank, the flames taking hold as they ate up the fuel.

A muffled explosion and then another as a figure staggered forward, barely recognisable – the major was also on fire, screaming and writhing. I could see his uniform burning. That hated uniform. Hear his agonised cries.

I took aim, squeezing the trigger as I murmured some kind of prayer. It was only when he, too, hit the ground, motionless, that I realised what it was. The Kaddish. The Jewish prayer I'd heard so many times in Auschwitz. I wasn't saying it for him but for all the people he'd killed, all those souls he'd taken, all the ones he could no longer take.

'Rot in hell, you bastard.'

I fired a final shot into his charred remains, then looked up to see Jack limping towards us, Marianne holding out her hand to him, the squadron of four now running towards us too except that one was evidently badly hurt, his mates half-carrying him as they ran, pistols raised, pointed now at us.

As they drew closer, I could make out the insignia on their uniforms – a dagger with what looked like two pale wings rising either side of it, the words 'Who Dares Wins' emblazoned across it. The SAS.

'It's OK,' I called out. 'We're British.'

'Thank Christ for that,' said one. 'This is our captain. He's been hit. Can you help him?'

As they hoisted him higher, his face came into view. My heart plunged.

'Jamie,' I whispered.

Blood was seeping from his torso as well as his left arm and leg.

'Get him in the ambulance. Is that tyre mended?'

'Good as new.'

'Then let's get him out of here before another unit comes along.'

They hoisted him in the back of the ambulance as gently as they could, and I strapped him down, grabbing a pair of scissors and cutting open his clothes so I could see how badly he was wounded. It didn't look good.

'We'll leave you to it,' said his mate. 'Can you get him to the Allied lines?'

'That's where we're headed.'

'Us too, but we have a few things to do on the way. You'll look after him?'

'Of course.'

Easier said than done. If I didn't get that wound cleaned up and the infection under control, he would succumb to sepsis within hours.

I grabbed the emergency kit and snapped it open – bandages, disinfectant, sulfa powder, needle and thread. Good. I heard the rear doors slam, but I was already trying to stem his bleeding with compression, cleaning his wounds as I felt around for bullets, murmuring, 'It's alright. It'll be alright,' as I began to stitch.

His left arm needed to be set – a volley of bullets had smashed into it, shattering bone. He was chalk white, mumbling something unintelligible. I would have given anything for chloroform, but there was none. All I could do was murmur soothing words, glancing at his face now and then to see if the pain was too much, sprinkling sulfa over the sutures when I was done. It wasn't penicillin, but it would have to do for now.

My hands were shaking by the time I was done, as much with shock as anything else. What the hell he was doing out here was anyone's guess, but questions would have to wait for later. Right now, I needed to keep him alive. He'd lost a lot of blood. Too much.

I gently picked up his right wrist and took his pulse – it was thready and faint. I scrabbled through the ambulance supplies as it lurched and jolted along, grabbing at a bag of saline, managing to insert a needle and tube into his arm so that at least he had an IV drip keeping him hydrated.

'You can do it, my darling – keep fighting,' I murmured.

His eyelids flickered – a nerve tremor maybe.

'Can you hear me? Oh, Jamie, please. Just open your eyes.'

A tiny sigh escaped his lips, and then he was motionless once more, lost somewhere far away, beyond consciousness. Even so, I would swear he'd heard me and recognised my voice.

As we neared the outskirts of the town, we came upon bodies hanging from lamp posts and trees – men and one woman. Around their necks were signs scrawled in German: 'I have been hanged here because I am too cowardly to defend the capital of the Reich. I have been hanged because I did not believe in the Führer. I am a deserter and for this reason I shall not see this turning point in history.'

'The SS,' I murmured. 'I'm glad I killed him.'

I only wished I could have done the same to Mengele. One day, I promised myself. One day soon.

'Bravo.'

I felt pressure on my hand, the one I was using to hold Jamie's, a squeeze of my fingers. He said it again. 'Bravo.' Barely audible, his voice cracking on the word, but still he'd uttered it.

'My God. You're awake. Jamie! Oh my love.'

His eyes were open, and he was looking at me in a way I would never forget. It was all there – pain, admiration. Love. Best of all, fight. I stroked his forehead, feeling it wet beneath my palm, his fever intensifying.

'Stay with me,' I whispered.

But he was slipping away again, sinking back into that place where I couldn't follow. All I could hope to do was pull him back and this time keep him with me. Forever.

FORTY-FIVE

White flags fluttered from windows and doorways, some of them white sheets, others tablecloths and rags. They were wrapped around the arms of the people stumbling around the town square – or what remained of it. The jagged ruins of buildings gaped between those still standing, while people streamed in the opposite direction to that from which we'd come. A few had horses and carts, but many were simply walking, carrying with them whatever they could, arms and backs laden with their most precious possessions, some heads bowed in defeat, others raised in hope that they would find sanctuary elsewhere.

We slowed as we crawled past them, the voice in my head urging Jack to put his foot down even as I could see there were so many it would be impossible to do anything else.

I heard Jack call out to them. 'Where are you going?'

'To the Americans,' shouted one.

'They've crossed the Rhine,' yelled another.

'They've crossed the Rhine? Where?'

'Oppenheim.'

'Nierstein.'

'Fool, they've crossed in many places. They keep on coming.

The war is over, my friend. We're finished. You might as well surrender too.'

'You hear that?' Jack shouted from the front as we sped away. 'They're here. Our boys are here.'

I wiped Jamie's forehead with the cool compress I'd made out of dressings and some of the water left in the canteen. The rest I saved to hold to his lips, to moisten them if nothing else. The saline was almost empty, and we had no more left.

'How far to Oppenheim?' I shouted back.

'Seventy kilometres. Maybe less.'

Another two hours by road, possibly more if we had to go at this pace.

More ravaged towns and villages. More people flooding from them. Crawling, then stopping, then picking up speed once more. I pressed my lips together, unable to speak for fear of breaking down, staring out the back window once more at the miles flashing past.

All the while Jamie's breathing grew shallower, his features beginning to sink into grooves and caverns that presaged death, or maybe that was my imagination. He looked more dead than alive now, his lips blue and cracked no matter what ointment I applied or the water I gently wiped across them.

I tried to will my own life into him, to transfer it through my fingers, through my hand holding his, but there was no strength in his grip. His hand rested in mine, lifeless, the tips of his fingers turning blue as well as all his blood concentrated in his organs, his body trying desperately to stay alive.

I watched him take a shuddering breath. Then another. Was this it? His death throes?

I dropped over him, placing my mouth against his, gently pinching his nose and breathing into his mouth. My life for his. My oxygen filling him.

He sighed, relaxed, his breathing once more even.

I sat up, gulping in air, ready to go again. That was when I heard a shout from up front. Heard it again. Marianne.

'Americans.'

More shouts, demanding that we stop. Jack shouting back in English, 'We're with you – OSS, SOE, SAS.'

An American voice, incredulous. 'What the hell...?'

Someone wrenched open the back doors and faces peered in – American faces smeared in muck.

'You're Brits?'

'Yes. Look – he's a captain with the SAS.' I held up the insignia on the clothing I'd cut from him. 'He's badly wounded. We need medics fast. And penicillin.'

More shouts passing along, a blur of movement. Then men climbed into the ambulance, men with armbands that bore red crosses, gently examining Jamie, one of them looking at me as I repeated, 'He needs penicillin. The sulfa isn't working anymore.'

Another man passed him a syringe, and he plunged it into Jamie's arm. A fresh bag of saline was hooked up and more blankets passed in.

'Let's get him out of here,' said the medic. 'You follow us to the field hospital.'

'Do you think he's going to make it?'

'He has as good a chance as any.'

Which wasn't much, but it was all that we had. And I would take it.

FORTY-SIX

24 MARCH 1945, US 7TH ARMY LINES, THE RHINELAND, GERMANY

'We're going to evacuate him today to Paris,' said the surgeon. 'I've done what I can, but he'll need more surgery. Possibly skin grafts.'

I tried to ignore his blood-spattered gloves. Jamie's blood. 'I want to go with him.'

'That shouldn't be a problem. You're a medic after all. I hear it was you that sutured him up.'

'I did.'

'You saved his life. If you hadn't done that so well and kept those wounds as clean as you did, he'd have died back there on the road. Good work, Nurse.'

'Actually, I'm a doctor.'

'Well then, if you ever need a job, look me up.'

'I don't think I will, but thank you.'

I turned to see Marianne hovering, her face creased with concern. 'He's going to be alright,' I said. 'They're evacuating him to Paris. The surgeon said I could go with him.'

'Want me to come with you?'

'No. You need to get back to Suzanne with the others and debrief. I'll be fine.'

I felt a tap on my arm, turned to see a sergeant saluting me.

'Surgeon says you're the doctor travelling with the patient.'

'That's right.'

'Transport's here.'

I engulfed Marianne in a hug, holding her tight. 'I'll see you when I see you.'

She held me a second longer. 'You look after yourself, Maggie. We'll see you very soon.'

Jack was next. 'I'm so glad you're back with us.'

I smiled. 'Me too.'

Then I was once more climbing into an ambulance to sit beside Jamie, only this time it wasn't all up to me to keep him alive.

'Maggie.' He was awake, groggy but smiling up at me. 'You're coming with me?'

'Only to make sure you don't get up to any more mischief.'

'I wish I could. With you.'

'You are incorrigible.'

He fell asleep then, the anaesthetic still in his system, his breathing deep and regular in a way it hadn't been since he'd been injured. I sat and watched him as we drove to the airfield, studying the swoop of his lashes on his cheeks, the curve of his mouth even in repose, the way his brows puckered now and then, as if he was dreaming.

'I love you,' I whispered.

'I love you too.'

'You bastard. You're supposed to be asleep.'

'How can I sleep when I can feel you looking at me?' His smile lit up his face, bringing the life back to it in a way that nothing else could. 'I'm glad you're here, Maggie.'

'I'm glad you're still here.'

He reached for my hand, his fingers fumbling until they found mine, weaving their way through them, holding on tight.

'Will you marry me?'

I gaped at him, dumbstruck. 'You want to marry me?'

'Yes. Very much. Is it such an awful notion to you?'

'No. Not at all. It's I who's the awful notion. How could you want to marry me?'

He looked at me then. Really looked at me, his eyes moving across my face and then staring deep into mine.

'You think you're damaged goods, don't you, Maggie? Well, to me you're perfect. Better than perfect. And it's those cracks and scars that make you so. I've never met anyone like you, so brave and yet so selfless, although you don't even know it. It would be the greatest honour if you would consent to marry me, but I understand if my own cracks and scars put you off.'

I laughed, an incredulous bark that sounded harsh even to my ears. 'Your cracks and scars? There's nothing wrong with you. At least, nothing that time won't heal. Me... I'm not so sure. I can't inflict that on you, Jamie. I love you too much to do so.'

'Then marry me. Time heals everything. Yes, even you. So does love, Maggie. And I love you so very much.'

Just for a moment, I started to believe it could actually be true.

FORTY-SEVEN

24 MARCH 1945, PARIS, FRANCE

Suzanne was there, waiting for me outside the military hospital when I finally emerged, feeling as if I hadn't slept for days. She looked me up and down, then pulled the scarf from her shoulders and wrapped it round me. 'Shall we?'

As the car set off back to Paris, a silence fell between us, pregnant with unspoken secrets. I could see her steeling herself to say something.

'Just tell me,' I said. 'What's happened?'

'It's Leah. She's sick.'

'Sick? How?'

'They think it could be typhus.'

'Oh God no. Not Leah.'

She patted my arm. 'Antoine is with her. We'll get you back to the Lutetia as quickly as we can and find out more. Your debrief can wait.'

The Lutetia was just as I'd left it, except that there were even more people sitting, traumatised, in the public rooms or wandering the corridors in search of a familiar past if not a future. Some looked sick, their eyes fevered; others as if they didn't know what to do. The helpers still bustled round them, but they too appeared exhausted or unwell. Worst of all was a smell I recognised from the camps, from Gross-Rosen. The stench of typhus, fainter here but still detectable.

I found Sophie in the library, patiently turning the pages for a young girl who stared at them without recognition, reading out the names of the illustrations: apple, butterfly, cat. I hated to disturb her, but I had to find out what was going on.

'Sophie.'

'Maggie. *Ma cherie*. How good it is to see you.'

'And you.' I kissed her on both cheeks. 'Is Antoine here?'

Her eyes dropped and, in that moment, my heart did too. 'He is at the hospital with Leah. The Necker children's hospital.'

'How is she?'

'She's very sick, by all accounts. Antoine is there day and night.'

'It's definitely typhus?'

'Yes.'

I looked around the room, at the people milling around so close to one another – some recent arrivals, others who'd been there for weeks. 'It's spreading. How many are already sick?'

'Thirty. Maybe forty. We send them to the hospital, but there are more cases each day.'

'You need to separate them all out and sterilise this entire building. Take everyone's clothes and burn them. Burn the sheets and blankets too. We need to spray the rooms with DDT and delouse every single new arrival, stripping them completely naked and applying louse powder.'

Sophie looked at me as if I'd lost my mind. 'We can't do that. It's degrading. These poor people have already been treated worse than animals.'

'I know, but we have to. Trust me, this is how typhus spreads. It's the only way to eradicate it. It's how Leah caught it, from the others here. If we don't stop it now, there'll be an epidemic.'

I didn't mention this was how Mengele had brought it under control in Auschwitz, although his methods had been far more ruthless.

'We have so few sheets and blankets already. Barely enough. And the clothing supplies are also running low.'

'Sophie, we can get more sheets and blankets for these people along with more clothing. What we can't do is resurrect them once they're dead. Don't you think they've suffered enough? We have to give them the best chance now of having a good and healthy life, or as much as they're able.'

She quietly handed the book to the young girl. 'You're right. This one here is Polish. She was sent from the ghetto to the camps. If she survived all of that, we owe it to her to do this. We owe it to all of them.'

'Exactly. Can I leave you to start doing that while I go and check on Leah and Antoine?'

'Of course. You go and give them all our love.'

'Before I do, I'm going to wash my hands thoroughly and change. We need to get those basic hygiene measures in place. Segregate anyone who seems sick immediately. We have to be very strict.'

'We've been trying to get those who are sick to stay in their rooms until we can get them to the hospital, but it's hard to spot who's ill until it's too late.'

'I know. You're doing your best. We all are. So let's keep doing it.'

These people had gone through too much to get here, to a place they thought of as safe. There was no way in heaven or on earth I was going to let them be struck down by a disease that could spread like wildfire. I'd seen it in Auschwitz. I wasn't going to let it happen here, even if we were on the back foot, playing catch-up. It was a miracle more people here hadn't contracted it, although there would no doubt be more cases in the days ahead. But if we could stop it in its tracks now, we stood a good chance of stamping it out altogether. If we didn't, then many would die needlessly, just when they thought they'd been saved.

I wanted to kick myself. Why hadn't I stayed here, where I was needed? But then, if I had, I would never have been able to save Jamie. So many impossible choices. An endless series of them. All I knew was that two of the people I loved most needed me here now. Jamie wasn't out of the woods by any means, the surgeons here muttering about amputation. As for Leah, my baby, there was no knowing what would happen. Typhus rarely killed children, but she was so very young that there was no knowing if she would be one of the lucky ones or not. She might not actually be my baby, but I'd brought her into this world, and I'd promised her mother I would look after her.

Hold on, Leah – I'm coming, I began to chant in my head. *I'm coming and I'm never leaving you again.*

It was a promise I prayed I could keep.

FORTY-EIGHT

I found Antoine by her hospital cot, his head slumped forward onto his folded arms, which were resting on the side of it, as close as he could get to her in sleep.

I touched his shoulder. 'Antoine.'

He stirred, mumbled something.

I turned to the nurse with me and murmured. 'How's she doing?'

The woman gave me the kind of shrug that said only time would tell.

I bent over the cot, gently pulling aside the sheet covering her. The rash stood out, livid, on her torso, her limbs hot to the touch. Her eyes were half-open, but she wasn't looking at me. I so wanted to sweep her up in my arms and hold her close. Instead, I checked the drip going into her little arm.

'Has she taken any milk?'

'A tiny bit, but she spat it out again.'

I looked at Antoine, now sitting up straight, blinking at me.

'You look like shit,' I said.

'I could say the same for you.'

We smiled at one another, the wan smiles of people meeting in the worst of circumstances.

Leah let out a cry, although it sounded more like a bleat.

'She wants to be in on the conversation too,' I said. 'That's good. She's refusing to give up.'

'You think so?'

'I know so. Look at her, Antoine. She might be small, but she's tough.'

'Like her mother.'

'Which is why she's going to make it. Your daughter is one hell of a fighter.'

At that, Leah opened her mouth and let out a proper bawl. It was such a wonderful sound to hear that I laughed.

'That's it, my girl. You tell us how you feel.'

Antoine gazed at the rash on her chest. 'It's still there.'

'Yes, but it will go. Has she had any seizures?'

'None.'

'That's good. Vomiting? Diarrhoea?'

'Both.'

I checked her chart. Her last recorded temperature was nearly forty degrees. Still too high. If they could keep her hydrated, she stood a chance, but the next twenty-four hours or so were crucial. Although Leah had let out a cry, her breathing was still fast, her abdomen tender to the touch. Typhus had her very much in its grip, and it wasn't going to let go without a fight either.

'Antoine, why don't you go get some proper rest? I can sit with her for a while. I'll send for you if necessary, but it won't be necessary.'

He ran his hand through his hair, which was limp and in need of a wash. He must have been here for days. There were shadows under his eyes that looked more like bruises. 'I want to stay,' he said. 'I would never forgive myself if... if...'

'I understand. Then why don't I sit here while you go and get some food from the canteen and maybe have a quick wash?'

'We tried to get him to go and rest in a side room, but he wouldn't have it,' said the nurse.

'I'm all she's got,' muttered Antoine. 'And she's all I've got.'

I looked at the nurse. 'It's alright. I can look after them. I'm a doctor.'

Her eyebrows shot up.

'I am. Really. Ask the doctors at the 189th Hospital if you don't believe me. I've just escorted a patient there. They said I saved his life. That he wouldn't have made it if it wasn't for me.'

I was aware I was rambling, probably sounding half-crazed. No wonder she didn't believe me. I was in as much of a state as Antoine, in spite of scrubbing myself from head to toe and putting on fresh clothes.

'Who was this?' asked Antoine.

'Jamie.'

'Your Jamie?'

'Yes. He was on a mission, in Germany, heading for the Allied lines, as we were after we left Gross-Rosen. We stumbled into his squad quite by chance when we all got caught up in a skirmish. Jamie was hit but we got him out. He's here right now, in hospital, but he's badly injured.'

'Did you get him? Mengele?'

I shook my head. 'We cornered him at Gross-Rosen, but he got away. We did manage to get his notes, so at least that's something.'

Antoine gave my hand the briefest of squeezes, but it was enough to know that he understood. Of course he did.

'So here we are,' he said. 'Both of us. Both of them.'

'Yes, and how I wish we weren't.'

I looked at Leah again. 'She's fast asleep. Go on. Scoot.'

'You'll call me if anything happens?'

'I will.'

He stumbled off, and I took his seat, watching her as she slept, her little body twitching now and then, trembling with fever.

'That's it, darling, you sleep,' I murmured. 'It will help you get better.'

I must have dozed off too, because the next thing I knew, Antoine was back, a cup of water for me in his hand.

I glanced at Leah – still sleeping, but her colour was a little better, although perhaps that was wishful thinking.

'Antoine, I'm sorry. I must be more tired from the journey than I thought.'

'Don't be sorry. You're exhausted.'

'So are you. You look as if you haven't slept for weeks yourself.'

He sighed. 'It's not just Leah I'm worried about. The hotel is getting fuller by the day, and people are getting sick.'

'Don't worry about that. I was there. I've already asked Sophie to put measures in place. With any luck, we can prevent an epidemic.'

'Maggie, what would I do without you? Truly, you are an angel.'

'I don't know about that. Wrong hair colour for a start.'

He looked at my hair, now curling well below my ears. Soon it would be back to shoulder length and then, perhaps, I'd feel more like myself.

'I think it's the perfect colour for you. Bold. Bright. Unmissable.'

I laughed. 'You're making me blush.'

'We handed that woman over to the authorities. The one you called the Beast. They'll keep her in prison until they can try her for war crimes.'

'Good. I wish we could have done the same with Mengele. Marianne and Jack have gone back in on their other mission, trying to locate more of them. Of course, that means they're not at the Lutetia.'

Antoine sighed. 'Besides the typhus, I'm worried there'll be more like her and Victor. People are flooding in now, from all over. It can only be a matter of time before there's more trouble from someone trying to sneak through. That's another problem with my being here. The others are on their mission. There's no one to question the arrivals and make sure they're not collaborators. Or worse.'

'Why don't I question them?'

'On your own? You're already running between two hospitals and trying to prevent a typhus epidemic. Look, Maggie, we'll be alright here. You focus on making sure no one else gets sick.'

'We don't have to do this on our own for long. The others will be back soon. It was so good being a team again. I'd forgotten how it felt, being out there in the field, even if we did lose Mengele.'

'You'll find him. It's only a matter of time.'

'That's what Marianne said.'

'She's right. Just like old times, eh, Maggie?'

A memory flashed through my mind, my legs pumping as I rode my bicycle for miles through the countryside, delivering messages, my radio set hidden in the basket, my heart resolute. Until the day they'd caught me sabotaging that railway line, my bicycle on the ground, its wheels still spinning. No time to grab it and try to get away. The SS had been on me like starving rats swarming over a piece of meat. That was how they'd treated me – not as a human being but a lump of flesh to be degraded and devoured by the hell that was Auschwitz.

It was my medical skills that had saved me. Once they'd realised I was a doctor, I'd had a use. Those same skills had helped save Jamie too, and now, with any luck, I could use them to save others at the hotel from suffering the same fate as Leah. Typhus could be eradicated, even in a hellhole like Auschwitz. If I could do the same, if I could stamp it out at the Lutetia, then maybe that fragile sense I could be myself again would grow and become stronger too. Then I could spend the rest of my life healing rather than hurting. A life I wanted to spend with Jamie, whatever happened. If they had to amputate, then so be it. He was still my Jamie and always would be – the man I longed to marry with all my heart. The heart he'd captured the moment I saw him.

FORTY-NINE

31 MARCH 1945, PARIS, FRANCE

Jamie's bed was empty, the sheets pulled drum tight, the blankets too.

I marched back to the nurses' station where a ward sister was measuring out medication. 'Where is he? Captain Maclean?'

She peered up at me from under her cap. 'Outside, taking some fresh air.'

I looked in the direction she was pointing, taking in the open French windows in the recreation room beyond the ward and the garden beyond that. The hospital to which Jamie had been transferred was old but spotlessly clean, its corridors broken up by archways that were reflected in the shape of the windows and the courtyard cloisters. It sat in the shadow of Notre-Dame, but here, in the interior, was this oasis that felt like a secret garden with patients in chairs and wheelchairs dotted around it.

Jamie was sitting under one of the arches, staring out over the box hedges and flower beds, a book lying face down in his lap. A blanket was tucked around his legs, one of which was propped on a board that extended from his wheelchair.

He looked up, saw me and smiled. 'I still have two legs, as you can see.'

'So I can. And you're here, out of bed. How are you feeling?'

'Much better now that you're here.'

He reached up, pulling my face down to his, planting a lingering kiss on my lips.

'You are feeling better,' I murmured.

'All thanks to you.'

'Not just me. I'm sure the staff here can take some credit.'

'Ah, but they don't have your special touch.'

'What special touch is that?'

He dropped me a wink. 'I was hoping you might show me.'

'Outrageous.'

'Isn't that what you love about me?'

I smiled, stroking the back of my hand across his cheek, feeling him nibble the tips of my fingers as I caressed his mouth. 'That and many other things.'

'Maggie, can we get married as soon as possible? Why wait? We don't need some big, fancy wedding. All I want is to know that you and I are bound together, forever.'

His eyes were dark with sincerity, his gaze unwavering.

'I'd like that too.'

His smile lit up his whole face. 'Wonderful. Then let's organise it. I'm sure your friends will help.'

I thought of Marianne and Jack, Suzanne too. And Antoine. Dear Antoine. 'I'm sure they will, but I'd like to wait until I know that Leah is going to be alright. I couldn't celebrate knowing she wasn't yet recovered. Once she's out of the woods, we can get married.'

'That's how I first saw you both, running out of the woods, you and Leah. Of course we'll wait. I know how much she means to you.'

'It may seem odd, but it really does feel as if she's a little bit my child too. I know she's not, in reality, but I delivered her, and I kept my promise to Eva to bring her to Antoine.'

'So you gave her life twice. She's bound to be special to you. I understand. I really do. And I hope one day we'll have children of our own.'

I brushed the lock of hair from his forehead that flopped stubbornly over it, leaning forward to kiss the same spot. 'I hope so too. I can't think of anything more wonderful than to raise a family with you. To watch our children grow.'

'Would that be enough for you, Maggie?'

He was studying me intently, eyes still dark but this time with something else.

'What do you mean?'

'I mean after all this. The excitement. The adventure. Would a life of domesticity really be enough after everything you've done?'

I stared out at the garden, taking in the flowers just coming into bloom – scarlet and purple, yellow and blue. All the colours of the rainbow. A symbol of new life, of promise. I wanted rainbows in my life, not grey mists or brown fields littered with the fallen. No more white flakes falling on my face or smoke belching from a crematorium. I could not – would not – forget, but the best way to remember and to honour those who were no longer here was to live in full colour, to feel every moment. Even if at times those moments were too much.

I might never find Mengele, but I had the evidence that would convict him, that would prove to the world what the Nazis had done. Marianne and Jack were out there even now, hunting down more of them. When this war ended, we would make sure they were brought to justice. All of them. But it didn't need to be me out there anymore. We'd had one last mission; I'd had one last mission. They would carry on as the brilliant team they were, but for me, a different future beckoned. One I could see sitting before me in this garden, the man who'd saved my life in so many ways. Who was still saving it now.

'I can promise you, hand on heart, it will be more than enough. It's exactly what I want, and I want it with you. Besides, I could ask you the same.'

'Here.'

I looked down. He was holding out a flower, a spring rose he'd plucked from the shrub alongside him. It was perfect, its petals coiled in cream whorls tinged with pink. I held it to my nose and inhaled. Its scent was strong and deep.

'That rose is like you,' he said. 'It looks so delicate but then you see the thorns that protect it.'

He pressed his finger against one of those thorns and I watched as a tiny drop of blood welled, scarlet against his skin.

'You see? It can draw blood, just like you. But it can also bring joy with its beauty, its fragrance. Just like you, Maggie. You are truly the most beautiful being I've ever seen. Inside and out.'

I could feel the tears running down my face, see them drop onto the petals. 'No. No I'm not,' I whispered. 'I'm tainted. Dirty. I don't deserve you. Or this.'

'Is that what they told you? Those bastards in Auschwitz?'

'Every day, but it isn't just that. I'm alive, you see. I'm sitting here with you, in this garden. So many aren't. They'll never see another flower bloom or a rainbow in the sky. That's what I can't bear. That I'm here and they're not and there's no sense to any of it. I'm not better than any of them, and yet somehow I survived.'

'You did, and I'm thankful for that every day. As are so many other people. Look at you now – helping at the Lutetia, looking after others just like you always do, ever since I've known you. You're here now, looking after me. I want to look after you too, for the rest of our lives together. And I want that life together to start as soon as possible.'

I heard it in his voice, the same urgency I felt, that so many of us felt. To live. To love. To seize the day because there might never be another.

'It already has,' I said. 'It started the moment I saw you. And I hope it never ends.'

'It won't.'

FIFTY

Leah was sleeping peacefully in her cot, her cheeks pink with health rather than fever, the rash all but gone from her torso and tiny limbs.

'She looks so much better,' I breathed.

Antoine smiled. 'Doesn't she? The doctor said she can probably go home in a day or two.'

It hung in the air between us, that awful, unspoken sense that home was no longer where it used to be and that it contained just the two of them.

'That's good news, Antoine.'

'What about you? How's Jamie?'

'I think you mean my fiancé.'

Antoine seized both my hands. 'Maggie, that's wonderful. I'm so happy for you.'

He glanced at my left hand with its bare ring finger.

'He's still in hospital too, don't forget,' I said. 'A ring and all of that can wait.'

'Then allow me to lend you one in the meantime, just until he can get you one. It would be improper not to have an engagement ring. You must, after all, let your other potential suitors know that they're too late.'

I laughed. 'I don't exactly see a queue of them. Thank you, Antoine, but I'm content to leave things as they are for now.'

'I insist. You would be doing me an honour,' he said, drawing a ring from his pocket. 'I keep this with me always. It was Eva's. She gave it to me for safekeeping the day they came and took her and the boys. I always think she must have had some kind of premonition. She said she didn't want to walk around with it on in case people noticed and tried to steal it to sell for food, but I knew that wasn't the real reason.'

I gazed at the ring in the palm of his hand, bearing a single, perfect diamond set in white-gold filigree. 'It's absolutely beautiful, Antoine, but I couldn't possibly wear it. This is Eva's ring. Not mine.'

'She would want you to wear it. I know she would. One day, I will give it to Leah, but, for now, I want it to be yours.'

How could I refuse? I could hear the longing in his voice, the ache to have her back, to see something of hers brought to life again.

'In that case,' I said, picking up the ring and placing it on my finger, 'I accept. I'll wear it for you both. For all of you.'

Leah sighed, a deep contented sigh, her arms flopping out in the way only a baby can sleep. A real sleep, one that was healing her by the minute, her mouth working as she dreamed, stretching now in what looked like a smile.

'You see,' murmured Antoine. 'She approves.'

I stretched my hand down to tug the blanket up over her stomach, seeing the diamond flash twice as bright, doubled by the tears that sprang to my eyes. If only I'd been able to save them both, to return Eva to Antoine as well. But there was nothing I could have done. I knew that I'd truly done my best. In that moment, I also knew that Leah wasn't the only one healing, that there was hope for me too.

FIFTY-ONE

A car was waiting for them when they landed, Suzanne emerging from it to greet them both.

'Just in time.'

Marianne returned her embrace. 'For what?'

'Maggie and Captain Maclean are getting married tomorrow and they want us all to be there.'

Marianne didn't know whether to laugh or cry. A whirl of emotions engulfed her as she glanced at Jack and then back at Suzanne. 'Married? What, here?'

'They wanted to do it in Paris so Antoine and Leah could attend too. I think after everything that happened, they wanted to do it sooner than later.'

'I can understand that. How is he?'

'He's on the mend. It could have been a lot worse. But on top of that, Maggie's had to cope with an outbreak of typhus at the Lutetia. Little Leah caught it, but she, too, is almost fully recovered.'

'Thank goodness. Poor Maggie. She's already gone through so much and then to have all that to deal with...'

Suzanne nodded. 'She has, which is why I'm so happy for her. This wedding means so much to her – you can see that.'

'Then we must help make it as special as possible,' said Jack.

Marianne threw him a smile. 'We will. What about Maggie's family?'

'I don't know. From what I understand, she's had trouble tracking them down. They went south, to Marseilles, when their place in Normandy was requisitioned. She also has two brothers in the French Army. No word on them either.'

'Can you put any feelers out?'

'I already have. As has Antoine, I believe.'

'And if that doesn't work, she has us as her family,' said Marianne.

It was true – they were family, although something told her this would take Maggie in a different direction, to a place she would far rather be. She'd seen it in Maggie's eyes when they were leaving Gross-Rosen, an expression not of defeat but of resignation, as if she'd accepted there were some battles she could not, or no longer wanted to, win. Mengele had represented everything that was evil to Maggie. Probably still did. He was her chance to avenge all those he'd murdered. And yet, when it came to it, she suspected the real revenge for Maggie was in living well, which was what she would do with her Jamie. Starting with this wedding tomorrow.

She felt Jack's hand brush against hers, as light as a moth's wing. Even so, it sent shockwaves through her. He didn't need to say anything. She knew what he meant. They were family too, bound together every bit as much as Maggie and Jamie. A wedding was just a formality. They already knew they would be together forever. Or as long as forever lasted in a world where everything could change in the split second it took to pull a trigger or pull a pin from a grenade.

FIFTY-TWO

I emerged from my newly appointed consulting room to find Sophie greeting the latest arrivals, a weary line of people filing into the lobby, pinched with fatigue and that peculiar patina that the camps left on everyone, the sheen of having lived alongside death for so long that it leeched all the blood from your skin.

'Welcome,' I cried, my eyes automatically sweeping the line, searching. Most of these people had come from the DP camps in Germany after they'd been liberated from other camps by the Soviets. They came from Auschwitz and Gross-Rosen as well as prisoner of war camps. Each time, I looked for anyone I might recognise, including my brothers. I had no idea if they'd been captured or not, but in this war, as I well knew, anything could happen.

I'd yet to see anyone I knew, but more and more were arriving, along with people who were also looking for their loved ones, bringing with them pictures of mothers and fathers as well as wives and husbands. It was the photographs of the children I couldn't bear, especially as I knew they were almost certainly dead, executed by the Nazis as soon as they got off the transports, sent into the showers innocently clutching their bar of soap, unaware that they were about to die in the most unimaginable way.

As they came through the hotel door, a couple of the volunteers sprayed them with DDT powder. I could see the surprise on their faces along with the fear.

'It's just to prevent disease,' I called out. 'It won't harm you.'

Truth be told, we had no idea if DDT was harmful or not, but it was all we had against the far greater risk of typhus.

'This way,' cried Sophie, ushering them into the room off the lobby which we now used as a waiting room while we medically screened each arrival. In there, soup awaited them, a gentle start to refeeding. For the few children there was milk, and for everyone there was a kind word and a smile. Once they'd been checked over, they were sent to be deloused and to take a shower. For this most sensitive task, we provided them with an individual bathroom which we allowed them to inspect beforehand if they wished. Some begged us to leave the door open as they showered and we, of course, complied.

I beckoned to a woman who sat crumpled on one of the chairs, her eyes sunk so deep into her skull I couldn't tell the colour.

'Hello, my name is Maggie. Would you come with me?'

From the back of the room, I heard someone repeat my name and then call it out, louder. 'Maggie. Maggie, it's me.'

I turned to see another woman standing up, waving at me. It took me a second to register and then another to recognise her.

I excused myself and strode across the room, moving through the milling crowd until I was by her side. 'Hanna! Oh my goodness. How on earth did you get here?'

'Like everyone else – on a truck.'

She hadn't changed. That impish smile was still in place,

along with her energy, although she looked a little healthier than when I'd last seen her.

'It's so good to see you.'

'And you. But I didn't come alone – I brought a friend with me.'

She indicated another woman, who was also huddled on a chair, visibly weaker than Hanna, although there was something familiar about her. Then she looked up at me and I realised who it was.

'Eva. You're alive. My God.'

I staggered, half-fell, grabbing on to the arm of her chair to right myself. I had to look again, to keep on looking until I was convinced it was really her. Even then, I reached out and touched one of the blonde curls that now framed her face.

'Yes,' she whispered. 'It's really me.'

'But how? When I left you, you were dying.'

I realised that people were starting to stare so I offered her my arm, helping her up. Hanna accompanied us along the corridor to my consulting room, where I settled Eva in a chair, closing the door to give us some privacy and peace.

'Now tell me,' I said. 'What happened? How did you two find one another?'

'After you left,' said Eva, 'a doctor looked after me, a Polish man. He was kind. He knew you, and he spoke about you often. Dr Laba.'

I stared at her, remembering. Remembering too the way he'd looked at me the day Aleks died, the things he'd said. There were good people everywhere, even in the worst of circumstances and places.

'I know who you mean. He saved my life, in a way, and it looks like he saved yours too.'

'Do you know where he is now? Dr Laba?'

'In the same DP camp we were in. He insisted we take the

transport to Paris before him. Hopefully, he'll be here soon too. Such a good man.'

'He is. I can't wait to see him.'

She looked at me, her face naked with fear and longing. 'What about Leah?' she whispered. 'Hanna told me how you also saved her life. Where is she? Is she here? And what about Antoine? Is he alright?'

I reached forward and took both her hands between mine. 'Oh, Eva, I have so much to tell you. Antoine is bringing Leah to his apartment even now from the hospital.'

Her brow puckered. 'Hospital?'

'Don't worry. She's absolutely fine. She caught typhus, but she recovered. She's a strong one, your daughter. A fighter. Just like her mother.'

'Oh thank God. Where is his apartment?'

'I'll take you there, but first I need to check you both over and get you showered and changed. The last thing I want is for Leah to catch anything else. I feel awful saying that, but I hope you understand.'

Her eyes dropped to my hands holding hers, taking in the ring Antoine had pressed upon me. I slid it from mine and placed it on her finger, where it dangled, now far too big.

'Here,' I said. 'This is yours. Antoine insisted I wear it as I don't have one of my own, and my fiancé couldn't get me a ring because he was in hospital. I hope you're not offended? He meant it in friendship.'

'Of course! I'm so happy that you wore it. That you're engaged. But this is too much. My Leah. Antoine. All of you here. I can't believe it. Let's just get this over with. I can't wait another minute.'

I looked at Eva's tired, worn face, now alight with excitement and trepidation. My heart went out to her, but it ached too. Leah was her daughter, hers and Antoine's, and yet she also held a part of my heart. It would be so hard to let her go. Tomorrow Jamie and I were to be married. We would have our own children, God willing. Even so, I would never stop loving the child I'd delivered and then spirited out of Auschwitz. For me, Leah was a living reminder to never, ever give up.

FIFTY-THREE

I knocked once and then again. Behind me, I could feel Eva trembling. She leaned on Hanna's arm, scarcely daring to breathe. I could see the effort she was making to remain calm when all the while her senses must be screaming at her to see Leah, to hold and to touch her as well as to be reunited with Antoine.

'Antoine, it's me, Maggie. Open up.'

I could hear him grumbling behind the door and then, finally, he opened it.

'I'm sorry. I was changing her. You would not believe...'

His words trailed off as he saw who was with me.

'Eva?'

He sagged as his knees gave way. Eva was simply standing, gazing at him as if rooted to the spot. Then Leah let out a hungry cry and she pushed past us into the apartment, her maternal instincts taking over as she looked for her baby.

'It's alright, Leah, Mama's coming.'

I took Antoine by the shoulder and steered him back in.

'The kitchen's there,' I said to Hanna. 'Could you make us all some coffee?'

Eva was bending over Leah, picking her up and rocking her with that age-old rhythm parents everywhere somehow knew, swaying gently as she murmured, 'There now, is that better? Are you hungry, little one?'

Leah gazed at her, rapt, then reached up to touch her nose, her hair, her tiny fingers grasping as she crooned in delight.

'Do you think she recognises me?' whispered Eva.

'Of course she does. You're her mother. She knows that, and she knows you.'

Antoine let out a sob and then another, all restraint falling away as he moved to her side and took them both in his arms, resting his head on her shoulder as he cried his heart out.

'First Leah, then you,' he gulped when he could finally speak. 'My two miracles.'

Eva held Leah in the crook of her arm as she caressed his face, his mouth, his hair, her fingers tracing every feature as if to prove it was really him and that he was really here.

'I never stopped thinking about you,' she said. 'Not for one minute. Every night I would dream of you and Leah too. Now we're together again and I can't believe it.'

He took her hand and kissed it. 'Believe it,' he said. 'Even if I don't.'

He was gazing at her as if he would wake up at any moment and she would no longer be there.

'She's so beautiful,' said Eva, staring at her daughter.

'She looks like you.'

The tears were falling down both their faces now, and I knew they were thinking of the children they'd lost.

I looked at Hanna emerging with a tray from the kitchen. 'I think we'll leave you alone now,' I said. 'I'll call for you later.'

Antoine tore his eyes from Eva's. 'Maggie, you're getting married tomorrow. We can call for you.'

'Married? Oh, Maggie, that's wonderful.'

Hanna's face was suffused with delight; Eva's too.

She brushed aside her tears. 'Maggie, I'm so happy for you.'

'Thank you. I'm happy for you too. For you all. Really, there's no need to call for me. I have everything I need, and it's only going to be a small wedding. His parents can't travel from Scotland, and I have no idea where mine are.'

My voice caught in spite of my best efforts.

'I'm so sorry,' said Eva.

'Don't be. Really, I must go. You two have so much to talk about.'

'Not least how you saved my life and Leah's.'

I waved away her words. 'That wasn't all me. It was down to you and your spirit as well as hers.'

Hanna held out her arm. 'Shall we? I think we have plenty to talk about too. For one thing, you have to tell me all about this man you're marrying. It's not the one who held the dance for us, is it? Your captain?'

'The very same.'

She clapped her hands. 'I don't believe it. How romantic. Come – you can tell me the whole story on the way back to the hotel.'

'I want to hear it too,' said Eva. 'Later.'

She was already gazing down at Leah again, glancing up at Antoine to share a look that said everything. I could see him taking in her face, her pallor and extreme slenderness. She wasn't the Eva he'd known but, in time, they would come to know one another again, perhaps in a different way. We were all scarred by this war, some more deeply than others. But love and patience would help to heal those scars so that they united rather than divided us even more. At least, that was what I hoped for all of us. For me and for Jamie.

FIFTY-FOUR

The door to my consulting room flew open.

'Put your stethoscope down,' said Marianne. 'You're done for the day. You're coming with me. That's an order.'

I wrapped my arms around her. 'Oh my God. You're back. Where's Jack? Are you both here? Do you know I'm getting married tomorrow?'

'Suzanne told us on the way from the airfield. Now get your coat – we have things to do.'

'Where are we going?' I asked as she hustled me along the corridor, slinging my coat on as we walked.

'To the Ritz.'

'Why?'

'You'll find out.'

Outside, a cab was waiting. I glanced out the window as we drove away. Something caught my eye – a huddle of two men sharing a cigarette. Ordinary enough except that one of them looked awfully familiar. The other too, now that I looked again.

No. It couldn't be.

It had been such a long day already, what with Eva and Hanna arriving. Being reunited with Antoine and Eva. I was tired. Maybe I was imagining things. I couldn't help but let out a yawn.

Marianne laughed. 'Lightweight. You'll perk up once we get to the Ritz.'

As soon as we got there, she marched me to a lift that had only one button marked 'Imperial Suite'. I looked at it, then at her, but she stayed schtum, an enigmatic little smile the only clue she was giving me that something was going on.

As the lift doors opened, so did the door to the suite. I caught a glimpse of a magnificent salon beyond and then all the people gathered there – Suzanne; Antoine and Eva sitting on a sofa with Leah at their feet in a bassinet, Hanna alongside them; Sophie smiling at me from a corner by the window, as was Joseph beside her.

'You're all here,' I cried as I was passed from embrace to embrace. All except one.

At that moment, the door to the suite opened again. A wheelchair lay beyond – an empty one. And then Jamie hobbled in, leaning on Jack's arm.

I gasped. 'You're here. Oh, my darling, you're walking.'

He planted a kiss on my lips. 'You bet I am. I'm walking my girl down the aisle tomorrow if it kills me.'

'Sit here. I'd rather it didn't kill you, thank you very much.'

He sank into the nearest chair, the effort he'd made all too visible.

A man appeared at our side bearing a silver tray on which two glasses were perched. 'Welcome to the Ritz. Champagne, madame? Sir?'

'May I introduce Monsieur Meier,' said Suzanne. 'He's a great friend to us all as he was to the Resistance throughout the occupation. It's thanks to him that we were able to get you this suite for tonight and tomorrow.'

'Thank you so much,' I said. 'It's an honour to meet you.'

'The honour is all mine, madame. The Ritz hotel is also honoured to host your wedding reception.'

I gaped at him, then at Suzanne. 'We're having a reception here? But I thought...'

'You thought wrong. Only the best for our Maggie.'

My eyes filled with tears. I dashed them away as I looked at them all, at their smiles and the affection written across their faces. 'I don't know what to say.'

Marianne handed me her handkerchief. 'Say nothing and drink up. We have something else to show you.'

'More surprises?'

'Don't worry. You'll like these too, I hope.'

She was once more holding out her hand, impatient I should come with her. Over her shoulder, I could see Suzanne beaming. Most unusual. What on earth was going on?

I dropped a kiss on Jamie's head. 'I'll see you in a minute.'

A pair of double doors led from the salon into a bedroom. I stepped through the doors and stopped dead.

It was the most beautiful room I'd ever seen, its canopied bed draped in oyster-coloured silk, a gorgeous bowl of flowers set on the Louis XIV table at its foot. But it wasn't the bed or the bouquet that stopped me in my tracks. Hung on the door of the wardrobe was a wedding gown, its flowing lines deceptively simple.

I walked over to it and stroked the cream silk, the lace of the veil that hung next to it. This time, I couldn't find the words. I just looked at them both, a sob escaping from my throat.

Marianne's face creased in concern. 'You don't like it?'

'I love it. Truly.'

'Then hurry up and try it on. I can't wait to see it on you.'

It fitted like a glove, as if it were made for me.

'You can thank Suzanne for that,' said Marianne. 'She has an excellent eye for measurements as well as everything else. How about the material? You like that too?'

'I do. I love everything about it.'

'It's parachute silk, made from the parachute Jamie used to drop into Poland. In a way, it saved your life too. He had it sent over, and Suzanne gave it to a couturier friend of hers here. See, she sewed both your initials into the hem.'

Marianne lifted the hem to show me our intertwined initials inside a heart, all of it exquisitely embroidered in silver thread. The dress hugged me at the waist and then flared out, its skirt embroidered with the same thread and tiny pearls.

'There are just a couple of things missing,' she said as she placed the circlet of flowers on my head to which the veil was attached. It floated around my shoulders, a fairy-tale cloak cascading halfway down my back, rivulets of lace flowing into the dress.

Marianne unclasped the string of pearls from her own neck and placed it around mine. 'One final touch. There we go.'

She spun me round so that I was looking at myself in the mirror, a vision in a cloud of cream, my unadorned face soon decorated with a slick of lipstick and powder too. Once she was satisfied, she called Suzanne in to admire the finished result.

Suzanne gazed at me and then her eyes filled with what looked suspiciously like tears. 'You're just perfect. And the fit. Perfect too.'

She opened the wardrobe and took out another dress on a hanger, a deep blue cocktail dress this time that skimmed my body, with fluted sleeves and a draped neck. 'This is for you to wear tonight,' she said. 'Let's get you out of your wedding dress and into it.'

'Careful as we take it off,' Marianne commanded, easing it over my head so I wouldn't smudge my make-up on it.

I slipped into the cocktail dress, then looked down at my left arm. The sleeve didn't cover my tattoo.

'Here,' said Suzanne, sliding the wide silver bangle from her own arm and up mine, adjusting it until it fit perfectly.

'Don't ever feel ashamed of that,' said Marianne. 'See it as a mark of your strength and endurance. You're still here when so many are not.'

I stared at the bangle and then at her. 'I know you're right, but it's hard not to. I'll get used to it in time.'

'You can also cover it with make-up. Here.'

She sat me down at the dressing table and slid the bangle down so she could apply foundation and powder to conceal the tattoo before artfully coiling my hair into a chignon just like the one she habitually wore. With her pearls around my throat and the lipstick, I looked every inch the lady as I stared at myself in the mirror, unable to tear my eyes away.

'Quite a transformation,' I said. It certainly was, from the blood-stained doctor with a stethoscope around her neck instead of pearls.

I touched my hair, patting it as if it wasn't quite real. 'It's long enough to put up now.'

'It is,' said Marianne, her eyes also glittering.

She brushed them with the back of her hand and then let out a shaky sigh. 'I still can't believe you came back to us, Maggie. And now you're here and you're getting married tomorrow to the man who helped save you from that death march. It's like a dream.'

'Some of it was more like a nightmare,' I whispered.

'I know. Actually, I can't begin to know. None of us can except those who were there with you. What I do know is that you're probably the bravest person I've ever met. You came through all of that, and yet you show such care for others. I know it haunts you, Maggie, but you don't let that stop you. I only hope that one day those ghosts will leave you alone. That you'll find peace.'

I looked at Marianne in the mirror, at Suzanne standing with her, two women who'd risked their lives again and again to try to win this war. We were so close now, our troops over the Rhine, into the heartland of Germany.

'It was worth it,' I said. 'Now let's go and join the party. I'm getting married tomorrow and you're my bridesmaid so let's drink to that and to victory. Doesn't love conquer all?'

'It does, Maggie. It certainly does.'

FIFTY-FIVE

8 APRIL 1945, PARIS, FRANCE

The church was dimly lit, its Gothic arches framing the aisle stretching ahead of me. I could smell the flowers – lily of the valley, roses, a faint spicy undertone. The pews appeared full. Surely not. I'd expected perhaps twenty people at most, but there were over a hundred.

Marianne smoothed out my dress, while Hanna handed me my bouquet, also made of roses and lily of the valley. Antoine stepped forward, ready to lead me down the aisle. Or so I thought. Then I saw someone else emerge from the gloom, someone I recognised immediately.

'Papa!'

'Maggie, *ma cherie.*'

His face creased into that smile I knew so well as he pulled me into his arms. I nestled there, unable to believe it was really him, that I was once more in his embrace.

'But how?' I whispered. 'How did you get here? Who found you?'

'Your friend Antoine.'

I blinked over Papa's shoulder at Antoine, mouthing a 'thank you'. Antoine smiled and slipped away into the church.

'Where have you been all this time?'

'First Marseilles and then Toulouse. I'll tell you all about it. Your *maman* and sisters are here too.'

'You'd better. What about my brothers?'

'All I know is that they're both with the First Army, fighting.'

'But they're alive?'

'The last I heard.'

'Oh, Papa, it's just marvellous that you're here, all of you. And for my wedding.'

Papa gave me a final, gentle squeeze. 'I must be careful of your dress,' he said as, reluctantly, he let me go. 'You look like a princess. No, a queen. You have grown so beautiful, *ma petite*.'

'Nonsense. I look like me but skinnier. Now where is Maman? And Charlotte and Emilie?'

He waved towards the front of the church. 'Up there, waiting for you. As is your groom, I believe. Shall we?'

The organ burst into life as he crooked his arm for mine, looking at me with such love that I felt buoyed up, ready to float down the aisle on it. Reunited at last, after so long, and yet it was as if we'd never been apart. Papa was just the same, his suit rumpled, his hair too. No matter how hard my mother tried, he always looked as if he'd just stumbled out of bed, and I loved him for it. He might come from a long and noble line, but any fortune or title had disappeared along with the crumbling chateau. One thing that remained aristocratic was his profile, and I admired it now, catching glimpses of the people in the pews as we passed.

They were all there – Sophie and the volunteers from the Lutetia along with some of the guests. I saw Joseph dabbing a tear from his eye and several of the others standing ramrod straight in their best clothes donated by the Red Cross, pride at being here shining from every pore. Then there were officers and men in uniform, from Jamie's regiments I guessed as well as from OSS. Goodness, even Steed was here. Hanna gave me a little wave, and I noted Eva cradling Leah in her arms, who cooed as I passed, with Antoine at their side.

Maman was sitting beside Suzanne, my sisters next to her. At the altar, Jack stood by Jamie's side, supporting him. Papa slipped in beside Maman as Marianne – my other sister – also took her seat. I turned and smiled at her before moving to Jamie's side.

'Dearly beloved,' the priest began.

Yes, they were, I thought. All of them. So dearly beloved by me. But none as much as Jamie.

I gazed at him through my veil. He looked like a mirage, a dream. Except that this was no dream. It was real, and we were here, our hands joining, our hearts too, united in holy matrimony.

'You may kiss the bride.'

'Try and stop me.'

As Jamie lifted my veil, the congregation broke into applause while Jack whooped in delight.

That first kiss as husband and wife was so sweet, the honey that soothed away the memories and the fears. It was enough that we had today – and we had one another.

'Here.' I took Jamie's arm as the organ struck up the 'Wedding March' and we turned to walk back down the aisle.

'I can do it,' he muttered.

'Don't be an idiot. Lean on me. Isn't that what we're supposed to do, support one another?'

He glowered at me and then grinned. 'Is this our first fight?'

I smiled. 'The first of many.'

Together, we walked back down the aisle, pausing so Jamie could rest a moment before we continued, taking our time as everyone cheered us on, moving in behind us to form the most unlikely procession. Here we were, soldiers and spies, refugees and the reunited, beloved brothers and sisters and friends, along with my parents. I knew Jamie wished his could have been there too. Well, we would make up for it.

As we emerged from the church to a guard of honour from Jamie's regiment, someone threw petals over us while others cheered and clapped.

And then I heard it. A shot. Then another.

'Get down!' I yelled, pulling Jamie down beside me, back inside the door of the church, looking to see if he was alright and seeing only blood soaking through my dress.

FIFTY-SIX

'He's over there.'

'Get the bastard.'

Feet thundering past me, people screaming. Looking at the bloodstains on my skirt, then my hand, dripping from the cut I'd sustained when I'd pulled us both to the ground.

Jamie scrambled to his feet, using the pillar to pull himself up.

'Jamie, be careful!'

'Careful be damned.'

He signalled to his men to spread out across the street. Jack and Antoine were already there, ducked behind a car, scanning the rooftops while my bridesmaid covered them with her drawn pistol.

'Stay back,' I yelled to everyone behind me, still in the church, trying to comprehend what was going on. 'Close the doors.'

'I see him. There he is!' someone shouted as a figure broke cover, leaping from one balcony to the next, pausing only to fire at us again before ducking behind the balustrade. In that split second, I got a good look at his face and gasped.

'Victor.'

Another bullet whizzed past my head and slammed into the font behind me. Jamie pulled me back inside the porch.

'Who the hell is Victor?'

'One of the DPs from the Lutetia. You saw him once. You didn't seem to like him.'

'I've no idea who he is, but I sure as hell hate him for this.'

He signalled again to his men, a hand gesture that told them to cover him.

'No, Jamie,' I hissed as he stepped forward.

Sure enough, Victor opened fire. But he had to peer above the balustrade to do so, and at the exact moment he pulled his trigger, so did Jamie. There was an agonised howl, and then Victor toppled from the balcony and fell to the street below, where he lay still.

Jack sprinted over. 'He's dead,' he called out.

'Get him out of here before everyone sees him,' snapped Suzanne.

Jamie's men hurried to help Jack cover the body and heave it out of sight. As they did so, Jamie got a good look at Victor's face.

'I remember him now. I also remember seeing him at the Lutetia and not quite recognising him. It was the hair. He showed up at the DP camp when I was there wanting to see his mate, that Auschwitz Kapo you recognised. They must have been going to work the ratline together. Kicked off when we said he couldn't. His mate was already in custody, thanks to you. It was me that dealt with him. Thought I'd teach him a lesson he wouldn't forget. Obviously, he did.'

'He was helping Nazis escape justice. I hope he rots in hell.'

'Don't worry, sir – we'll take care of him,' said one of Jamie's men as they hauled him towards a waiting jeep.

The others stepped smartly back into the guard of honour as if nothing had happened and opened the church doors once more. This time, our guests flooded out into the street after us, many none the wiser.

'A car backfiring. Nothing to worry about. We just had to check,' Suzanne tried to reassure everyone in the church.

Some didn't look too convinced, but they were far too used to the ways of war to say anything.

I moved the folds of my skirt to cover the faint stains that remained, my handkerchief pressed into my hand as I smiled for photographs. All the while, I was back there, hearing those shots, my legs trembling under my dress with shock.

Yes, but I didn't freeze. I reacted as I should. There's hope for me yet.

Maman appeared in front of us, stretching out her arms to embrace us both while Papa beamed beside her. My younger sisters hovered shyly, their eyes darting to Jamie and then to me. In the two years since I'd seen them, they'd grown up so much.

'Welcome to our family,' said Maman, dropping kisses on Jamie's cheeks before doing the same to me.

'I'm sorry your parents couldn't be here,' said Papa, shaking Jamie's hand. 'But I hope that you feel we're your parents too now.'

'Thank you, sir. It's an honour and a privilege to be a part of your family and even more so to be married to your daughter.'

Maman's lips wobbled as she embraced him once more, the way she looked at him as she patted him on the cheek saying more than words ever could.

'Look at you two,' I said as my sisters took their turn to hug us both. 'So grown up. So beautiful.'

'You're the one who's beautiful,' said Charlotte, while Emilie merely blushed. She'd always been the shyer of the two.

People were starting to move towards cars and cabs for the reception. There were just a few more hands to shake and cheeks to kiss. Then we'd be able to forget all about Victor and concentrate on our wedding day.

Would we ever be truly at peace? I had no idea. I only knew it was what I wanted above everything. To spend time with Jamie as a normal couple, living a normal life. Today's incident had only brought home how inured I was now to violence. It had become my normal. And that wasn't right.

'Are you alright?' murmured Jamie, squeezing my hand.

'I'm absolutely fine.'

'I love you, Mrs Maclean.'

'I love you too.'

'What, no monsieur stuff?'

'We don't need that. I think we know who's in charge here.'

He burst out laughing, a moment I later loved to see had been captured in our photographs. 'You're irrepressible, my darling. It's what I love about you.'

'Just that?'

'That and everything else.'

'You don't know quite everything yet.'

'I don't, but I intend to find out.'

A shiver of anticipation rippled through my spine, turning into warm waves that washed through and over my entire body. I couldn't wait for Jamie to finally make love to me as his wife and I to him as my husband. It was about time. We belonged together.

FIFTY-SEVEN

11 APRIL 1945, PARIS, FRANCE

It had been three days since the wedding – three wonderful days that would stay with me forever. Now we were gathered in the Hotel Lutetia, packing things up ready for the Red Cross to take over. Marianne and I were lugging boxes from the office full of papers documenting the interviews we'd carried out with each new arrival. Their registration papers and other records would remain here so that the Red Cross could help reunite them with their families. Antoine would carry on sifting through for any potential collaborators, but, apart from him, our work here was done.

'I'll miss this place,' I said, looking round my consulting room one last time. The typhus eradication measures had proved so successful they were now carrying them out at every reception centre and displaced persons camp across Europe. More and more were springing up each day as we gained ground in Germany while the Soviets did the same from their positions in the east. The end had to be close. Yet still the Germans fought on. Hitler wasn't giving in. There was still so much work for us to do. For them to do.

I looked at Marianne. 'I'll miss you all too.'

'You'll see us soon enough,' said Marianne. 'Once you're back in London.'

'Jamie and I are staying in Scotland for a while, at least until he recovers.'

Marianne put down the box she was carrying and stared at me, hands on hips. 'You're leaving us?'

'For the moment.'

I was fighting back tears, trying to smile through them. I'd so dreaded this moment.

'Maggie deserves a rest,' said Suzanne, gliding into the room with Hanna in her wake. 'And Jamie needs to recover from his wounds.'

'God, what I would give for a rest,' said Hanna. 'Any chance I can come with you?'

I smiled. 'No chance, I'm afraid. We're going to be rather busy.'

'I thought you were having a rest?'

Marianne tutted. 'Don't be naughty. She'll be on honeymoon. An extended one, I hope.'

'Making babies of your own?' teased Hanna.

I looked down at the papers in my hand. 'Maybe.'

'She is, she so is,' crowed Marianne. 'You dark horse, Maggie. Who would have thought you'd be the maternal type?'

'First of all, I'm not intending to make babies, at least not yet. Secondly, what's wrong with being maternal?'

'Nothing whatsoever,' said Suzanne. 'Ignore her. She's just jealous.'

'Jealous of having to look after a screaming brat? Not likely.' Marianne hopped down from the desk where she'd been perched and sauntered out the door. 'I'll be sorting files in the library if you need me.'

'I bet she would secretly love to be married too,' said Hanna.

'I don't think it's so much of a secret,' I said. 'It's only a matter of time before she and Jack get hitched.'

'Jack's a lone wolf,' said Suzanne. 'Always has been, always will be.'

'I thought I was too. Until I met Jamie.'

'You're different, Maggie. You come from a stable, loving family. Some of us haven't been as fortunate.'

It was the closest Suzanne had ever come to divulging something about one of her agents. She had to be talking about Jack. I wondered what she meant.

Hanna glanced at me and shrugged. The subject was closed, at least for now.

A tap on the door broke the silence that stretched across the room.

'I came to say goodbye,' said Joseph.

He was dressed in the suit he'd worn to my wedding although the shirt he wore was new and pressed. Supplies of clothing were coming in thick and fast thanks to the Red Cross too.

'Joseph, my friend, I'll miss you.'

He gave me a hug and then held me at arm's length, his sharp eyes searching. 'You look happy. That's good. But if your young man ever does anything to upset you, you know where I am.'

I had to suppress a smile. It was evident he was serious. 'Thank you, Joseph. I'll remember that, although I intend to keep him firmly in line.'

'That's the way. My wife always did.'

His smile faltered. There was still no news of his family. I feared they'd perished in the camps. Then again, there was always hope. Hadn't I learned that?

'Don't give up, Joseph,' I said, holding his hand between mine. 'Promise me you won't.'

He clicked his heels together and gave me a little bow. 'I promise.'

As he turned away, I could feel my heart crack a little more.

He would always have a special place in it.

Someone else appeared in the doorway as he was leaving, an American soldier who saluted smartly. 'Message for a Madame Suzanne. I was told she would be in here.'

Suzanne took the envelope he was carrying. 'Thank you.'

I watched her face as she scanned it and then read it through again.

'It's from OSS Headquarters,' she said. 'Josef Mengele has been arrested in Poland.'

I felt my knees give way and leaned back against my desk, dropping the files in my hands.

'Are you alright, Maggie?'

'Yes. No. I just...'

I could picture them. All those innocents he'd killed. I was crying again, and I didn't care. There was so much to cry for, so many people. If I cried an ocean of tears, I could never cry enough for them. Yet, if I looked around, I could see some of them here, people who'd been saved. People like Eva and Leah.

Suzanne handed me a handkerchief, waiting until I was more composed.

'I also had word from Christine in Berlin. She's following a lead to the Dahlem Institute there that collaborated with Mengele on his experiments. With any luck, she'll be able to get more evidence to add to what you have already.'

'I need to go and see Eva,' I gasped. 'Say goodbye to her and Leah.'

'Antoine can go with you. He's in the library, I think.'

'It's hard to explain, but I want to see them alone. There are things we shared that Antoine may not know. Things that only we can understand. Once I've seen them, I'll come back here, but right now, I need to do this on my own.'

I saw the flicker of concern in Suzanne's eyes. 'If you're sure, Maggie.'

'I'm sure.'

There were also things I needed to say to Eva alone. Questions for which I needed answers. I hoped I might be able to answer any of her lingering questions too. It was time to speak the truth and to hear it, for both our sakes and especially for Leah's. She would always have that special place in my heart, but it was time to part, at least for now. I would no doubt hear about her over the coming years, from a distance. The distance I was choosing to create for my own happiness. My sanity. It hurt so much to leave them all, but it would hurt far more to stay.

FIFTY-EIGHT

Eva didn't seem surprised to see me. 'I thought you'd come,' she said. 'Antoine told me you're leaving tomorrow.'

'Not just France. I'm leaving the service.'

'Forever?'

'At least for now, although it may well turn into forever.'

I glanced at Leah, waving her tiny teddy in the air, giggling as she did so.

Eva followed my gaze. 'Come – let me make you a coffee. You look as if you could do with one.'

I sank onto the couch beside Leah and gently tickled her tummy. 'Look at you,' I whispered. 'You're becoming such a big girl. I'm so proud of you, Leah.'

She looked at me and laughed. Her eyes were darkening, no longer that clear, pale blue they'd been when she was born. The blue that had so enthralled Mengele. That had almost condemned her to death too. I choked back a sob. All those babies murdered the minute they were born. Another reason I had to go away, to heal. Perhaps to have a baby of my own.

'Here.' Eva handed me a coffee cup. 'Have a biscuit too. You need fattening up.'

I could hear the irony in her voice. Eva was even thinner than I was. She no doubt heard the same every day from Antoine.

'They arrested Mengele today – Suzanne just told us. They've caught him at last. Now he can face justice for his crimes.'

Eva placed her hand on her heart and bowed her head for a moment, her lips moving. As I caught the odd word, I realised what she was saying – the Kaddish.

'There will be other survivors like us who can testify against him,' I said when she'd finished.

'And so many more who didn't make it.'

We looked at one another. There was nothing more to say. We had seen it. Lived it. Survived it when millions had not.

'I wanted to talk to you about the day we left,' I began awkwardly.

She laid her hand on mine. 'Maggie, I don't need explanations. You did what you had to do. They would have shot you if you'd stayed.'

'But I could have tried harder to save you. That's what tortures me. I abandoned you there, and I feel so guilty about that.'

'Don't. You did the only thing you could and saved my daughter too. I'm eternally in your debt. If it wasn't for you, Maggie, Leah wouldn't be here, and I probably wouldn't be either. I was dying when I gave birth to her – I know that. Somehow you managed to keep me alive and Leah too. Don't torture yourself. Celebrate the fact that we're here.'

Her eyes were fierce, her tone even more so. It was the same fire she'd shown the day Leah was born, in spite of everything. The fire her daughter had inherited and which I knew would sustain her throughout her life. The life her mother had given her.

'When I took the Hippocratic oath,' I said, 'I swore to ensure that I would give my patients the food they needed and that I would do no harm or injustice to them. I couldn't do that in Auschwitz. Instead, my patients starved. Many were harmed, and every day they spent there was an injustice to them and to humanity. I broke my promise, Eva. I find that very hard to live with.'

'Listen to me, Maggie. You did your best. Think of that other doctor, the one who looked after me when you were gone – Dr Laba. He too took an oath that he had to break, but he did his best to make up for that. As you are doing now with all your work. As you will always do – that I know. But I also know that there is nothing for which you need to apologise or atone. You're only human, just like the rest of us. It was the Nazis who tried to take that away, not you.'

'They tried but they didn't succeed, did they? You're right. Thank you.' I felt Leah's foot kick against my leg, strong and vigorous.

'No, thank you. You gave us back our family. I will never forget my other babies, and Leah can never take their place, but we have a future now and so do you. Embrace it. Do what makes you happy. But remember that you bring much happiness too. You're a healer.'

I embraced her, leaning forward to take her in my arms. 'Thank you,' I whispered.

'Goodbye, darling,' I added as I stroked Leah's face one last time. She grabbed my finger with her fist and held tight.

'She doesn't want you to go,' said Eva. 'None of us do. But I think you must. You will always have a special place in her heart though – and mine. Come and see us whenever you wish, once you've had time to get settled and to heal. I want you to always be a part of her life, if you'd like that. And of ours of course.'

'I'd love that. Just give me some time.'

'Take as much as you need, Maggie. For you. You have your own wounds to tend. Scars that need to fade.'

She was right. First, I needed to heal myself. Once I'd done that, I could heal others. It was why I'd become a doctor after all, to alleviate suffering and to heal. My life's purpose. Except there was another purpose now and that was loving Jamie. Somehow, I would find a way to meld the two. There was always a way.

FIFTY-NINE

The table was laden with food, the candles and crystal gleaming. The Lutetia had done us proud, but I couldn't eat a thing.

'You know,' said Jamie, filling my glass, 'they're giving everyone else in the hotel exactly the same food as us tonight? I saw them in the dining room as I passed, tucking in. They know that they're safe now. That they won't have to save their bread for someone weaker.'

I glanced at him out of the corner of my eye and then down at my plate, lifting my fork to take up a mouthful, chewing and swallowing as all the while a voice in my head screamed at me not to.

I took another mouthful and another, each time drowning out that voice with a song I sang in my head instead, one of determination.

Jamie said nothing as I forced my food down, and I loved him for that. I loved him for so many other things too, not least his kindness.

He saw me looking at him as I finished what was on my

plate and raised his glass in a silent toast. Then he stood and tapped that same glass.

'Ladies and gentlemen, I want to propose a toast to you all. My wife and I would like to thank you for everything you've done for us. It's been an honour and a joy to get to know you.'

I, too, got to my feet. 'I'd like to propose another toast. To my husband, the best of men – apart from the rest of you of course.'

A burst of laughter around the table. Their faces were turned towards me, lit by the warm glow of the candles – Jack and Marianne, Hanna, Sophie, Suzanne, who'd left her own love behind in London. Somehow, we all managed to keep the fires of love burning across oceans, miles and years. It was what Antoine and Eva had managed to do too. He'd never stopped loving her, even when he'd thought she was dead.

'And to love,' I said. 'In all its forms.'

'To love,' they chorused, glasses once more clinking, eyes meeting. It was what we fought for after all. The love of one person for another, for a family, a country. The love of freedom and of choice. The love of what was right in the face of enormous wrong. Love would always win – or so I hoped. While this war raged on, it was all we could do. All I could do.

I could feel the tears welling. Let them come. I wasn't ashamed of how much I loved them.

'I'll miss you all so much.'

'We'll miss you too, Maggie.'

Marianne, my leader for so long and my friend, smiled up at me, her eyes glistening too, Jack beside her as ever, as Jamie was now by my side. They were all my friends and the bravest of the brave, off in the morning on another mission.

I had a mission too, one that would take me in a separate direction. I felt the tiniest pang for a moment, but only a moment. Perhaps one day we would all be together again like this. Perhaps not. As I sipped my wine, I drank in their faces too, imprinting them on my heart.

A LETTER FROM AMANDA

I want to say a huge thank you for choosing to read *The Midwife's Child*. If you did enjoy it and want to keep up to date with all my latest releases, just sign up at the following link. Your email address will never be shared, and you can unsubscribe at any time.

www.bookouture.com/amanda-lees

This was such a hard book to write in so many ways. I had the great privilege of knowing several people, chiefly Hungarian Jews, who survived Auschwitz and lived to tell the world of what happened to them. I vividly recall seeing the numbers tattooed on one elegant woman's arm as she drew back her sleeve to show me. Scarcely faded, they stood out as a stark emblem on her skin, a reminder that we all bear a responsibility to not only never forget but to ensure it never happens again.

I also remember sitting in rural Hungary, talking to the Jewish grandparents of the friend I was with, who described to me how the Nazis came to their village, lined up the men against the lip of a quarry and shot them all so that they fell backward into it. They too survived Auschwitz, being sent there at the same time as my heroine, Maggie, would have been.

It was the weight of those memories, among many, that sat heavy on me as I began to write this book. I so wanted to get it right without being salacious or denigrating anyone's story. I needed to find the right balance of raw truth and allusion while knowing that, as I hard as I tried, I could never really under-stand what it must have been like. And I'm glad that I can't – I don't believe anyone can unless they were there – because Auschwitz and all the other camps like it were unimaginable. The cruelty meted out by the Nazis was unimaginable. That is partly why, in spite of the reports bravely brought out by people such as Rudolf Vrba, Alfred Wetzler and Witold Pilecki, who escaped to try and alert the Western Allies to what was happening in there, no one believed them. When they finally did, they either did nothing or not enough.

The other great lesson I learned from my elderly Jewish friends who survived Auschwitz was hope. They couldn't have got through it alive otherwise. It was the quality I wanted Maggie to embody above all, along with the kind of love and compassion for her fellow prisoners that also saw so many survivors through, although the after-effects of what happened to them were often unrecognised at a time when PTSD was unknown or dismissed as 'combat stress'. We know better now, but we still have a long way to go before everyone suffering from it receives the help they need. In every great tragedy there are great lessons to be learned. I have learned so many in the writing of this book, and I hope that they, along with the story, resonate with and uplift you as they did me.

There is another true story that lies at the heart of this book and that is the love between Maggie and Jamie, who are based on a true story I came across of a Scottish commando who met a beautiful young woman who was in a displaced persons camp having survived a death march and invited her to a dance where he was too shy to approach her. Luckily, he got over his nerves and they got married, remaining so for over seventy years until her death in 2017, just after they had celebrated their seventy-first Valentine's Day together as a couple. I'm sure that Maggie and Jamie will do the same.

As with all of my other Second World War books, this one

is based on things that actually happened and people who existed. One or two of them still do, although, as time passes, we will lose them too. That's why it's so important that we retain and pass on their stories, fictionalised or otherwise. We must never forget. These people were brave beyond belief, enduring and overcoming situations and events that most of us could scarcely begin to imagine. I am constantly in awe of their courage as I write, and I hope I've done them justice. They certainly deserve it.

I hope you loved *The Midwife's Child,* and if you did, I would be very grateful if you could write a review. I'd love to hear what you think, and it makes such a difference helping new readers to discover one of my books for the first time.

I love hearing from my readers – you can get in touch on my Facebook page, through Twitter, Goodreads or my website.

Thanks,

Amanda

amandalees.com

facebook.com/AmandaLeesAuthor

twitter.com/amandalees

ACKNOWLEDGEMENTS

As ever, there are so many people I want to thank for helping me bring this book to life. First, there is my agent and friend, Lisa, who has exquisite taste, laser-sharp instincts and the heart of a lioness. I owe her so much, along with her amazing team in Patrick, Zoe, Jamie and Elena.

Then there's my brilliant editor, Susannah, and the team at Bookouture, who not only get my books out into the world but make sure they have gorgeous covers, are superbly produced and come in all kinds of formats, including audio. Behind the scenes, they crunch data, perform publishing wizardry and weave marketing magic. Peta, Saidah, Kim, Noelle, Sarah, Jess, Jenny, Alba, Alex, Ruth, Richard, Lauren, Marina and so many others, you're all fabulous, and if I've left anyone out, forgive me. There's simply so much talent under your roof.

I also have to once again thank my author buddies – Karin, Vanessa, Anne, Victoria, Lisa, Martyn, Susi, Anna, Diane, Vicky and, again, too many more to mention who've been endlessly supportive.

As ever, there is my constant inspiration, my daughter. I love you, and I am always proud of you.

Next, the friends and family who've been there for me through times dark and light – Julia and Phil, Andrew, Josa, Guy, Nina, Barb, Christian, Jackie and Sam, Marianne and Margaret, Claire, Charlie and everyone else who has helped in any way or cheered me on. Some of those names you may also recognise among the names of the main characters.

Above all, thanks to the women and men who served, and gave their lives in service for, their countries and our freedom. We will never forget you, as we will never forget all those who suffered in the Holocaust.

Printed in Great Britain
by Amazon

25307306R10169